'A remarkable book – perhaps [...] of a new scientific discovery, which is so plausible and ingenious that I had to ask if it was true or a fiction. It ranks with Ian McEwan's brilliant climate change ideas in *Solar* . . . Elegantly written, intricately and plausibly plotted with some stunning surprises. A page-turner, in fact. More, it is moving about miscarriage, about childbirth, in a way that is exceptional'   Craig Raine

'Fiction can go anywhere, as long as the writer is sufficiently skilled and brave; Maxwell is totally unafraid, and her precision-tooled descriptive powers make her an invaluable guide . . . This unlimited access is Maxwell's chief triumph . . . Wonderfully intricate plotting that capitalizes on Maxwell's formidable grasp of neonatal medicine'
                                                          TLS

'An obstetric tragicomedy, both harrowing and hilarious, about the traumas we experience and the pain we cause as we struggle to get into the world'   *Observer* Books of the Year

'She wields a feistily original brand of wit and maybe her life as an Oxford academic accounts for the way she marshals a capacity for ethical debate that feels so unstrained . . . Maxwell does evoke hospitals — that closed-off world and its sometimes ludicrous bureaucracy — with verve and authority . . . Wry, daringly visceral'   *The Times*

'It's a brave author who confines her subject matter largely to the workings of a large NHS hospital and, in particular, to neonatal ethics and politics. Julie Maxwell's second novel is written with waspish wit and is unflinching in its examination of an under-discussed area of women's experience – pregnancies that go wrong and babies born far too soon . . . interesting on the moral and political implications of work in neonatal medicine'   *Daily Mail*

'An original and witty writer who deserves to be better known'
                                                          Kavenna

Julie Maxwell is the author of a previous novel, *You Can Live Forever*, which won a Betty Trask Award. She is a Fellow and Lecturer in English Literature at Exeter College, Oxford. She is married and has two young children.

A set of questions and thoughts for reading groups
can be found at the back of this book.

These are Our Children

JULIE MAXWELL

Quercus

First published in Great Britain in 2013 by Quercus Editions Ltd
This paperback edition published in 2014 by

Quercus Editions Ltd
55 Baker Street
7th Floor, South Block
London
W1U 8EW

A CIP catalogue record for this book is available
from the British Library

ISBN 978 1 78087 714 3
EBOOK ISBN 978 1 78087 713 6

10 9 8 7 6 5 4 3 2 1

Typeset by Ellipsis Digital Limited, Glasgow

Printed and bound in Great Britain by
Clays Ltd, St Ives plc

In memory of Baby Maxwell, 21.01.07

In celebration of Jude, who survived and saved me

———————————

'Most of the time we're double, we can stand outside and see an event – hope, fear, anticipate, judge. And then something happens where – where we have no room for thought or imagining – where what happens is real and all that is real . . . We think that sort of single-minded grief is insanity, but it's only an acknowledgement of a factual truth. An intolerable truth.'

— A.S. Byatt, *The Game*

'I wonder how far doctors *can* push back the frontier. How long before neonatologists simulating the end and middle of pregnancy push back far enough to meet the experimenters trying to create and nourish human life in test tubes. What will happen then to even the earliest miscarriage, to the whole concept of miscarriage – ?'

— Peggy Stinson, *The Long Dying of Baby Andrew*

'THESEUS: You must love one of them.
EMILIA: I had rather both'

— William Shakespeare & John Fletcher,
The Two Noble Kinsmen

PART ONE

What Not to Expect

One

The last time she knew anything about herself for certain, Florence was thirty-one years old and six-and-a-half weeks pregnant. The pregnancy, which she had confirmed by tests taken a fortnight before, was planned but it surprised her anyway. After so many years of protected sex, it was faintly astonishing to discover that the method actually 'worked'.

'No surprise to me,' Robert had said, grinning triumphantly, when she emerged from the bathroom.

But to Florence it was as if a long-suspected theorem had finally been proven. Public opinion was right about something at last. The rumours were all true. In less than nine months, Florence Brown, curator of the museum that combined the treasures of Little Dillyford with those of Greater Dillyford, would have a baby of her own.

Now, however, the six-and-a-half-week pregnant woman found herself sitting in a hospital emergency room twenty-four miles away.

'One of your fallopian tubes may be about to rupture,' the consultant surgeon said.

He spoke quite casually. Then the consultant surgeon decided to take his patient's pulse. Placing his thumb firmly across Florence's left wrist, applying a pressure that was soon slightly uncomfortable, he glanced at his watch, closed his eyes, and after a short interval looked again at the watch.

'It's rather high,' he said. 'A high pulse can be a sign that the tube is about to erupt.'

(A high pulse can be a sign you've been told you might explode imminently.)

'What are the other signs?' Florence asked, as the surgeon took his seat behind the desk.

'Yes, what *are* the other signs?' echoed Florence's mother Lydia. An effort to contribute which only gained her an impatient look from Florence.

The surgeon, a second-generation Kenyan, tilted his head in the direction of speech like a mannerly daisy. His patient's hair was dyed a childlike white-blonde. She had very large breasts that were slightly squashed by her salmon pink shirt.

He answered her gravely: 'Severe abdominal pain.'

'But I'm not in pain!' Florence objected.

(And an absence of pain can be a sign that there is nothing wrong with you.)

The surgeon, however, only looked at his patient so very pityingly that Florence thought she must be deceiving herself.

'No,' he agreed, nodding, 'no you're not in pain, *as such*, but . . .'

Florence waited rather neutrally for the surgeon to explain. Not for the first time, she had begun to feel at some remove from her own life, as though it were all happening, in reality, to some other person. Who just happened to reside within the confines of her own body. As though she were merely a spectator of the farce rather than – as she had so often allowed herself to believe – its central participant.

'But,' the surgeon continued, 'it may be that you've got rather a stoic disposition. It may be that the pain is worse than you realize because you have such a high pain threshold. Sometimes patients are like that.'

Florence was in fact a naturally hypersensitive and alarmist

4

character. Momentarily, however, she was so pleased by these compliments about herself – her distant self, that familiar companion – that she felt almost convinced of the surgeon's judgement. She saw herself newly revealed: Florence Brown, woman of strength and fortitude.

'And tell me again about the bleeding. How would you describe it?'

Last night: Worcester sauce. This morning: mulled wine. Ten minutes ago: filmy, like the skin that forms on boiled milk.

'Tell him about the Roman milk pan,' Lydia intervened. 'My daughter is a curator.'

'Okay, well, I'd like you to be scanned as soon as possible, Mrs Brown. That all right?'

So Florence and Lydia were hurried out to wait in the corridor lounge. They resumed their seats beside the unstaffed emergency reception 'desk' – merely a stool and whiteboard with 'Urge Gynae' written in small curly green letters. Opposite were two doors: Ultrasound 2B and Breastfeeding Counsellor. Ultrasound 2B opened and shut regularly as patients were called to their appointments by the sonographer, a woman in a ballet cardigan, who smiled blindly at the waiting room audience, nose wrinkled like a small friendly mammal, and leant her left hand heavily against the door handle. Breastfeeding Counsellor, the other door, was permanently open and empty, allowing Florence and Lydia to observe a green carpet, two matching pictures of the seaside and a straw-weave basket whose homeliness was evidently considered an aid to lactation. Every so often, a large midwife sailed past.

'Well, you never know, you see,' Lydia said, referring to her growing certainty that the very next person to appear in the corridor would be 'that Professor' she had read about last Thursday in the paper. 'Didn't *you* meet him once?'

Florence nodded weakly. She could see that her mother felt vindicated.

'And he's a widower,' Lydia added. 'Which is very sad.'

But the Professor of Neonatology was out of the hospital, giving a press conference, so the scene that Lydia had imagined did not arise. Instead they watched as dismal refreshments arrayed on two brown tea trays – Cornish pasties with dinosaur spines, white bread sandwiches that sagged and smeared their cling-film wrappings over-intimately – were sold, or rather not sold, from an aperture with a redundant rain canopy. Florence had already eaten. They decided to share a pot of tea for one, and to stave off the terror with a little humour. As they took turns with the cup, each time positioning it to avoid the other's lipstick trace, they kept repeating, in significant whispers which slightly thrilled them both, what the surgeon had said. As though they had not both been there at the time.

'He said the high pulse could be a sign the tube is just about to erupt.'

'And the pain may be worse than you realize.'

Since they were both capable of going on like this for hours, days even, about the most mundane events, the pair had a sense of the remarkable luck, the heaven-sent gift, as it were, of this plentiful new material.

'Actually, Flo,' her mother teased, 'you may have quite a severe case of Stoic Disposition.'

But they were cut short forty minutes later by the announcement of Florence's name.

'Florence? Florence Brown?'

With a sense of having been called to the podium, Florence and Lydia rose.

Two

In the small dark room Florence sat by a desk with a Gestapo lamp and was asked to confirm her DOB as 22.03.92 and supply her LMP. The light was making her eyes water.

'1992!' Lydia interrupted with mild outrage. 'I'd have been *fifty* by then!'

'It's not '92,' Florence explained, blinking. 'My date of birth is 22.03.77. What's an LMP?'

'First day of your Last Menstrual Period,' the sonographer replied, offering Florence one of the small blue boxes of tissues – a new one for each patient – piled neatly towards the back of the desk.

Florence pulled away the cardboard oval – easy enough. After some further effort, however, she seemed to be holding only the remnants of a former tissue. Then a great clump of the tissues emerged all at once, in one solid impenetrable fold.

'Do you know what date it was? Your LMP?'

The woman looked up encouragingly from her notes, and smiled so hard she seemed to have to shut her eyes at the same time.

'Oh!' Florence was sure about this one. It was the twenty-third of April, the day the builders started.

'So that would make you . . .'

The sonographer took a second to calculate. She wrote down a strange fraction – 6/40 – then stood and walked to the other side of the room. Using both hands she ripped a very wide sheet of pea-green paper energetically from a dispenser on the wall. The action was almost unnerving. Laying it over a thin maroon plastic mattress, she directed Florence to lie down on the table and pull up her shirt. The paper was slightly abrasive against Florence's palms. The patient shut her eyes and heard a jangling sound. It was the skating of metal rings on the metal pole, almost indecently joyful, as the woman drew a shower curtain across the length of the room. Just in case, she explained, anyone should happen to come in. Then the woman washed her hands and there was something like a small foghorn blast as the leg of a chair was pushed back. Really, Florence wanted to think of something other than what was happening. Alas, this only brought her to thoughts of Andy.

Andy Hunt was the owner of MyBuild, the recently established local company that Florence and her husband Robert were employing for the renovation of their Victorian home. And MyBuild, as Andy had explained to Florence on the first day, were setting out not only to transform individual properties and sites into domestic dwellings of exceptional character, but to transform the building trade itself. Unlike other building companies, they would not fail to turn up for work without notice. They would not leave you in the lurch with unfinished projects. They would not spend half their time on another job. Florence was pleased and everything was promising: the builder's frankness, his way of nodding confidently and laughing loudly, of moving his head and long neck about, very deliberately, as though expressing his grasp of the whole scope of the undertaking and exactly what it would take to achieve it. And of course his name, Andy, which encouraged confidence in an inevitable 'handiness'. Even, indeed, the builder's unexpectedly thin legs, in particular his ridiculous bony knees in their ridiculous shorts (clean pale denim, with proper sewn hems, not torn-off ends), spoke an appealing vulnerability that seemed decently English and home-owning. He looked as if he were welcoming you to his family barbecue. In short – and this was what Andrew really traded on – he was middle class. He was not gruff and rough. Homeowners could feel that it was more or less their own, well brought-up son working away quietly at the new patio or porch.

But now MyBuild *had* failed to turn up without notice, left them in the lurch without a toilet or a shower, and spent half their time on another, more lucrative project up the road. The day before yesterday, Andy was good enough to call in long after working hours (twenty past three) to explain why.

Firstly, he re-emphasized, it was not because they were just like all the other companies around.

'I wouldn't want you to think that. Because that's really not it. And it would be such a pity if you thought that, after the good start we've had here. The thing is . . .'

The thing was: they weren't, *generally* speaking, like other companies. They had just – *exceptionally* – appeared to behave like other companies, in this one, particular, sad, unfortunate instance. She understood that, didn't she?

'Are you cross?' Andy asked finally. 'Because I'd understand if you are. Are you cross and you don't like to say?'

Florence had shaken her head as gently as she could manage. Andy's moods were delicate and she did not want to give him an excuse not to return at all. Two weeks before, he became depressed by one of the folding French doors that were being stored under tarpaulin. He took it badly when four panes of the 'historic' glass (they had paid extra for glass that deliberately warped the view) shattered following an accidental encounter with his drill. Then he left for the rest of the day. So, in the interests of forward progress, and because she had never been any good at confrontation anyway, Florence consoled him with coffee from her Thermos. She listened as he confided that he had recently become the victim of his own success: now that his small business was earning more than ever before and he could draw a larger salary, he would soon have to pay income tax at the higher rate.

'It's like,' he'd said slowly, frowning, as though trying to express a very difficult formula in words, 'the harder I work and the more I earn, the more I'm being penalized, you know?'

Florence nodded sympathetically at the injured party, poured herself another cup of coffee and moved onto a second chocolate digestive. She heard more about the victimization of the British entrepreneur, and about MyBuild restoring – or rather, introducing, perhaps for the first time in its history – customer relations, customer choice and customer power to a profession notorious for its rudeness, dogmatism and inefficiency. She wondered, not for the first time, whether a surly manner might in fact be necessary for success in the building trade. Whether class might be inversely proportional to competence, after all.

'Chris should be here soon,' Andy added. 'So hopefully we'll be able to crack on. I hope you don't mind me telling you all this. It's just that I want you to know there's a very good reason for what's been happening here.'

Or not happening. After Chris arrived, Florence had heard some drilling – that was good – followed by a great shout of 'Oh *fuck*! It's leaking *everywhere* now!'

Yes, it would be better not to think of Andy or Chris or what could happen on a building site. She thought instead of her GP, who had sent her here this morning after their brief telephone conversation. 'Yes, I'm afraid it *could* be a miscarriage, Mrs Brown, because of the bleeding, and in this early type of miscarriage' (there were types? Apparently there were types) the 'issue' would be much like an ordinary period. There would be no discernible body parts – the point Florence had particularly wanted to clarify. But it would be better not to think of her GP either. The woman was elegant but unreliable. All of the books on the shelves in her office were called things like *Medicine – At A Glance*, *Prescribing Without Peril*, and *Doctoring In A Day*. And her watercolours were of louring navy skies and unpredictable shafts of light.

Reluctantly Florence's thoughts now returned to the monitor on her right and the woman who was quietly looking, clicking, moving – sometimes perched on the high chair, sometimes standing in her ballet pumps. With the scan stick she applied varying amounts of pressure to Florence's belly: it was like being investigated by an unusually inquisitive roll-on deodorant. After a few minutes she switched to a transvaginal probe in the hope of obtaining a clearer image. Lydia occupied a hard plastic chair to the left and offered bolstering smiles whenever Florence turned in that direction. Surely, Florence reasoned, the consultant surgeon was wrong. Her alarm at his words, her shooting pulse, had been momentary. Hopefully, *hopefully* the ultrasound scan would show that she was, despite the bleeding, still pregnant. She felt a surge of weepy joy at the idea. On the other hand – she said to herself, thinking it might be best not to get her hopes up too much – perhaps it would show that she had miscarried. This news would be sad but she would do her best to think of the scan as a sort of reverse pregnancy test – and try again next month. She had always liked to think of herself as a pragmatist.

'And you were very sure about your dates, weren't you,' the woman said, 'which would make you about six-and-a-half weeks?'

Florence nodded apprehensively.

'Well, I can't see anything that would correspond to that. Look for yourself,' she said, almost challengingly.

And so Florence looked at the monitor for the first time. It was true that the image did not in any way resemble the six-week-old embryo like a cashew nut she had found a few days before on the internet. She could make out the large, upside-down, partial cone shape, like the area cleared by her rear windscreen wiper. But as for what lay within those parameters – well, Florence Brown could make no sense of that at all.

'The womb certainly looks pregnant,' the sonographer continued. 'But what I'm seeing . . .'

With the very tip of an elaborately painted nail she pointed to a tiny spotty white area around an even tinier black hole. Florence tried to peer more closely, even hunched her shoulders, feeling surprised that they were really making a serious attempt to look at such a confined and minuscule area of the image. Surely one might as well examine outer space without a telescope.

'That might be a pregnancy sac of about four weeks, okay?' the sonographer explained.

'But the test?' Florence objected for the second time that morning. How feeble her protest sounded. 'The test showed I was pregnant *then*.' Pregnant, that was, with her husband Robert's baby. A pregnancy that should now be six-and-a-half weeks.

'Was it a very faint line?'

'No,' Florence replied, feeling increasingly agitated.

No, it was not. It was a thick blue indelible cross. Then she'd tried another brand and it was two pink lines – the universal sign, she fancied, for twin girls. One line was, admittedly, ever so slightly weaker than the other: but that must be the twin with the hypersensitive disposition like herself. Or perhaps the thicker line was the one with the stoical disposition like herself. Finally, when she used the most expensive of the tests, it had made the unambiguous statement 'Pregnant'.

'To get a positive result you must have been at least three-and-a-half weeks at the time you took it,' the sonographer said thoughtfully. 'But . . .'

But: there it was again.

'But this could be another pregnancy.'

Suddenly the woman looked excited, she looked as though she might pirouette, and it was always worrying when you excited the medical profession enough for them to pirouette. Florence could see the words 'Case Study' shining in the woman's eyes, closely followed by 'Clinical Trial', 'Research Cluster', 'Conference Paper', and 'Peer-Reviewed Dissemination Streams'. She turned to her mother, who looked equally pleased. Whether it was a four-week or six-week-old granddaughter was surely immaterial.

'Is that – *possible*?' Florence asked in disbelief.

'Oh yes,' the sonographer continued, smiling as she had when she first opened the door. 'You could have been pregnant at the time of the test, and at some later point your body *absorbed* –' she laid strange and unaccountable emphasis on this word – 'that pregnancy and then you fell pregnant again.'

The woman seemed weirdly thrilled by this idea of Florence's cannibalistic, infanticidal womb machine, and repeated the word 'absorbed' in one or two further sentences to the same effect. Florence hadn't realized that such things were possible. And Lydia definitely hadn't. No, in Lydia's day, you had sex the once or maybe it was twice, you began to vomit, and nine months later you no longer had a bathroom but a small launderette dedicated to servicing terry-towelling nappies. Suddenly, however, impregnation seemed less like a bodily event and more like a complex legal proceeding, with unfamiliar loopholes. Florence regretted not having taken professional advice about all of the possibilities first.

If it was four weeks, then it was Thomas's. Thomas Marvelle – the Professor her mother knew only from the paper – and all the expertise that Florence could ever have wanted. And if it was Thomas's . . .

'Of course,' the sonographer added, cutting across these thoughts, 'I can't be sure that what I'm seeing even *is* a pregnancy sac. There are all sorts of explanations. All sorts of possibilities we need to look into.'

All sorts? How many could there really be?

'What worries me now,' the woman continued by way of example, 'is your right ovary. I can definitely see an eighteen millimetre growth there.'

She pointed to the evidence but again Florence could only take her word for it.

'So what we could be looking at in the uterus is not a four-week pregnancy at all, but a pseudo-sac.'

She paused significantly.

'A *what*?' Florence asked.

'A pregnancy sac that's empty, because the pregnancy – the real embryo – is somewhere else.'

Lydia looked perplexed by the idea that her grandchild might be discovered, in the end, up one of her daughter's nostrils or curled around an eardrum.

'You mean like an ectopic pregnancy?' Florence asked, beginning to realize her situation.

She knew that an ectopic pregnancy occurred when the embryo implanted itself in the wrong place. Usually, as the consultant surgeon had speculated an hour earlier, it misplaced itself in one of the fallopian tubes. Meanwhile another, empty, pseudo-pregnancy sac continued to grow in the womb, sometimes for several weeks. But just occasionally, when there was someone like Florence around to provide the medical profession with variety, an ectopic embryo was discovered in an ovary instead.

'Once,' the sonographer said dreamily, 'we found it in the bowel.'

Whatever the location of the ectopic pregnancy, it was a medical emergency and the embryo could not be saved. 'In nature,' Florence had often heard Thomas say, 'an ectopic pregnancy is a disaster; in science, however, it's a solution.'

'Yes exactly,' the sonographer replied. 'An ectopic pregnancy. You'll have to discuss your options with one of our surgeons.'

Three

Professor Thomas J. Marvelle was notorious for writing *F*ck On*, a popular bestseller in the science of sex with an accompanying video. It made him a fortune. However, he would be remembered for inventing Wet Incubation – one of the greatest advances in medical technology that the twenty-first century would see.

This new technology was the most important development in neonatal medicine for decades. Everyone in the department thought that the Professor would surely be a candidate for the Nobel Prize. In the early years of the Wet Incubator's history, however, before it was adopted in hospitals throughout the Western world, Thomas had no illusions of glory. Whether his work took the form of a clinical experiment, journal article, or even, like *The Survival of the Foetus*, a book for general readers published to coincide with today's formal announcement of Wet Incubation to the world, this rule held infallibly true: it was always flawless and always denounced. Faultless and at fault. Usually, as the regional journalist who was the first to get hold of the story would say, it had been *widely* denounced. That was the trouble with being a man of genuine brilliance and professional integrity: Thomas's enemies were like his skin tags – acquired with ease, self-multiplying, and never truly shed. But nothing in his long and difficult career would ever compare to the controversy that surrounded Wet Incubation.

The Wet Incubator solved the problem of lungs. Florence remembered his explanations, which were always lucid and very certain. Extremely premature babies – especially those born before the twenty-fourth week of pregnancy – could not survive outside of the maternal body principally because their lungs were undeveloped. The lungs were the last major organ of the body to reach an adequate capacity in the womb. There were other problems of severe prematurity, of course, like low immunity, but having nothing to breathe with was, he said, the main obstacle. Infant Respiratory Distress Syndrome (RDS) had been at the centre of neonatalogical research for over half a century. After RDS claimed the brief life of Patrick Bouvier Kennedy, the firstborn of First Lady Jacqueline Kennedy, neonatology had developed into a fully professional and well-funded branch of medicine in the US. Across the Atlantic in Britain, the rise of neonatology – one of the great success stories of post-war medicine – coincided with Thomas's own career path.

Occasionally, there were astonishing cases of survival that required very little medical intervention. Several years before, Thomas had witnessed the case of Maria Alexandra Ramon. Born only twenty-one weeks and six days into the pregnancy, Maria Alexandra measured less than a pencil's length. But she breathed rather well. Professor Marvelle was not, however, entirely persuaded that this *was* quite the exception it appeared to be. Ultrasound scans were used to make educated guesses about how long women had been pregnant. The resulting gestational estimates were exactly that – estimates. Only a glance at Maria Alexandra's sweet diminutive parents, who had given Thomas a bottle of Freixenet cava when their daughter was delivered and another, larger bottle, when she was discharged, told you why the baby girl was so very small. Neither parent was above five-feet-two. Thomas had once treated a newborn with a hereditary form of pituitary dwarfism who was no more than eleven inches by the end of her first year.

Still, whether Maria Alexandra was twenty-one weeks or twenty-two or as much as twenty-four, she was clearly a very young baby. And even after the twenty-fourth week of pregnancy, foetal lungs were so severely underdeveloped that almost all premature babies needed help to breathe as soon as they were born. Many continued to suffer from respiratory problems for life. If they were lucky, they were sent home with oxygen tanks several times their own size. If unlucky, they were transferred in due course from the neonatal unit to a paediatric ward. There they would serve out the rest of their life sentence – ventilated, tubed, suctioned – behind the bars of a hospital cot. Sometimes visited frequently by their parents. Sometimes not.

But helping a baby's lungs to breathe was one thing. You couldn't help what didn't even exist. As Florence understood it, ordinary neonatal incubators were of no use in such cases and the picture had not changed in more than a dozen years. It was just bad luck if you were born a fortnight too soon. The boundary of human viability seemed pretty well-established. Foetuses born before the twenty-fourth week of pregnancy were highly unlikely to survive. And even less likely to avoid debilitating health conditions, whether mental or physical or both. Twenty-four weeks was the point at which the foetus had a fifty per cent chance of long-term survival. Experts accordingly spoke of the limits of foetal viability as having been 'reached'. The British Medical Association described, with more latitude, a 'threshold of viability' between twenty-two and twenty-six weeks. There was increasing reluctance to name a particular week. Not because there had been a few unexpected survivors like Maria Alexandra. But because of the ethical significance of those exceptions in legal rulings and arguments about abortion.

A foetus could not be legally aborted once it was capable of surviving outside of its mother's body. Except, that is, in very rare circumstances like endangerment of the mother's own life. But 'capable of surviving' meant capable of surviving *with the help of technology*. 'Albeit with artificial aid' was the phrase used in the landmark *Roe v. Wade* trial in the United States Supreme Court. In the UK, abortion had once been permitted up to the twenty-eighth week of pregnancy. Now it was permissible only until the twenty-fourth. Not because babies had got any better at surviving a delivery between the twenty-fourth and twenty-eighth weeks of pregnancy on their own strength. Only because the technology now existed in neonatal units to support such early life. There were incubators and ventilators and phototherapy machines. Pro-choicers, Thomas had told her, worried that improved neonatal care would continually push the boundary of viability backwards and soon women would not be allowed to have abortions at all. In fact, the EPIcure study had shown that the more sophisticated neonatal interventions of recent years improved the life prospects of those born at twenty-four weeks and later. But it made no impact on younger foetuses. It was the problem of lungs that prevented any further movement backwards. A problem that was now going to be solved by Thomas Marvelle and the Wet Incubator.

Other doctors were still working to refine the existing technology. Oxygen saturation level trials, for example, were currently underway. Today, however, Florence's lover was announcing his new invention to the world's press. The Wet Incubator was designed to replicate conditions inside the uterus favourable to the development of human respiration. Lungs could grow to the desired capacity. A nice honeycomb, wet with surfactant, could develop before the foetus was transferred to an ordinary incubator. Or 'dry' incubator, as they would from now on be known. As the name suggested, the Wet Incubator kept the foetus immersed, in a state analogous to its uterine experience, rather than taxing underdeveloped lungs with air or even pressure-controlled oxygen. It was 'a sort of artificial ectopic pregnancy, if you like,' she had heard Thomas say at least a dozen times. Deliberately engineered to allow human gestation to continue 'outside the womb' – the literal meaning of 'ectopic', and an irony that was not lost on Florence Brown as she sat waiting to talk to the Kenyan surgeon again.

Behind Lydia, a wall of windows gave onto a small concrete courtyard. A single plant in the central pot, with wide, once-spiky leaves, had collapsed from dehydration and now looked like a dead sea monster. Lydia was riffling through the reading material on the coffee table – magazines for anyone who wanted to hold views on garden gnomes, or the optimal number of bridesmaids. A moment later a smiling Indian woman emerged from Ultrasound 2B with her husband, carefully cradling in her palms what was evidently a scan image of her baby. Florence returned to her own thoughts.

An artificial ectopic pregnancy was of no help when you were dealing with a real one. The Wet Incubator could not do anything for an embryo of a mere four or six weeks. The new technology was, however, going to push the boundary of human viability back to twenty weeks. Perhaps a little further, it was too soon to tell. A huge bioethical debate would erupt, Thomas said. But it would just have to be borne.

It was at this point in his explanations that Thomas often became irritated. His stormy chat, his pacing about Florence's house (or, sometimes, the pied-à-terre he kept near the hospital) and particularly the stories he told of his misunderstood career, were intimate and compelling. Having no very strong ideas herself on the subject of neonatal intervention – or hospital administration, or ethics committees – it was easy for Florence to side with Thomas's views. To be sympathetically outraged, to nod, to agree that he was absolutely right. And he was so much cleverer than her that she was flattered, even long after they had become lovers, to be taken into his confidence like this. She thought of it as an aspect of his love for her: generously he assumed that she was his equal and spoke as though curating the local history museum was really an equivalent career to his. Or would be, one day.

Her mind wandered back inevitably to the present situation. What if it wasn't an ectopic pregnancy? What if she really *was* pregnant with his baby? It wasn't difficult to guess what he would want. But what did she want?

She imagined him now, blinded by the photographers, a little nervous and pink-faced, yet controlled and clear as he explained something useful. Perhaps that Wet Incubation would not replace the use of prenatal corticosteroids. Nothing could be better, not to mention cheaper, than keeping the baby inside its mother for as long as possible. However, the technology could be used in cases where it was too late to delay labour by administering tocolytics. Or in cases when those drugs would not gain the lungs enough time to develop adequately. For time was what lungs needed most. Lungs began like a child's drawing of a tree. A mere trunk and main branches. Trachea and splanchnic mesoderm, that was all. But give them time and they sprouted with the complexity of inlaid medieval carving. Lobes, terminal bronchioles, distal airways, epithelial cells and, finally, alveoli. Or, to use Thomas's preferred analogy, lungs began as stumps. But time revealed them as the stumps of angels' wings and then the incredible thing happened at last: lift-off.

Four

While Florence spoke, the Kenyan surgeon held his head delicately aslant, nodding fractionally as though listening to an especially fine passage of music.

'So an ectopic pregnancy is what?' Florence asked. Despite – or rather because of – the circumstances, Florence caught herself behaving like her mother again, and almost enjoying all the drama for a moment. 'The appendicitis of gynaecology?'

Obviously it was nowhere near as grave as appendicitis. But it would be nice to be able to say afterwards, when the anecdotes were being told.

'I'm afraid it's much worse than that,' the surgeon replied. 'It would be like your aorta rupturing. There would be . . . well, let's just say, *massive* internal bleeding. That's why we need to act quickly.'

'Her *aorta*!' Lydia gasped. It sounded bad.

Florence felt herself go pale and looked away. Her eye caught the shelf behind the surgeon's head, where her urine sample had been placed. More blood than urine, and foaming around the edges, it looked like a tiny lava explosion.

The surgeon was busy explaining that they could take a conservative approach to intervention and measure her blood levels over a forty-eight-hour period.

'But I don't believe we have time for that,' he said, smiling. 'In fact

I would like to operate as soon as possible. Have you eaten anything this morning?'

'Only a *pain au chocolat*,' Florence replied. *Deux*, actually.

'Okay, well as I say I'm pretty sure this is ectopic, and if it is . . .'

The surgeon jiggled his shoulders painfully. Thomas always said that surgeons erred on the side of not being sued – better too many operations than too few. And she had no desire for unnecessary surgery. One of her stepfather George's phrases came to mind: *Never let them cut you open. Not if you can help it*. But when the Kenyan added that there was a seventy per cent possibility of death if Florence did not consent to an immediate operation, it seemed not in Florence's own best interests to urge the counter-view.

'All right,' he offered, standing up to leave the room, 'I'm going to give you five minutes to decide, okay?'

The women looked at each other.

'Well, my darling?' Lydia enquired theatrically, taking her daughter's hand into her own, with a sense that this was her moment: Robert was bound to turn up sooner or later and then her importance in the situation would be correspondingly diminished. But for now, she was the one who had answered the early telephone call, the one who had driven Florence to the hospital this morning, the one who was sitting here in this room, where it was all happening.

Less than two minutes later, the surgeon was back again. 'It's a surgeon's five minutes,' he explained. 'Have you decided?'

They nodded.

'You're going ahead?' he surmised correctly. 'Good.'

He sat down behind the desk.

'So. Assuming we find an ectopic, we'll remove the whole ovary.'

The surgeon continued to speak as he took out of the drawer a

23

mint-green sheet of paper with pre-printed columns. He began to write in flowing black letters.

'All I need to know now is what you want to do about, we call them, "the Retained Products of Conception".'

Florence frowned.

'Yes I know,' he said, mistaking her incomprehension for offence. 'It's a diabolical way of putting it, but we've never been able to come up with a better one. There's a very small chance that if our diagnosis is wrong and we *don't* find an ectopic, that it might be a four-week-old pregnancy sac instead. So do you want us to leave it, or do you want us to clear the uterus? Because if we leave it and it isn't a viable pregnancy – it's unlikely to be viable – I'm afraid you may have to come back for a second operation in a couple of weeks.'

This second operation, a D&C (dilation and curettage), would be necessary to evacuate the uterus of 'the Retained Products of Conception' as they were known, and thus prevent infections that could affect her future pregnancy prospects. Florence pretended to confer with her mother, as if it were *University Challenge*.

'Do you want to phone Robert?' Lydia suggested.

'No.'

'I really do have to know,' the surgeon urged. 'The thing is, if we find out that it's not what we think, I can't exactly wake you up and ask you what you want!'

'Will it be you doing the operation, then?' Florence asked.

The surgeon checked his watch. 'Yes, I'll still be on. And I think it would be much more humane for you, Florence. But please,' the surgeon hurried them, making no offer to leave the room this time, 'I have to know what you want.'

He rested his elbows on the table, making a prayerful wedge of his hands, and looked at her intently.

24

At last there seemed to be an element of choice, a matter that Florence Brown could actually do something about, a decision that she was, in fact, required to make. Once again she cast her mind back a fortnight. She saw Thomas, pink and happy, coming through the front door. It was mid-afternoon. The builders had gone and Robert was at work.

'Hello,' she'd said. 'I'm pregnant.'

He beamed. 'I thought you might be. Hello,' he added shyly, touching her belly very lightly with an index finger.

'It's Robert's.'

'Ah. You're quite sure? Because it can be difficult—'

'I'm sure.' In fact, she had made sure. 'You were away for two weeks.'

'So I was.' His next words were sad. 'And a little ambiguity would have been so nice.'

But there was no ambiguity. Not that day. Upstairs they removed their clothes, as usual, without ceremony. On the satin stripe pillows they said 'hello' again, laughing fondly, for this was where they really found each other. She said at least there was no need to be careful any more. He tried to warn her that it was never safe, in his experience, that he had only to look at a woman with lust in his eyes . . . but she just laughed. And then it had aroused her to think of him, yes, as her impregnator. The term was deliberately chosen. She liked to think of words to come to. She remembered that, entering her, he had spoken very gently – and so what he said was all the more surprising, and stirring. 'Now try to stop me. Close your fanny up. But I'm coming in anyway.'

This tender violence had brought her to the destination. That day, the next day, and every day (until the arrival of the inevitable thrush) for about a week. And now there was ambiguity. Lots of it. Four weeks, six weeks, the wrong man's baby, not a baby at all.

'Well?' the surgeon pressed.

'Can thrush cause a miscarriage?' Florence asked instead of answering his question. 'I had thrush soon after I conceived.'

'No,' he replied. 'Not unless it's left untreated and leads to a urine infection. Then there's a possibility . . . Are you still experiencing symptoms?'

'No.'

'Well, that's all right then. Now what do you want to do?'

I'm sorry, little person, Florence Brown thought. Loving another man was one thing. Planting a cuckoo in your husband's nest was quite another. Procreation was permanent. Damage that could not be undone. It involved other people. Not least, the procreated. Lydia's husband George Morley was not Florence's biological father and she knew the difference it made. Most of all, though, it was Robert's baby that she really wanted. And she had fallen pregnant so fast – in the very first month of trying, when she had been prepared for a long wait – that she took her fertility for granted as she made the decision. She wasn't a woman who was desperate for a baby at all costs and having Thomas's would, she feared, bring with it too many complications. However, here was an immediate solution, presented under the guise of a sensible medical decision. If she asked them to clear the uterus now, she would avoid the small matter of the second operation and the large matter of bearing another man's child if the pregnancy turned out to be viable after all.

She would never have to know, and nor would anyone else. That was what made the decision possible, even easy. It wasn't like asking for an abortion, when you knew for certain that you were pregnant. And if she let this opportunity go, she doubted that she would manage to go through with an abortion, should one be needed, at a later stage. In fact, she knew she would not. She loved Thomas. She would not destroy their child in cold blood. Instead she might have to end the affair (but how strange to call it that!) as the only possible way of reconciling herself and Robert. Because she loved Robert too, of course, and she could already feel the guilt and the jealousy poised to engulf the happiness of her life.

The surgeon twisted the form around for her to read and Florence Brown quickly signed her consent to the surgeries about to be performed on her and her acceptance of the hazards – infection, surgical damage, reaction to General Anaesthetic – that could leave her infertile or incontinent or something worse: vegetative, perhaps.

'As long as you're quite *sure* . . .' Lydia said doubtfully.

And at the same time Florence Brown signed, technically speaking, the death warrant of the four-weeker who might be inside her. In fact, not technically speaking, in the eyes of some – particularly the pamphlet distributors of the Society for the Protection of the Pre-Born she had seen on her way into the hospital that morning. Not technically, but literally, deliberately, unforgivably. She was sorry but all the same she was going in for an undercover abortion, for what effectively amounted to a termination. However, she reminded herself, *no one would know.* Even her left hand could not be certain what her right hand was now doing. Not even, or especially not, Thomas. He was safely away giving interviews. Instead, everyone would simply believe she had miscarried. So at least something was going to be simple.

Yes: amazingly, fortunately, fucking luckily, in fact, no one – not even the surgeon who performed it – would ever suspect.

Five

There were times when Florence Brown thought that her whole life had been determined by the outcome of the Post Office/Berol Pen Letter Writing Competition she had entered in 1986 when she was nine years old. As though the events that would one day lead her out of that Kenyan surgeon's office, and on to all the horror and scandal that lay beyond, were part of an already perceptible pattern. The papers would try to investigate her early life, of course. They would even interview school and university acquaintances. But what they discovered was scarcely worth the reporting.

In 1986 young Florence waited many weeks to learn the result of her competition submission, each morning patiently dismayed by the arrival of George's gas bills and Lydia's catalogue parcel orders – until the day in 1987 when the Certificate of Merit arrived in a hard-backed brown envelope with a trim. But it was neither the splendid triumph she had been dreaming of, nor the woeful failure she had been dreading. It was something else altogether. The document certified, not her talents of letter composition, but the skilfulness of her calligraphy. (All entries had to be written with a calligraphy pen.) 'In the opinion of the appointed judges, the handwriting demonstrated by Florence A. Morley on the occasion of the 1986 Post Office/Berol Pen Letter Writing Competition was worthy of merit.' Florence hadn't even known that the calligraphy was going to be judged, so at first she didn't know whether she felt more disappointed or pleased by the unexpected bonus. Pleased, she soon decided. And also slightly puzzled by the enclosed advertising pamphlet for Berol calligraphy pens.

She told the news only to Selena Johnson from school, and then they resumed conversation about the machine. The machine, which was always spoken of in urgent, furtive whispers, was the one with wooden spoons and other apparently innocent apparatus that parents in fact used for hurting their children. Florence, who had never been chastised by either parent, could not remember who had mentioned the machine first – only that they both talked about it immediately, incessantly, and with utter conviction. These conversations were restricted to one of two locations: either the grassy incline to the rear of a corrugated-roof carport used for pushchairs and bicycles, or the end of a long, low, rectangular shrub bed, with burgundy plants, at the furthest point of the playground. Each day the technology and the rules for its operation got more elaborate. And each day they thought of more daring things to say to each other about it. The machine smacked you with your knickers off. It could do it with them on, of course, but knickers off was the proper procedure, Florence said, looking across the school field to the closest and most significant landmark – a gigantic hedge encircling a tree. In the summer months they were allowed to play on the field and it was possible to run in and out of the hedge. A few weeks before, for a combination of esoteric and ecological reasons, Florence had appointed herself Guardian of the Chief Portal – a hole in the hedge used to access its inner warren. The idea was that the joy of the hedge must be preserved for future generations. The trouble was, this meant stopping anyone, including herself, from enjoying it now. Worse, there wasn't even very much stopping to be done. She had envisaged great battles, with the forces of the future and of culture pitched fiercely against the reckless libertinism and philistinism of the present, right up until the very moment the teacher's whistle should blow. Instead, whenever she said, 'I am Guardian of the Chief Portal and ye shall not enter!' the other children replied agreeably, 'All right, then!' and skipped on. She never even got to deliver her speech. She could only stand by and watch as everyone else ran around and skipped and shrieked and enjoyed themselves as far away from the hedge as possible.

The smacking machine was much more fun. By the next day the machine had a sophisticated audiovisual monitoring system so parents could see even when their children were being naughty in secret. Did the one at Selena's house have the same functions? Florence asked, spreading her arms and helicoptering down the incline. Solemn and excited, Selena nodded. Yes and it was dreadful, simply dreadful, that such a machine existed, they murmured feverishly to each other for the rest of the lunch break. But what were they to do? they said, wide-eyed, sighing, happily aghast. They were simply powerless while the machine did things to them.

It was only a few days later that Florence made her remarkable discovery about Enid Blyton. The authoress had written a book that went quite beyond her usual remit. Florence was a long-time admirer of the Famous Five and even of the Fabulous Four. In fact, she had noticed that when Blyton concentrated her efforts on fewer characters, or, better still, limited the number of books within a series, the results were markedly better. Florence's two favourite Blyton series were the Naughtiest Girl in the School and The Magic Faraway Tree. These consisted, so far as she was able to judge from the shelves of the school library, of only three volumes each. But now a standalone Blyton volume had come into her hands and Florence had the sense of stumbling across the masterwork.

Indeed, it was not even a whole volume. *Tales of Long Ago* divided into two quite distinct halves. The latter was about some Blyton characters Florence had not come across before, like Sinbad the sailor, and who did not hold her interest quite as intensely as the first half had. For that part was a small miracle. When Florence read of a mortal boy riding the chariot of the sun, of a king whose touch turned everything to gold, of a sculpture that came to life, she knew she was in the presence of an incredible talent. Sometimes women called on a goddess called Lorna to help them have their babies. Powerful gods kiss-chased beautiful and unwilling girls. They chased them hard, Blyton explained, because they were so keen to marry them. They had to catch the girls up before their bodies were transformed into rivers or trees. This seemed to be the way of the world: before you could ever quite get there, it had changed into something else anyway. In Florence's experience of the game, if the boys ever *did* catch up with you, they simply became embarrassed and ran away. These gods seemed more determined about the pursuit. What a genius Blyton was! What a triumph!

By the time Florence realized her mistake, her own kiss-chasing days were quite over. Puberty came early and dealt the usual death blow to another promising sexual fantasist. She even stopped watching *Carry On* films. Finally, in her thirteenth year, Florence fell unsuccessfully in love, one lunchtime, with a boy who was clever and curly haired and said the most astounding things. For instance, he said that Emmanuel Blasco, whom practically no one had heard of, was a very much better painter than his famous cousin Picasso. Later Florence learned that this was quite untrue, but at the time such unconventional judgement impressed her deeply. And the curly boy was very free with the word 'orgasm', which she heard for the first time from his rosebud lips. Learning that Florence was in love with him, he promptly punched her in the arm and, just to be clear, arranged for his best friend to repeat the action in the mathematics corridor, a site of particular anarchy, the following afternoon. Florence was further pained when, in their fifteenth year, her curly boy began fucking his way through a pile of bodies which were discernibly uglier than even she appeared in the mirror. Pained and wholly baffled. Still, Florence understood that being on the pile was not necessarily pleasanter. Selena Johnson was quite high up the pile and would sigh each time he came around for what she termed – with a bitter, daring candour that left Florence marvelling – 'a casual fuck'. And that was how Florence knew that Selena must adore the curly boy utterly too. Her own severance from the male half of humanity was, however, certain. A fact to be borne, like any other terminal illness, and without indulging unlikely hopes of remission.

When she was seventeen and ugly, Florence applied to read Fine Art and Museum Studies at the University of St Andrews. The rambling Victorian house where some of the admissions candidates were accommodated overnight had enormous stack chimneys and a series of late and disfiguring architectural additions that had Florence and other pious interviewees bemoaning the loss of the building's 'integrity'. Interview timetables were Sellotaped to two large green chalkboards in the centre of the waiting room. Candidates were advised to consult them frequently in case of last-minute changes. In the event there were no changes, last-minute or otherwise, only a continual flurry of checker-uppers obscuring Florence's own view of the board.

Then a rival candidate leaned forward and opined that it was really only a matter of showing them how 'nice and friendly' you were. He was wearing a black blazer with cream chino trousers, and had spent his summer holidays travelling Wales by tandem. Instantly and rather shrewdly, Florence thought, she had penetrated his false lead and as he sat back she wondered how the wastrel thought he stood a chance.

She won a scholarship. The following September, she met the boy in the blazer again, this time at a champagne-and-haggis reception for freshers convened in an eighteenth-century music room.

'Of course!' he grinned, beckoning and standing up. Florence started. 'I knew you would be here,' he said, dropping to a whisper. '*You told them what I told you to say.*'

Florence frowned as he continued.

'Don't you remember, how I suggested that you come back to my hotel room? And how we had a glass of wine? And then we discussed, oh, what would it have been . . . ?'

He had been talking with his head bent but now looked up enquiringly in a way that said, quite unambiguously, *Over to you*.

Florence swallowed. She had no social talent, nor even competence. She had analysed social discourse for how it was done and arrived at certain conclusions. For starters, she was willing to admit freely (to herself) that she could not do it. But then she would insist with equal force that she did not especially *wish* to do it. After all, why would you? At a formal reception like this, for instance, so far as she had been able to ascertain, conversation was a game of cards. Generally, it was a matter of Snap! One person mentioned an unfortunate incident once with quail in France and you mentioned yours. In its favour, Snap! was an easy game. It was clear what you had to match – although chicken in Portugal might have to do, and though it was perplexing why you should want to anyway. Generally the chosen topics were not very interesting, and it was difficult to see how multiplying the examples could assist. Not in its favour, then, was the fact that Snap! was dull.

But sometimes, social conversation was not Snap! Sometimes,

it was Poker. The rival candidate's demand that Florence should remember going to his room, where she had never been, to discuss whatever it was they didn't discuss, was a clear case of Poker. And no amount of listening to other people's conversations had ever taught her the rules of Poker.

'Yes, that's right,' he was saying, when Florence failed to reply. 'And tell me: do you still hold to your view of Ovid?'

Florence was unaware that she knew Ovid (even in bowdlerized form) at all. Still less that she had ever formulated 'a view' of the Roman poet from which to have the luxury to depart. She replied that he must be mistaking her for someone else. The wastrel in the blazer was very insistent, however, that he was not. Several of the candidates – successful and unsuccessful – were well known to him. In fact, one of them, he said, pointing to a very beautiful Ethiopian girl, was his girlfriend. And they had plans to marry, but only after Finals and getting jobs of course.

Florence immediately recognized her as the girl who lived in the tiny study bedroom directly above her own. People who had been at boarding school with her said that she was troubled by dreams and voices, which sounded rather grand and fashionable. On the first day Florence had called around to share loneliness. Superfluously, as it turned out, because Miss Fiancée had a visiting friend called something like Clementine. Photographs of other friends lined the shelves like Christmas cards. These gave evidence of the girl's frequent presence at such events as parties, skiing holidays and picnics – and of the giddy happiness of all those involved. Already Florence knew they would never be friends. Eventually Florence would discover that she preferred lovers to friends, but her insecure eighteen-year-old self could hardly foresee this as she watched Miss Fiancée and 'Clementine' busily unpacking a large CD collection.

Somehow the little plastic boxes exuded the coolness of second-hand vinyl. An emerald throw flaunted itself on an iron bedstead that would otherwise have been identical to the one in Florence's room. Later, in privacy, Florence ventured a pathetic rivalry with a thin navy scarf. She scanned the room for other comparisons – absorbing, in particular, the impact of a nicer kettle.

'No.' The wastrel in the blazer was screwing up his eyes now. 'No, I really can't remember what you said about our Publius Naso.'

Then he added, as though it were his own accomplishment, that Fredericka's father worked on the first three seconds of the universe. In a mental trade-off for dignity, Florence made a solid determination: read more classics. It was certain that the blazer was playing games with her, and as she turned off the reading lamp that night and failed to sleep, she felt desperate to think of something clever to say the next time she saw him. Some terrific intellectuals' put-down. Some wry misquotation of T.S. Eliot, perhaps: 'I am struggling to hear the footfalls we never made echo in my memory.' Some snappy reply: 'Actually, I find the last three seconds of the universe more pressing.'

But it was too late for that and besides, Florence Brown knew she never would.

The blazer was never so boldly fictitious again. But if he met Florence in the street, he would enquire elaborately as to whether he might carry her books. If they met in the university library queue, he would ask her why she looked so furtive (*he* looked furtive), and whether she was taking 'any dirty ones' out. Florence knew she should have laughed. She should have said, 'You have an optimistic view of the library holdings.' Instead, incapacitated by shame, she managed nothing. These questions must be a mockery of her sexual status: viz., well beyond the bounds of consideration.

Meantime the fiancée lived on, exquisitely, upstairs. One Saturday afternoon Florence saw her returning to her room with pink and orange paper shopping bags. Two minutes later, however, she was back downstairs, knocking on Florence's door, and somehow Florence was then upstairs. Really it was all quite extraordinary. 'Clementine' was not there. Florence had an idea of her always being there, handily available in the wardrobe, for friendship as required, but in fact she wasn't. And then, for some reason Florence could never recall, not so much as a moment later – because what succeeded it was so extraordinary – Florence found one of the girl's art postcards in her lap. The girl must have put it there. Florence must have gazed long at the message on the reverse.

A love inscription: fulsome, devoted – even – so far as the handwriting went – *curly*. Florence commented, with an awe in her voice that conceded she was no judge of these things, on the splendour of the relic. And Miss Fiancée (most extraordinarily of all) replied lightly that he was her boyfriend – fiancé, in fact – and yes it was 'all very sweet' of him . . . oh! Florence's brain was just gasping! To be in a position to *condescend* to a love token was a magnificence (Florence knew no other word) such as she had not hitherto observed but perhaps, now, would! What treasuries of love letters must the girl have! What munificence – like change casually left, the amount unchecked, for the waiter. Miss Fiancée wasn't merely 'having sex'. And oh to be *merely* 'having' it. Or indeed in any other grammatical relationship to it. No, she was having *cultured* sex.

There were other evidences. Chief among them, the ownership of the red satin strapless bra. Florence knew about this because of an occasion, some weeks before, when they'd met in the laundry. Finding Miss Fiancée glamorously there, sprinkling washing powder into the top loader like a celebrity pastry cook, Florence had confided that it would cost at least twenty pounds to buy underwear suitable for an off-the-shoulder ballgown. The engaged girl paused and volunteered to lend hers.

'I don't know if it will be any good,' Miss Fiancée remarked, 'size-wise. I'm only an A cup.'

Of course, Florence could not use it. It was in the genius of this girl, however, to make small breasts seem the advantage. One sensed that she existed on a different scale from all other girls. Like a great gleaming statue, she had huge intense eyes and long strong legs surely designed for bounding over mountains.

In her dealings with Florence, the fiancée seemed to lurch between kindness and contempt. She advised Florence usefully on their university tutors: the art lecturer Gerald Rutkin was past his sell-by date, she said, in fact he was due to retire. So Florence wasn't to worry about what Rutkin said, nor the junior lecturer who had pondered the difference between Modernist and Modernism. The boy in the blazer agreed. It was all just mental masturbation, merely 'an intellectual wank', she'd overheard him saying once, and this sounded very advanced to Florence (somewhere in the territory of ESP) although she could tell that was not how he meant it.

In fact, Florence hadn't fished about down there *at all*. But then a couple of awkward moments with Rutkin forced it on her.

Practically every week, Gerald Rutkin talked about orgasms in art. The rapt expression on the face of Bernini's Theresa was an inevitable favourite. Then he would make his way over to Florence's easel and ask her questions (about orgasm in art, or orgasm in general) that she couldn't possibly answer. Really it was difficult to see what relation orgasm bore to Florence's pencil study of the sarcophagus and canopy of the tomb of Mastino II della Scala at Verona. Even when she moved on to her Gryphon bearing the North Shaft of the West Entrance to the Duomo, the connection remained tenuous.

All the same, Florence thought her work might begin to suffer if she did not at least find out what the celebrated sensation was actually like.

Like?! Nothing else ever! her body sang in reply.

It went like this. Florence drew the floral curtains. (Her breathing became more rapid.) She locked the outer bedroom door and the inner. She pulled up her skirt and pulled down damp knickers, sloughing her tights off with them. Then she sat on the bed leaning her back against the ice cream coloured wall. Florence had read twice over *The Pink Book: A Female Undergraduate's Guide To Sex* and now, to avert 'the trouble that so many women experience of "letting go"' – a comment she confused with Christian's burden in *The Pilgrim's Progress*, which she knew particularly well from GCSE – Florence imagined hurling away her backpack. That done, she prepared herself to tumble most deliciously over 'the precipice'. Forty-three minutes later, Florence had discovered

Everything. Her index finger was at the centre of an explosion, from which the universe radiated outward.

Florence was busy for a good six months. She had discovered the secret of life and naturally it took up all of her time. Her work began to suffer. For the first time in her life, she did not achieve an A-grade in the end-of-year exams. Semi-permanently at 'the plateau stage', as the guidebook called it, what did she care for the interruptions of essays, or, indeed, the cleaner?

'You're looking happy these days – things going well?' he asked half-scornfully as he bent to empty the small bin outside her door one day.

He was wearing short trousers with a pleat and turn-up, and had a social habit of saliva-slicking his eyebrows. Florence nodded non-committally as he tucked the white bin liner back into place.

'Well, anyway, you wouldn't believe it if I told you what's happened now!'

Florence raised her eyebrows to the all-ears position.

'I've been asked to do another building.'

Florence was briefly hopeful. 'Really?'

'Oh yes.'

'Instead of this one?'

'Instead!' he scoffed at such simple-mindedness. '*Instead!* They can't get anyone, can they, so they come to me, they say can *I* do that one *as well*? *I don't know* – I'm run off my feet as it is!'

And there he stood, arms akimbo with indignation, elbow propped on a Hoover tentacle.

'You want any Hoovering?' he asked, dangling the nozzle propositionally.

'It's all right, I've got my own Hoover now.'

'Well, tell me how you are anyway. Did I tell you it's my birthday tomorrow?'

Yes, what did she care for him!

Or, for that matter, the marriageable Ethiopian who lived upstairs on skinny slices of reconstituted turkey and individual bottles of Strathlomond mineral water. Occasionally Florence would hear screaming in the middle of the night. *Sexual delight? Or the old dreams and voices come back to trouble Her tragically beautiful Majesty?* Florence would think impatiently as she put a pillow over her head and tried to sleep. Sometimes the girl asked Florence whether she wanted to go with 'them' into town. Whoever *they* were. Florence didn't. When it *was* absolutely necessary to go out, it now astonished her to see so many people shopping for bread and other trivia (and what a deal of time they spent pulling packets off the shelf, groping their softness, weighing earnestly whether indeed this was the loaf for them!) when they might have been in their beds on the plateau or even the precipice instead. The engaged girl also asked Florence (rhetorically – she liked giving Florence rhetorical instruction), didn't she think that people were just *meant* to be together and wasn't it all terrifically natural? And several times a day Florence would see the girl and the blazer walking about, arm-in-arm, or hand-in-hand, grinning ecstatically, like an advertisement for this new creed. When they got to their first class with Gerald Rutkin's replacement, however, the girl behaved unforgivably and thereafter Florence took pleasure only in finding more reasons to hate her.

Everyone had been asked to write short essays about symbolism in High Italian Renaissance painting. The new tutor told them to look out for things like finches in images of the Madonna and Child: why were the birds there? What did they mean? Florence already knew they were symbols of Christ's later death. As though the painting were shaking its head gloomily and predicting: 'Well, Jesus may look like a cute little babby right now, but there's bad stuff coming up, you mark my finches.'

With luck, she wouldn't be asked about the meaning of the Cyclops. According to *The Penguin Dictionary of Symbols*, 'One eye in the middle of the forehead betrays either the ebbing of the intellect, or its burgeoning.' Well – which? They might as well say: 'We know it means *some*thing, we just haven't a scoobies *what*.' Then Miss Fiancée suggested that Florence come to her room after supper (they called it supper), the night before the class, and discuss what they'd written. Or mostly, as it turned out, what Florence had written. Florence sat on the emerald throw, while the blazer took the window seat. She said she found such symbols a little ridiculous, but that one could hardly

40

expect Realism (she brought this textbook word into conversation shyly) back then, right? Miss Fiancée nodded encouragingly. Thank goodness! – Florence thought – for Miss Fiancée! She carried on talking, expecting the girl to know whether the argument sounded suitable. And again Miss Fiancée nodded and murmured approvingly as though it did.

When Florence duly trotted out the same points in the class, however, the bitch now sighed deeply.

'What are *you* sighing about?' the new tutor, noticing, demanded immediately.

'Oh,' she said hesitantly, 'well, I wasn't . . . aware of it. But what I wanted to say is . . .'

And what she said was just like how she dressed and walked and even screamed: immeasurably more sophisticated than anything Florence could manage.

'These symbols *are* realistic. So when you get a little finch fluttering by the baby Jesus, the finch is meant to represent His Passion. But it still looks just like a lovely little finch. In other words: it's a symbol, yet it's also realistic – ravishingly so. It's like,' she added superfluously, 'two things at once.'

Their new teacher nodded, pleased by this pretty little paradox – which was, Florence soon discovered, exactly the sort of thing that really got people going at university, but for some curious reason she could not so easily discover. The tutor exchanged a glance of mutual excitement with the blazer. As much as to say, '*Terrific* shot, huh?!' And when Florence checked the expression on the blazer's face he was, indeed, grinning away at the pure intellectual pleasure of it too. Florence was very much mystified but she liked their tutor being pleased almost as much as she liked him rebuking the girl for sighing. And every so often, Florence would remember the inscription on the reverse of the engaged girl's postcard, and sigh a little to herself. Ah! To be loved like that!

But that was before Florence met Robert, the love of her life.

Or Thomas, the other love of her life.

Six

I wrote to you before.

It was after we left the bar and stood outside looking at each other in the street. After we didn't kiss. After I didn't run after you. After I regretted it. And then I went home.

Home to you. And I didn't regret that.

Another day I was trying to cross the road. And there you were. As though by the grace of the universal choreography. Some chess manoeuvre of the angels too complex to fathom.

Without a word you took my arm and then, as if we were waiting for the beat, you said, 'not now' – there was a bus, a cyclist, a coach – 'yes now'. And in the narrow interval we escaped.

'Can I buy you a drink?' you said.

'Will it take long?' I replied.

Only a lifetime. You might have warned me.

Either of you.

When Florence met Robert she was living on the top floor of an olive town house that faced onto one of the city's central promenades. Inside the tiny apartment the floorboards sloped unevenly down towards a tiled Victorian fireplace, giving an experience that was much like walking on the deck of a ship, she liked to say to people, thinking this made her every step sound full of excitement and risk. Robert, in his turn, assured Florence that he worked in some significant capacity for 'rather an exciting' advertising agency, Red & Radley. They handled accounts for United International Pictures (*James Bond*, *Mission: Impossible*), Philip Morris, and Ford (Galaxy and Puma cars). They didn't have Coca-Cola but they did have Dr Pepper. The truth was that Robert was a cleaner who sat on the chairs in the boardroom, his socks resting on the thick cream pile, only out of hours.

He dreamed of creation and beautiful faces. His adoptive parents had offered to fund a university education provided he commute from home, where they wanted to keep him, cheaply and for ever, safe with toy cars. And provided he study, not Fashion Photography as he would have liked, but something 'useful' like Earth Sciences or Politics. This dismal prospect he declined. Instead he moved into a shared studio apartment in Brixton and took books of art photography he couldn't afford out of the public library: Man Ray, Mapplethorpe, Sieff – a different one each week. These were the days before digital photography and he took photographs he couldn't afford either. He photographed weddings for free providing the cost of his materials was covered. There was a brief moment when Red & Radley agreed to let him use their empty basement for a photographic shoot. He got hold of friends who wanted to be models and lacked a make-up artist. The photographs came out very well. But then someone worried about Health & Safety and he was told not to do it again. A few weeks later he took a photograph of the Queen which was accepted for publication by the *Mayfair Times*. They made a particular point of checking how he wanted his name to appear (he had decided on Robert E. Brown) – and then failed to use it.

It continued like this. The photographs were always good, the name was always checked – Robert *A*. Brown? Okay, I get it, *R.*

44

E. Brown – sometimes two, or even three, times, but the name was never published. Robert was anonymous in *Marketing Week* and *Campaign*, both trade magazines, and did a lot of unpaid work for the National Advertising Benevolent Fund, a charity for anyone who had once worked in the advertising industry and now fallen on harder times. It wasn't the most heart-wrenching of causes. In fact, it was arguable whether Robert's own times were not in fact harder. But, provided they paid for the photographic film, he always volunteered his services. He needed the practice and besides, he felt good when the pretty, ditsy, young girls in their first jobs asked him if there was any possibility that he might – they would be ever so grateful – help them out again.

At the charity dinners, a junior boxing ring was erected in the centre of the ballroom so that eleven- and twelve-year-old boys could beat the crap out of each other for the pleasure of bow-tied execs eating quails' eggs and capers. On these occasions Robert's photographs circulated as souvenirs and did not appear in the local papers. At other times he charged a modest £25 for directors' portraits. Once there was a charity calendar job: in January a boss pretending to be Bond had his trousers down and two ladies dangling from his ear lobes. By November he was naked but for a beret and string of onions.

What Robert liked best, however, was to photograph the UIP film premieres. He burned his own film for this and was getting together a portfolio: a braless Kylie, a blurry Stephen Hawking, Robbie Williams and Noel Gallagher at enmity on opposite page mounts. He should have been an architect or designer. He could never see a car go past without mentally correcting the line of the bodywork. He made it more beautiful, more precise, and, at least until his thirty-fifth year, when car shapes began to catch up with his early ideas, something far beyond any contemporary car designer's vision.

But a sideline in photography was, for a long time, all he amounted to. As a child his parents had enthused about his abilities – how he had put up the next-door neighbour's Wendy House by the time he was three! How, at four, he had selected a red pepper at the greengrocer's and thrust it (with, they thought, counter-intuitive genius) into his mouth as if it were a piece of fruit. And he had, of course, been the one child who knew there were exactly 367 jelly tots in the jar at the fair. But Robert's adopters – it surprised no one that they were not his natural parents – had never done anything about these talents; had, indeed, actively prevented him from developing any sort of interest. He was disallowed membership of the inter-school cross-country running club because it would have cost them money (though very little) and have taken up time that he should devote to helping them. Robert's mother ran an Oxfam shop. His father had worked in local government and continued to rant. Originally they had moved away from the good area with the good school so that Robert's father could be nearer the office, which was making the world a better place. When Robert wanted to learn the piano they gave him a toddler's keyboard that had been donated to the shop and featured a farmyard of sonic effects, multi-coloured flashing lights and touch-sensitive plastic animal decorations that catered very well for all of the needs he did not have. His pocket money was always irregular and when it did come, he was expected to give a cut to good causes. It wasn't that Robert wasn't sympathetic to good causes (witness his later work for NABF): it was just that he would have preferred to buy a Twix and that he didn't want to wear T-shirts with poor reproductions of African women and the words 'If this woman goes to the well, she will be raped. If she doesn't, her 24 children will die of dehydration'. His mother wore a fleece to save on heating costs and usually a velvet skirt. (A lot of velvet was

46

given to Oxfam.) The jelly tot jar he had been obliged to donate to a Christmas raffle.

Robert's parents were horrified by his move to London, where he worked next at Churchill Bingford, one of the largest privately owned chartered surveyors and property management companies. The business dealt with big portfolios of property, like shopping centres and hotel chains. Robert's main distinction was in the company softball team. His height and strength suited him for out-fielding. A fellow player made him feel good, every time he turned up late at the pub, by not asking where he'd been (helping his mum with the larger Oxfam deliveries) and instead asserting with a wink, 'He's always shagging, our Robert.' Then Robert would grin sheepishly, and hang his head like the bad dog he thought he would have liked to have been. He 'crashed' (as he preferred to phrase it) on friends' floors overnight and had once made it to the guest room of the girl he most fancied. He wanted to fuck her, she wanted him to fuck her, and accordingly stood chatting to him at the end of the bed for over an hour before he spent the rest of the night repenting his inaction.

Then one day he took a later tube than usual. He was wedged between a woman reading singles ads in the *Metro* and a man eating an egg sandwich. There was only one more stop to go before he would change trains. Suddenly, however, Robert heard a voice behind them, a man, who announced to the carriage, 'Ladies and gentleman, I'm getting out at Baker Street.'

The carriage fell silent at this breach of etiquette. Something was wrong. In the public space of the train people behaved privately: it was not a social occasion and they were often scowling silently, just as they might on their own sofas. Certainly they did not address the congregation of fellow travellers. The woman beside him tensed and Robert began to feel for the Swiss Army Knife he carried in his left trouser pocket. He could not detect an Irish accent in the man's words, which ruled out the IRA, and who else was there? A random nutter? The words themselves sounded horribly symbolic, as though to say that they would all be getting out at Baker Street – once the bomb went off. They would all be exiting this life.

Then the man continued to speak. 'So I was just wondering if anyone might be able to spare any cash? As I say, I'll be getting out at Baker Street, so if you think you might be able to help, I'll be walking through the carriage till then. Thank you!'

The woman exhaled and Robert, in a moment of insight that took in, all at once, her perusal of the singles column, the glorious life that stretched ahead of them both now that the 'terrorist' had been revealed as a beggar, and the potential (sideways) loveliness of her tits, turned to her and asked, 'Would you like to have dinner with me?'

The moment she accepted, Robert decided it was time to make some money. Inspired by Churchill Bingford, he discovered property development. His first house – a three-storey Georgian affair that had pigeons nesting in the largely absent roof when he bought it – sold for a terrific profit. Then he reached the quarter-finals of *Masterchef* with a difficult mode for fish and chips, and a talent for plating up that bordered on a minor installation art form. He had new ambitions to become an organic food technologist and eventually to set up his own restaurant. In the meantime he set about educating the palate of the woman from the tube, Florence Brown, whose idea of tasty was the smart of salad cream. Sainsbury's own for preference.

The first time they went to bed he told her what he knew: that women quite often did not come but still enjoyed the sex. And that if they *did* happen to come, they might well lose all control and wet themselves. (He'd heard.) And if that happened, she wasn't to worry, he wouldn't mind.

There was nothing erotic in the suggestion. Sincerely he meant to spare her any pain. And Florence, certain that her risk of disgrace was nil, listened to this little speech with touched amusement. She couldn't fault him. She couldn't hurt him either. So she made up her mind to fall in love with him.

And then there was Thomas.

When Florence Brown discovered that there were people in this world – a whole two of them, in fact – willing to love her back, she took hold of love with both hands. It didn't feel wrong. It felt miraculous.

It was only eighteen months after the wedding that Florence met Thomas. The interdisciplinary conference, 'Medicine: Its Histories and Futures', interested her as a curator. Thomas was giving a paper on the implications of ectogenesis for premature pulmonary function. When the afternoon plenary session broke for tea they joined the queue for coffee. Florence recognized the Professor from television and had read two of his books, classics of modern science writing in which complex ideas met the common reader. The idea of simply complimenting him ('I love your books?' 'I adore your voice?') either did not occur to her or was quickly dismissed as foolish. She felt she exuded all the social significance of a toilet brush, whereas Marvelle's achievements stood in front of everyone like boulders. It would be like saying: there is a boulder. Or: the Sistine chapel ceiling is a darn good thing, I think. Instead he did the talking, then listened with interest as she managed to tell him that the modest archives of the Dillyford museum contained at least one birth anomaly – conjoined baby rabbits preserved in a bottle with an elegant glass stopper.

After a few more meetings it seemed impossible to resist. Or if not impossible, because it is never impossible, certainly thankless and crazy. To find herself, within a mere two years of her marriage, happily in love with this other extraordinary man *as well*, was a blessing that filled her with astonishment and gratitude every time (and there were many of those times) she paused to consider it. She stood in quiet awe in front of piles of washing-up, and laundry, and her new life. She'd never even had a lover before Robert – only a series of crushes, increasingly hopeless, on men who turned out to be gay, or emigrating – and now she had two! However.

However, however. Here was the thing. *A woman must not love two men at the same time*. At least, not unless there were very special circumstances. In films, for example, one of the men had to be beating her, while the other man effected the rescue. Loving two men was merely a transitional phase – allowing her to discover that it was nicer not to be beaten. Alternatively, one of the two men had to be dying. Florence had once watched a case on the True Movies channel of a woman who loved both her dying husband and her new lover. In the circumstances the two men felt able to become buddies, and went for a flying trip together in a small uncertain plane before the end came. But if a woman were able to find two respectable unterminal men and love them both – what then?

Florence quickly appreciated that every convention of romantic love was against her: it was always one guy and one girl who got it together in the end. In fact, every rule of sexual morality and of social order and of 'His and Hers' embossed towel design was against her. The whole of evolution, the entire process of the natural selection of species, was against her.

Frankly, it was all a bit of a strain at times. But those were the rather rare moments like the morning in the Kenyan surgeon's office. Had adultery been mostly about the soul-searching, the moral agony, the *ethics*, it would not have been for her.

Only once had Florence said to Thomas, 'But don't you think I'm being unfaithful? How can I carry on like this?' And even then she had expected to be contradicted and reassured.

'I think you're *very* faithful,' Thomas replied, almost indignantly. 'It's just that you can be faithful to more than one person at a time.'

This answer was even better than she'd hoped. In a flutter of discovery Florence Brown had sat down to write the first love letter she'd ever composed to two people at a time. This would be the letter that would explain to all parties involved, but particularly Robert, the good sense of her emotional choices. This would be the revolutionary and ambitious epistle that would rewrite all the rules of love. The one that would show that Robert and Thomas were not rivals. The main point on which each man would want reassurance (yes, *of course* your cock is bigger than his – and better – and really, in every respect I can think of, more delightful) would be tackled somehow. Indeed, far from being rivals, Robert and Thomas were two men with a massive experience in common: loving Florence Brown.

Dear you, she began. *Dear you two*.

It had taken a very long time to decide on an opening sentence, but once it was done, she felt pleased by its bold and masterful declaration:

Dear Robert and Thomas:
This is the longest love letter and if everything was written down I do not believe that the world itself could contain the scrolls.

No, not the world itself. But then Florence looked again at the longest love letter addressed to two people the world had ever seen. And when, awkwardly, no more seemed to come (she'd drunk much too much) . . . When, instead, the page declared itself the shortest skimpiest missive in the History of the World because if she risked another word she did not imagine that the Milky Way itself could find a spot sufficiently large (or ventilated) to accommodate the full descriptive blazings of her passion for two men at the same time . . . When all that happened, she replaced her head on the desk.

Perhaps, she'd thought, Robert would understand her need to be loved by more than one man as a kind of emotional insurance. Or as a compensation for having been rejected by so many of them before. Or perhaps, even better, he would understand the simpler and less psychoanalytical truth: it made her happy. After all, it wasn't as though she was going to leave him. Robert was the keeper of her core identity, the person she felt most herself with. She knew she was better suited to him than to Thomas in almost every respect. But Thomas loved her too and she found she could not walk away from that. Naturally enough, she longed to tell Robert all about the other man she loved. But in the end it was too great a risk to try him out.

She did, however, google it once: 'love letter to two people'. Not a single search result. Then she tried 'longest ever love letter'. Several examples. One was 114 pages and no doubt full of repetitions. *And did I mention that I love you?*

Seven

Once Florence Brown signed the surgical consent form, it wasn't very long before they were using her for voodoo: sticking a needle into the back of her hand, taping it down, and even tightening a tiny screw. She witnessed the whole procedure (to wit: the installation of the cannula) in some disbelief. Her hand hurt badly, she longed to snatch it away, and it seemed almost unaccountable that she could not. If only these events could be delegated to someone else. *Any*one else. She was sure that Robert, who was sweetly reasonable about everything, would volunteer if he could. So why couldn't he? she asked herself, desperately, watching a little of her blood long-jumping the junior doctor's tight ivory gloves. He was holding her hand down very hard. At last he released her, rolled back the gloves, quickly put out a foot, and a bin clanged.

As they walked out into the corridor again, Florence felt mildly depressed and acutely conscious of her arm, which hung like a dead weight terminating in a swollen and now useless encumbrance. She kept her distance from other passers-by, as though they might swerve recklessly into her hand, causing worse pain and irreparable damage. In the toilets everything had to be managed one-handedly: the lowering of her tights, the lifting of her skirt (which she was able – just – to keep in place at the top of her back by leaning very far forward), the hooking of her thumb around each side of her bikini string so the knickers could be brought down by stages. There were some Marmite patches behind the white mesh of her sanitary towel, and a little pale pink rained-on confetti evidently unable to make it through this barrier. But nothing you could call red. She inched further forward as the trickle began. Hygienically aloft the actual toilet.

When she emerged Lydia was watching herself in a long chipped horizontal mirror above the sinks. It was that way she had of trying to correct the image, to toss back her head and attempt a more dazzling smile that would set everything straight and restore her to the rightful twenty-five. Or forty-five, anyway. Again she flicked back her hair, again she flipped it forward, even quicker this time, as though the element of surprise might work better on the mirror glass.

'Are you all right, my dear?' she asked.

'Are you in a lot of pain?' asked the nurse who was going to escort them to the ward.

'Yes. It's my hand.'

The nurse looked puzzled. 'Well, do you think you can walk all right?'

Florence opted for the wheelchair anyway. Some people were brave in adverse circumstances. Florence Brown was a natural coward and proud of it. It's an aspect of my humanity, she praised herself, as the nurse readied the foot flaps. *Be afraid* – that was one of George Morley's mottoes – *and you'll live longer*. She would happily delegate all of this to any passing stranger for a fee. Or intimate friend, or favourite relative. Yes, it was all the same to her now as she said her goodbyes to Lydia and passed on a last message for Robert, as they whisked her unreturnably down the yellow corridor, as she lay on the trolley in the antechamber to the operating theatre and sought a solution somewhere in the wall-mounted telephone, file holder and pinboard with posters that warned of diabetes, suicide and the

54

surprising ease with which house fires might be started. It wasn't Lydia or Robert or even Thomas she was worried about never seeing again. It was herself.

Then a man in a sea-green tunic and dinner lady's hat wanted to know what Florence Brown had eaten for breakfast. As death seemed imminent she made a full disclosure of both *pains au chocolat*, and the Kit Kat, adding that she was afraid of never waking up again. The anaesthetist laughed reassuringly. So did his portly colleague. There was no sign yet of the Kenyan.

'Is that really what you're afraid of? Is that all?' the anaesthetist asked.

Yes, yes, that's it. She nodded vigorously without actually speaking this time. That's everything.

'If you were a very old lady with a shaky pulse . . .' he said, smiling and bringing his nice tea-coloured face close enough for Florence to kiss, 'I might be worried. But you're young. Actually,' he said a moment later, looking up incredulously from the sticker on the front of Florence's medical notes, 'you're really *really* young. Can we just confirm your date of birth again as 22.03.92?'

'I told them already, the year is wrong. It should be 1977.'

'Ah,' the anaesthetist smiled. 'That makes sense.' But he had no pen to hand and made no alteration.

'What about the *pains au chocolat*?' Florence asked.

'Don't worry about that. It's more important to get on with the operation than to delay because of a little puff pastry.'

Seeing that Florence still looked worried, however, he added kindly, 'I'm just going to give you something to calm you down, all right?'

He took her hand as he said, 'It'll be like injecting three glasses of white wine instan . . .'

Eight

*I remember I was waiting for you. Watching the bodies entering and vacating
space. Endlessly and endlessly. Three sets of traffic lights at red. In the noisy
silence, the bustling solitude, I watched for you. Willed you there. I wanted,
more than anything, the flicker of your face, the certainty of your folded arms.
I began to despair at the sight of so many people who were not you. And then,
almost impossibly, as though my mind could really summon a lover into being,
there you were again. Summoning too.*

You were looking for her. You were looking at me. But how to say, Yes,
here I am, come again to you?

'*Where've you been?*' *you said, almost reproachfully.*

'I want you to know,' I said, 'that I'm not unhappy with Robert. In fact,
I'm very happy with Robert. So I don't exactly know why—'

'*It's because,*' *you said,* 'you want to be happy with me too.'

Yes. With you two.

Something had been done but Florence Brown didn't know what it
was. She could make out the oiled tail of a rat behind the cistern . . .
Now there were people talking about a new restaurant in town. Oh
yes, I've been there too! she tries to say, longing to join in, for once,
and prove that everything is normal again. The mackerel is really
rather good, and the chicken with the dill. But somehow it's quite
impossible to say anything. Because yes, *something* had been done.

Something had been discussed, something decided, something had definitely been signed for, even: although what and why, Florence couldn't exactly . . . It wasn't *exactly* on the tip of her tongue. Laparoscopy, salpinectomy, proceeding to . . .

Florence opened her eyes. The recovery room was larger than she'd expected. There were shelves at a distance and someone seated to her left looked up for a moment, smiled warmly, and then continued writing in a mustard-yellow ring-binder. There were other people near the shelves. Doctors in royal blue pyjamas. Rather comforting, actually, in its way. Especially with the stethoscopes slung quite casually like that around their shoulders. The operation must be over, but she wasn't about to ask, not about, you know, *that*. Whatever *that* was. For the moment she was glad she didn't have to know. It would all come to her, she supposed, soon enough. Indeed it was coming to her now – there – in that clock on the opposite wall. The clean white round face was enclosed in a neat steel circle and there were two red arrows for hands. It all seemed reassuringly simple now and she could work it out quite easily. (Polyamoury. Rhymes with Jackanory.) If that clock was above that doorway (and it was) on the wall opposite, and if she was looking at that clock (and she was) above that doorway on the wall opposite, then she must be living. It was a good start. In fact, an excellent one, and suddenly she felt in the most incredibly joyful mood. She was a*live*!

Just as suddenly she remembered Robert.

'Does my husband know I'm . . . ?' Alive?

'Yes,' said the person to her left.

A woman, Florence now discerned, whose scrubs were arsenic-coloured. The long sleeves of her beige thermal vest were visible and rolled back on her writing arm. Her other hand toyed with the end of her stethoscope.

'Your mother telephoned him. He's on his way.'

'Ah.' Florence waited to hear more. But some minutes passed in silence. The woman seemed only to respond to direct questions.

'And did they find it?' Florence asked at last.

The woman shook her head happily. No, it wasn't an ectopic pregnancy, after all. No salpinectomy needed. Florence still had two ovaries. More good news. It seemed astonishing that no one had volunteered this fact straightaway. *Yes, we* were *going to cut pieces out of your body. But then we didn't have to*. And not a word of it? Florence was surprised to see that her hand was now attached to a drip. The translucent udder swayed as the woman moved about, now adding to the previous information that Florence might even still be pregnant. She might not be miscarrying. Florence could not quite remember why this apparently good news was really bad news. But anyway, the woman said as she left, her surgeon was coming to explain.

It was Robert who arrived first.

'Hello, sweetie!' he said. 'You do know that you're only a very small and delicious sweetie, don't you?'

Florence, who liked to be infantilized, nodded silently.

'Look left!' he instructed. So she did. 'Look right!' he added, as he took the opportunity to peck her lips. 'Sight test, my sweetie.'

She smiled.

The surgeon – in fact two surgeons, neither of whom Florence had ever seen before – were fervent on arrival four hours later.

'What took you so long?' Robert demanded protectively. 'She's been waiting for *ever*. She's worried.'

The women nodded their apologies. The first was a young Chinese woman who spoke her clipped and broken English rapidly. The second and evidently senior surgeon, an earnest anxious woman in her early forties, wore a surgical cap bearing the emblem 'BRAINS

ARE BEAUTIFUL'. This was held in place with Kirby grips which she touched and adjusted in moments of agitation. Indeed, the conversation turned out to be mostly about this woman's feelings.

'I was very unhappy,' she said softly, 'with the idea of performing a D and C once it was clear that the pregnancy was not ectopic. I know that's what you agreed with my colleague this morning. However . . .'

However, this woman surgeon felt differently about it and she glanced reverentially between Florence and her lawful wedded husband Robert for confirmation of the truth of her feelings. Florence looked at Robert, checking his face for any recognition of the meaning of 'D and C'. Fortunately, there was none. Robert knew that his business here was to look firm and supportive and, whenever the surgeon paused gravely, to mirror her gravity as closely as he possibly could.

'So I discussed it with Mr Harris,' the elder surgeon continued, 'and he felt—'

'*Who?*' Florence asked.

'The registrar. Mr Harris.'

Someone else Florence hadn't met before.

'Master Harris,' the younger surgeon added, 'noticed that you are still in your teens, very good, so your future prospects for pregnancy were very excellent . . .'

'I'm thirty-one,' Florence murmured, too hopelessly to be heard by anyone but Robert.

'But all the same, Mr Harris felt just the way we did,' the elder surgeon said.

'Yes. If we believe that there is any possibility of viable pregnancy, we should not perform what would – ' the younger woman frowned as she tried to recall the registrar's exact phrase – '"effectively amount to termination".'

So, they didn't. *Because they had discussed it with – Mr Harris!* Oh boy. The three of them – Mr Harris, the special fried noodle, and the woman of feeling – all hell-bent on the survival of the foetus. Florence wanted to tell the surgeons to step right away from the end of the bedrail. To take their silly caps and pins and evacuate the fuck out of the – the – Aztec curtain cubicle. Or whatever the fuck that fucking pattern was supposed to be. However, with Robert there, giving her encouraging glances, Florence restrained herself to the most pertinent objection.

'But the bleeding? I'm still bleeding.'

'Sometimes women bleed because they have not enough hormone. Bleeding is not necessary bad sign, okay?'

The woman broke into a smile. Winning, irrepressible, she was clearly so happy about Florence's prospects for a healthy pregnancy that Florence could not help smiling herself. Instantly Florence saw the scene that must have taken place around the operating table: the women excitably calling the others to look through the surgical camera for themselves, and watch the small delightful homunculus who was swimming lengths in the bubble. The pleasant anaesthetist was beaming paternally, and even the more hardened members of the surgical team felt such a swoop of joy in their hearts that they would be obliged to disguise it for the rest of the day with the most savage of frowns. No wonder they had decided not to follow her instructions! Thank God they had not! Oh life – it was good!

'Will it be all right?' she asked them, suddenly anxious for her baby.

'Yes,' the elder surgeon replied confidently, now smiling too. 'You may find that the bleeding continues, or that the bleeding stops.'

'It won't affect the baby?' Florence asked.

'No. Spotting is – common,' the younger woman said.

'Spotting?' Florence repeated, dismayed, a moment later.

'Yes, spotting. Spotting is only blood. There is no loss of tissue.'

'But there *is*,' Florence objected. Dismally she saw before her this morning's urine sample on the shelf in the Kenyan surgeon's office. The little cupful, *draped* with tissue. Frothing over like a TV lab experiment.

The surgeon's statement now turned into a question and the smile slid rapidly off her face. 'There is loss of tissue?'

'Yes!' Florence replied.

Again, this was one they had discussed earlier.

'Oh very dear!' she said, surprised.

Oh. Exactly. Florence could see that changed everything. The surgeons hadn't seen any lane swimming after all, had they? Florence felt the spice of new tears starting up in her eyes. Robert moved from the visitor's chair to the edge of the bed and put his arm around her.

'Well,' the elder surgeon fudged, twiddling a hairpin, 'we never know. Sometimes women surprise us.'

Florence wondered what she said when there was a fuck-up like this in A & E: *Well, you know, the thing is, we* never *really know. Sometimes people surprise us. All the blood comes out of their body and then they just get up and start walking.* Florence felt almost insulted when the surgeon added that an appointment had been arranged to check the embryo's growth, in a week's time, at the morning clinic of Mr Harris.

The kid was bleeding to death and everyone was chatting as though he was going to make it and start playing football with his father — whoever that was — fairly soon.

Nine

And now the big decision was when and how, exactly, to move off the bed. Lydia had gone home soon after Robert arrived. Then Robert had gone too. Hospital rules. Florence braced herself and rolled slowly onto her side. Drawing up her knees, she got her left arm ready to take her weight in the manner demonstrated earlier by a kindly nurse with a grey ponytail. Then she pushed herself to a sitting position. Somehow Florence Brown got her legs to dangle over the side of the bed. Her thighs felt hot and sore from the tops of the surgical stockings cutting into them. They had to stay on for two days and she anticipated the delicious relief of removing them in what now seemed a far-off future.

She slipped the few centimetres to the floor and steadied herself on the IV pole, which she began manoeuvring across the pale mud-coloured linoleum. The contraption benefited from two-wheel drive and terminated in the cannula and trocar that was still pinned, taped and screwed into the back of her left hand. It was like carrying around your own hat rack. Or being stapled to one. The udder itself appeared full to bursting and she didn't like to look at it.

To the rear, Florence's improperly tied surgical gown exposed her knickers to the hopeless gathering in ward A498. She was conscious that she did not care. At least she was moving again. Moving, it was true, like an hour hand or fate. Slowly, even imperceptibly, but unstoppably nonetheless. As Florence continued her millimetric progress a surly nurse confronted her.

'You want the toilet?' she asked suspiciously.

Florence admitted as much with a nod but did not stop moving.

'All right,' the nurse said, as though relenting and letting Florence Brown off this time. 'All right, well, I'm going to check you for infection, so leave what you do in one of the pans above the toilet, okay?'

How Florence would transfer her wee, or extract it, from the water of the toilet bowl to a pan above the toilet was one of the logistical difficulties that Florence decided to defer.

'But anyway, you haven't got any bleeding, down there, have you?' the nurse asked.

'Yes.'

'*Bleeding?!*' The nurse sounded horrified.

Florence couldn't think why. After all, 'It's a *miscarriage*!' she said.

'Okay, I'll look in your file.'

'It's a miscarriage!' Florence repeated crossly and too loudly. Wasn't it?

Actually, Florence resented the term *mis-carriage*, which implied there was something wrong with the way she was carrying the baby. As though she were slinging it around quite recklessly and had only herself to blame if it clattered to the floor. No one spoke of the suicidal foetus. Or even the damn careless foetus. According to Thomas, foetuses were always wrapping their umbilical cords, playfully but dangerously, around their own necks.

The nurse went to find the file. Florence continued moving slowly forward. So slowly, in fact, that the light sensor in the bathroom didn't even pick her up at first. She could make out nothing but its red pinprick of light in the blackness of the windowless room. This morning there had still been windows, she was fairly sure: but here, now, deep in the entrails of the city hospital, there were none and she found herself imagining what the museum tour guide might say.

. . . reminding us of Dante's Paradiso, *where God is a pinprick of blinding white light. By painting, therefore, a red light sensor, the artist means to show us that* the Devil *is here . . .*

Exhausted, Florence tried to wave her free arm in the right direction — whatever *that* might be — as the delirious tour guide continued. Failing to attract the sensor's attention she reversed herself and her metal companion, her non-identical Siamese twin, back through the doorway, then attempted a faintly speedier new assault. Still failing, she thought that maybe if she stepped continuously forward and back, forward and back, if she supplicated the light strip, if she hoped . . . The light plinked on. In the longer term Florence aimed to make contact with a disposable grey cardboard toilet pan, a device still new to her. There was a stack of them like overgrown egg boxes on the shelf above the toilet. So that was what the nurse had meant. Rigidly the top one resisted her efforts to separate it from the pile. A minute later she had it positioned on the toilet seat. At last she began to sink, slowly, gratefully, uncertainly. The cardboard device looked more suitable for stabilizing takeaway Cokes. And she'd lost the non-adhesive sanitary towel provided by the hospital to the floor.

However, here was progress.

Seated at last, Florence lifted her head with mild satisfaction. And in this slight daze, this faint euphoria, she imagined what she would like to say to the two men she loved most in this world:

Dear You,

I'm sitting again, anyway. That seems to be the main thing now. And that I still have two ovaries, and may, therefore, one day have a baby. Or even two. Allow me to re-phrase:

Dear the-both-of-you. Dear You Two:

I'm sorry about, you know, earlier. But I think that's what I'd like, in the end: one of each, as they say. One little Robert, one little Thomas. Just as soon as loving two men becomes all the rage among the moralists. And as soon as Robert sees it's no threat to him, and all the world can live with it . . . yes, just as soon as we can get those last remaining details sorted – then I'll be ready.

The thing is, you two, you're the only two for me.

You're two in a million!

I know I'm the luckiest woman alive in that respect, and if Miss Fiancée could see me now, she'd never believe it. I wish I could see you. (Either. Both.) I imagine you either side of the toilet. Just the three of us. Because I've always thought it's one of the chief reasons for getting intimate with someone – that while you're on the loo there's someone to discuss your progress with. So that's why this declaration is also proper to my love letter:

I long to wee.

I was hoping for a decent puddle, actually, but my bladder feels like it's been pounded all afternoon on a lemon squeezer. And whenever I do manage anything, like just now there was a little bit, there's an involuntary pause, which worries me. I think I paused mid-stream deliberately, when the nurse took me to the toilet the first time, just to test my powers, and now I seem to have instituted something. Either that or it's damage from the operation. And I can't tell you how much I want to fart! There was a time when I hoped, naïvely, for a shit, but now I would settle joyfully for the alternatives. (A wee. A fart. Either. Both. The time I had my appendix out, you'll both remember, it took me days to reach the affirmatory state of shitting.) The fart will have to be carefully managed, I know, to avoid strain on the navel. So I'm thinking Fairy Liquid bubbles, gently dispersing to the sway of bells in high alpine meadows.

65

I'm trying for a fart right now, actually. Cautiously. A bit less cautiously. Nothing. But every time I shift my weight, there's hope.

I think I'm going to be shifting my weight rather a lot.

Actually, if you want to know the truth, when I think about you two, I can't imagine why more *people aren't in love with you. Why more or less* everyone *isn't in love with you. Either of you — or the pair. It seems the only reasonable thing. But you, Robert, are much too modest to realize it. Sometimes I think that if you were told a more important man needed to sleep with your wife, and it had been ascertained that I would be happy about it, then you would be too.*

Whereas you, Thomas, are simply relaxed about being hated. 'Sweetest: they all think I'm a cunt.' And I can imagine myself, six decades hence, venerable in pearls, quoted in your unauthorized biography:

And sometimes I would pass him in the street. That was before we knew each other. He always looked so, sort of, *tremendously* stern! But in fact he was a great laugher with the most remarkable laugh. *To think!* (I used to say to him) *you were only across the street, ten years away.* I was borrowing from Seamus Heaney, of course. He was a great poetry lover, you know. We both were. People were in those days.

'Look, you funny girl,' I remember you saying once, and kissing my cheeks, 'there isn't going to be any biography! You picked the wrong guy! They'll just be glad the fucker is dead. Shut up at last. Anyone got any spare nails?'

I was laughing helplessly by then.

'The Wet Incubator,' you said, 'will be received about as favourably as the tsunami. "Another great catastrophe from T. Marvelle." Look what happened with Roses*!'*

Roses, your television documentary series — based on a book you'd dashed off in less than a month, a sort of natural history study grafted onto cultural history — should have been disaster-proof. Didn't everyone love roses?

'It is true,' I agreed, 'that you're the first man in history to have made roses unpopular.'

But I love you anyway — and you.

Your

Florence.

As the imaginary letter came to its pleasant close Florence looked straight ahead but didn't register what she was seeing. Then, too late, and with a gasp, she saw it. There was death in the umbilical cord of the IV drip: right in the middle of the long plastic tube, a two-centimetre gap was apparent in the saline solution.

An air bubble, she deduced. Perhaps she had even caused it, somehow, when moving the stand, but no one had warned her. All she knew was that the air bubble was progressing steadily down the tube toward her hand, where it would shortly enter her bloodstream. Florence looked to the tiny sink for help. There was a sliver of very dry green soap like a thick cracked nail. It took thirty seconds before she saw the cord that said Emergency and pulled it.

Anti-climatically, the cord that said 'Emergency' lit a 25-watt candle bulb in a red box on the ceiling.

'I'm, ah, worried,' Florence told the surly nurse, having no choice of interlocutors, two minutes later.

She was endeavouring to strike the tonal balance between panic and sense as she pointed a finger cautiously at the drip. Everyone Florence knew, but especially her stepfather George, was full of cheery advice like, *You can drown in a teaspoon of water*, and, *Margarine kills*. An air bubble in your bloodstream seemed like an especially bad one. This morning's events and the talk of her insides rupturing now seemed like some kind of warning. A dark prophecy she had failed to heed properly. There – Florence pointed again – there was the invisible bullet, the lethal dose of nothing. With a finger she continued tracing its terrible path as it inched inexorably down the tube toward her. It was like watching a slow motion replay of the disaster that was about to occur. It could not be very much longer before it was actually in her bloodstream. Yes, *there* was her early demise, there her death by vacant space . . . Or perhaps it would not aim for her heart and kill her straight off. Perhaps it would go for her brain, and by the time the crash team intervened, her grey matter would be so much grey mush. Goodness, couldn't the woman *see*?

The nurse frowned, unable to see, and yanked the drip towards the light. Naturally, this sped things up. Together they watched as the bubble hurtled round its last Wet'N'Wild corner and plunged down the chute. Then it was in Florence's bloodstream.

'I think it's okay,' the nurse commented indifferently, which was a lot of comfort, and shifted the subject. 'But – are you doing much more now? A good amount of urine?'

Florence shrugged defiantly. What was a good amount of urine these days, anyway?

Listen, nursey, Florence longed to say, *I'm productive where it counts.* And to hear her say, *Oh yes, and how is that?* And then Florence would say, *Oh yeah, you'd better believe it. I'm writing the First and Longest-Ever Love Letter addressed to Two People at a Time. So there!*

But of course Florence didn't say anything like that. Or anything at all, in fact. Instead she shut her eyes in obstinate resignation to her fate. A moment later she heard the nurse sigh and leave. *Bitch.* She opened her eyes briefly to check that the woman really was gone.

Thinking of Robert, then of Thomas, Florence murmured, in the voice of a movie trailer, 'And only two men can save her!' But as neither of them was there, it seemed best to keep her eyes shut. So that was what Florence Brown, museum curator, did in the end.

PART TWO

Surviving

Ten

In one of Florence's favourite movie moments, from the film *As Good As It Gets*, waitress Carol Connelly (Helen Hunt) said to misanthropic writer Melvin (Jack Nicholson), 'Okay, we all have these terrible stories to get over, and you—'

'It's not true,' he objected. 'Some of us have *great* stories, pretty stories that take place at lakes with boats and friends and – *noodle salad*. Just no one in this car. But, a lot of people, that's their story. Good times, noodle salad.'

In times of exasperation, Florence imagined she was stuck in the long self-service queue at the non-noodle end of the salad bar. The doom that she felt wasn't tragic; it was ironic. And it was a conscious decision. It meant that no matter what happened, her life would never become a terrible story that had to be got over.

But Helen Donald, she had terrible stories to get over. She was still young: she didn't know what else to do.

As a child Helen was so serious that her mother used to say she was at least nine years old on the day she was born. Her mother was an alcoholic who preferred the hedonism of her son, who was younger than Helen by a year and liked to Pritt-stick cornflakes to the carpet. The domestic chaos, which reigned most acutely in the kitchen sink, was, however, largely attributed to her daughter's presence in the household. Helen was 'the eldest', her mother would say, her nose appearing redder and larger than the day before. This nose was the sign the small girl learned to live by: its grim radiance an unfailing register of emotions just about to be released. Rage, hysteria, or sometimes an evanescent heartiness that Helen was meant to enjoy but which seemed, whenever she was sentimentally crushed into her mother's arms along with her brother and a beer can, hardly less alarming.

The turning point in Helen's life was her mother's third pregnancy. Helen did not know who the father of the baby was, nor who her own father had been, nor even, at this point, that men were absolutely requisite to the business. The pregnancy had been planned to get them out of the two-bed flat and into one of the three-bedroom houses on a nearby development that was forty per cent social housing, sixty per cent private ownership. It had a children's park with a newfangled climbing frame and, more importantly, a newsagent's within easy walking distance. However. Breakfasts of Silk Cut cigarettes, Mars Bars and shandy, followed by bouts of vomiting that often did not stop till late in the evening, left the pregnant woman exhausted, dehydrated and finally ill enough to be frightened. Hysterically sure that she was dying, she ordered a taxi to her sister's house and demanded to be taken in.

During the tense pause Helen expected a row in the street. But the cul-de-sac had never witnessed one, and did not now. Instead the aunt, whom Helen did not remember ever having seen before, brought them into an oasis of beige calm. How it was all managed Helen could not at first begin to fathom but gradually, during their six-month stay, the miracle was revealed.

In the early weeks Helen's mother kept mostly to 'her' bedroom, where she wore size eighteen Minnie Mouse nightshirts and was brought meals on a Buckingham Palace tray she had expressed a preference for. Whenever curiosity or emotion brought one of her children to the bedroom doorway, she said she needed to sleep.

And so Helen began to watch her mother at a distance. From the hallway she could see her try to eat a tomato quarter or a lettuce leaf, instead of sausages with HP Brown sauce. Thus framed, her mother seemed a less daunting figure, simply the occupant of a single room in a large house with three storeys. When she was not watching her mother, Helen trailed her aunt. Once a week the aunt changed all of the bed linen. The freshly laundered sheets and duvet covers she took from the airing cupboard were stiffly papery and it seemed that as soon as they began to lose this quality, to soften and to slide grimily about in the way that Helen had been accustomed to, that was the cue that they needed changing back to paper again. But there was more.

One afternoon her aunt disclosed the steps by which the principal business was effected: showed her how you put the corner of the duvet inside a corner of the cover that you held in your hand, and then did the same on the opposite side. After that you held the whole thing up, with your arms stretched out wide, and shook it as vigorously as you could. Gradually the cover cascaded to almost the bottom of the duvet. At that point it was possible to lay the duvet on the bed and turn to the final task: the pressing of the poppers.

The small girl was astonished. That an item so large was, after all, so relatively manageable! And that an undertaking which had previously seemed so far beyond her scope, should in fact lie within her comprehension!

When the baby was born and the three-bedroom house duly made available to them, Helen was equipped with everything her aunt had taught her. She was eight by then. The baby, another girl, whom their mother named Kayleigh, was the tiniest human she had ever seen. She fell instantly in love and became the one to mother her. True, a baby was much harder than a duvet cover. But a baby was also more responsive than a duvet cover. Helen learned that the tiny person stopped crying because of her and started crying because of her. As Kayleigh grew up she hero-worshipped Helen, and as Helen grew up she knew that this was what she wanted to do for ever. In her teens she took on various babysitting jobs, but disappointingly her charges were rarely, in fact, babies. With less intelligence she might have become a nursery helper; with considerably more, a paediatrician. Instead she became a neonatal nurse and then – because she thought that having children, like her mother, out of wedlock, would not do – she got married.

She wanted to do everything right.

It was just that everything went wrong for her.

It was early one morning about a year into the marriage, and raining lightly as the car turned into the hospital cemetery. There was a small brick building to the right. The chapel, they assumed, although it looked almost too small to hold any public service. Grave-tenders, three in all, raised their faces in unison as the couple got out of the car. Helen was dressed neatly in her uniform and had washed her hair. Joseph wore his wedding shoes. He'd parked in front of a notice board, which she was anxious to read – wishing to be diligent and also hoping for a map of the cemetery. Something, perhaps, in the order of a hypermarket directory, with old Mrs Feefe on aisle fourteen, and the suicides on the wrong side of the northern picket fence. Helen was instead disappointed by directions for the disposal of flowers, and a prohibition of dogs, fireworks (*fireworks!*), or bicycles on the grass. Joseph waited for her, then they linked arms under the umbrella and took a path down towards what seemed to be a rose garden.

'I think it could be this,' Joseph said as they got closer. 'They did say something about a garden.'

'It won't be this,' she replied.

'This' was a border encircling a neat lawn located at the principal entrance to the burial ground. On inspection the roses were actually peonies and the ground was, in any case, undisturbed. They were looking for something quite different – a grave that showed signs of being opened regularly. It might be the peculiar entrance into the earth they discovered around the corner, which had two metal doors with black buckles and a chain. Sinister but plausible.

'There should be some kind of marking, though,' Helen said. 'I think we keep looking.'

So they continued, against the rain, down the slope. Joseph dipped the umbrella like a shield. A new possibility was coming into view: a privet hedge, at the bottom of the cemetery grounds, which seemed to enfold a memorial garden and screen off whatever else was inside. Joseph knew immediately that they were in the right place at last; Helen was less certain, even after they read the handful of small square plaques lining the grass.

Our Angel 10.11.2000

Baby Jones 29.04.03

Thomas Eliot 16.05.05

'Look at the single dates,' Joseph said. 'Because the date of birth is the same as the date of death.'

She mused anxiously over the grey, green, blue slates.

'I don't know,' she said, running a hand over her dark cropped hair.

Although Helen had worked in the neonatal unit on Level 2 for some time, she had never been to the hospital cemetery before.

At first there had been no reason. Then, for the last few months, she had often thought about this place but avoided it. These slates might be children's memorials. Or babies' memorials. *Proper* babies, who had actually lived a short time, not mere foetuses, as the unviable were usually termed. Admittedly she didn't recognize any of the names. They were not, then, former patients of the SCBU (Special Care Baby Unit). Even so, perhaps what they were looking for would still turn out to be somewhere else, separate from these others. Really she expected some kind of classification system. Circles of the afterlife. Or something like the new table of recommendations from the Nuffield Council of Bioethics on the treatment of premature babies. Bodies arranged with legal exactitude. With the same meticulous prejudice as the law which stated that a woman who delivered a baby which was alive (however briefly) before the twenty-fifth week of pregnancy, was entitled to full maternity rights. There was a famous case of a sixteen-week-old foetus who breathed for half an hour. And anyone born after the twenty-fourth week, whether dead or alive, got a death certificate too. Legal recognition as a person. But anyone born dead too soon, like her baby, the one they were looking for, didn't count. They were simply called miscarriages. A miscarriage was, by definition, a foetus who couldn't have survived alone. The new Wet Incubator was going to change all that, no doubt – but not yet. So she didn't presume on her baby's inclusion here in this memorial garden either. She heard the voice in her head that said, *Don't be ridiculous!* Perhaps they still had to keep looking.

But at the end of the path the monument was unmistakable. A narrow granite cone topped with a star, it read: 'Fleetingly Known But Remembered For Ever, These Are Our Children, Now And Always'. And even before she'd read it she'd seen what lay behind the monument. A muddy bit of field, with several rectangles of more or less recent excavation, the one in current use covered roughly with a piece of plywood for easy access.

These were mass graves. Every foetus, wanted or unwanted, born before its time in the hospital behind them, was buried here. They were all Level 7 cases and there was an inhumation once every two months. Helen tried to picture what lay beneath the ground: the unclassified stacks of tiny wooden boxes, enclosing the tiny wilted bodies. She tried, particularly, to think of their own tiny child, who would have been due today had he not been discovered dead in her womb some four months before. It was Friday when she found out – at the twenty-week ultrasound scan. He stayed inside her all of Saturday. On Sunday he was stillborn. Except you couldn't, until the twenty-fourth week, call it that. Dozens of tests had been done – she remembered the phials of blood samples from her arm, lined up like organ pipes on the hospital bedspread. A full autopsy had been conducted as well, but no reason had ever been found. He was simply a perfectly healthy dead baby – unlike the sickly, sometimes deformed infants she cared for every day. No chromosomal abnormalities were discovered, indeed no problems of any kind, and even the suspicious swelling on the right side of the baby's head was caused merely by the violent speed with which he had, at last, dropped through her cervix. When they told her that, instinctively she felt relieved for him. He would be all right, then – apart from the fact that he was already dead. But excepting that moment's relief, it had continually tormented her, not to know what had happened to him. What had he died *of*? And *why*?

Colleagues on Level 7 had given them a photograph of the baby, in a green cardboard folder which they kept in the secret jewellery drawer of the bedroom chest. Helen had never managed to look. Joseph had looked. Looked and felt so sad. Looked and cried. But although Helen hovered around the chest, finding things to do there, always hoping to feel her child nearby, she had not looked. Afraid of what she might see. Also afraid of what she might not see. Not what she remembered, perhaps. Or worse, much worse, a body so pathetic it would not seem enough to justify these past months of grief. From the beginning she had been afraid that other people, her colleagues especially, would consider her grief disproportionate, and had therefore kept it sacredly hidden from everyone but Joseph. Wasn't she a nurse? she imagined the other people thinking. Wasn't she a nurse, a neonatal nurse no less, and fairly inured to these mishaps anyway? She was a nurse but still she had been afraid of exactly what, by the end of labour, she was going to see.

Initially she had asked for surgery instead. Because in surgery you could be unaware of what was happening to you, a gap opened in your consciousness and you never had to fill it. She had asked – twice – and been refused. Because it was marginally safer and, though no one would have said it, cheaper, to deliver vaginally. So she had gone along with this protocol and given up protesting. They took her to a room with a laminated wall poster that said NEVER leave your baby unattended. NEVER allow a member of staff you have not seen before to take your baby for a test. ALWAYS ask for ID first. A delivery suite, naturally. She remembered how her face had looked both red and grey in the mirror and the powder in her compact took badly to the damp skin. Her finger ends were as puffy as her eyes by then. Bitten down to boxing gloves. The abortifacient, the pill to kill the placenta – Mifegyne, 200mg – sat on the made bed and the thought went through her mind that if the sonographers were somehow wrong, after all, and there was a heartbeat, after all, then taking this pill would be the end, after all. And then, unable to bear the uncertainty, she swallowed it anyway. Finally she went home and waited.

As long as she kept quiet on the topic, however, people would not be able to think to themselves, *Oh, there she goes again*. Or rather, she would not have to think of them thinking it to themselves – and in this way insult the memory of her baby. But what if (worst of all) she should ever arrive at the same conclusion herself? That her grief had been – that it still was – somehow excessive? What if even in her very grieving she was in the wrong? So instead of looking at the photograph she preferred to believe that inside that thin green folder with a lip there lay The Answer, if she should ever absolutely need to know what it was. But it was not a theory she could see herself testing.

The field was unremarkable. Not the underworld. Nothing in any way alarming. Helen turned round and round but saw only green grass and brown mud and the empty arms of the winter trees. She saw the way other people grieved – with dried chrysanthemums, baby Christmas trees, wind toys and small teddy bears. A mini Mother Mary, in folds of baby pink and blue, gazed on serenely. Helen wanted to say: *I don't forget you*. (Not, *I can't forget you* – although that might be true too, she didn't know, not having tried – but, 'I don't forget you', as a conscious act of will.) But again the voice objected, *Don't be ridiculous!* All right, she agreed, it did seem a little too deliberate, too melodramatically contrived, to start speaking aloud to the dead. Immediately another voice sneered, *See – you are ashamed of loving your own baby.* A pause. *Don't be ridiculous – we all know she never cared about that baby. She only cared about herself.*

That's enough! she cried silently, and then, to Joseph, said, 'That's nice.'

'Yes, that's nice,' they said to each other, referring to the things other parents had brought. They were determined to admire everything about the baby graves and it lasted them several minutes

81

– the discussion of the durability of plastic, of the authorship of the messages on the monument (there was another, equally assertive, on the reverse), and the meaning of the placement of the chrysanthemums at the head of one of the rectangles. Whoever had put them there must have attended a burial, must know in which rectangle their child lay. Helen and Joseph had stayed away, and now she didn't know. But perhaps some kind of rudimentary system did operate down there, after all. Perhaps there was a record of burials, a list of names, something corresponding to her own sense of professional orderliness. She wondered if they might be able to ask someone, belatedly, which rectangle was theirs. Where had all the January babies gone?

'Our whole life changed,' Joseph said.

'Did it?' Deep inside her own grief it almost surprised her that he felt like this too.

'One moment we were all geared up for kids and the next you were saying . . .'

Not like her, then. He wanted a baby, babies. Sons and daughters, actually. She looked at him: Joseph was a vigorous man with very large eyes. Intelligent but modest. Enthusiastic for life. He was always meant to be a father. But she wanted this baby. This baby and no other. Her womb was the small boy's shrine. So how could she allow someone else to trample on it?

'I'm sorry,' she explained, 'it's the only way I can cope. That day, when they said . . . I couldn't do anything to change what was happening, the only thing I could do was promise myself: *this ends here.*'

Except: it hadn't. She found herself going over it, again and again, everything that had happened between the Friday and the Sunday. How the baby drifted limply on the scan, as though he had drowned.

How she tried to think the best for those first few seconds. Even fancied herself saying to him, years later, when he was all grown up, that the first time she'd seen his face she feared he was a goner. But he had to be all right, she'd reminded herself, because any time she was really worried that things weren't all right, they always were. And then it was not all right. Their measurements indicated that he had been dead for a fortnight. He should have been twenty weeks. Now he would always be eighteen.

She looked again at Joseph. Standing around redundantly. Waiting for her to give the cue that they could go. Retrace their steps, pass the sons and daughters who slept with the angels, the families gathered together in a single grave, the 'A true and courteous KNIGHT, who fell full knightly with his armour on' – a foot soldier in the First World War with a penchant for medieval romance – and finally walk by the high-gloss obelisks of the new burial plots, a miniature Chicago of the dead.

So she reached for his arm and they began to turn back the way they had come.

Eleven

Upstairs, Florence Brown had woken to a new day. Flowers from Robert dominated the small bedside cabinet.

'Don't worry,' she said, following her mother's gaze. 'It's nothing.'

There were two splashes of blood on the floor that Lydia was inspecting with a mixture of horror and distaste.

'It was only from my arm,' Florence explained.

'Well, thank goodness for that! But how on earth did it come from *your arm*?'

'Where the drip went in. Some horrible nurse wrenched it out in the middle of the night. I tried to stop her and there was a bit of a tussle, that's all.'

'Why were you trying to stop her?'

'Well, I was asleep. I thought I was being attacked or something. And then when I realized she was a nurse I wasn't sure she knew what she was doing. And judging by the state of my arm this morning, she didn't.'

'How long ago was that? You'd think someone might have cleaned the floor by now, wouldn't you?' Lydia tutted.

'I wouldn't think anything by now,' Florence replied drily.

She was alive and it looked as though she was going to stay in that condition for the foreseeable future. Sleep had restored reason and Florence had decided that an air bubble – if it was an air bubble –

would have struck within the first twelve hours. Robert had sent a reassuring text message in reply to her panicky enquiry of the night before: *dont think its a bubble, just a vacuum*. It was about as far from fatal as you could get.

'When's Robert coming?' Lydia asked.

'Not till tonight.'

'Why aren't they giving him compassionate leave?'

'I suppose they're not very compassionate.'

'Well, my dear, *I* have some good news for you.'

'Oh?'

'*Very* good news.'

Florence waited.

'Yes, and it's all because . . . Well, you wouldn't believe who *I* saw!'

Lydia looked around, as though fearing or rather hoping to be overheard, but she was disappointed. One oldster had died in the night and the other two beds were now empty. She turned back to her daughter.

'Who was it?' Florence asked obligingly.

'Professor Marvelle,' Lydia replied. 'He was here. *Actually* here! Going out of the hospital – we used the same double doors, or it may have been the revolving . . . let me think . . . no no no!' she cried in delight. '*That's* right. *He* was using the revolving door, although I didn't know, of course, at that point, that it was *him*. I was *going* to go through the revolving doors, but the timing of those things is always awkward. I never feel as though I'm quite in step with them – you know what I mean? Then he stopped to talk to someone and then I stopped him and he *did* remember you, my dear, and he said he'd come and look at your file just as soon as he has a moment. Apparently he has a radio interview this morning. *Radio!*' Lydia repeated excitably.

'And then I went through the double doors, and they were fine, or *more or less* fine . . .'

'To look at my file?' Florence repeated.

'Well, I don't think he's coming to look at your fanny, my dear!' Lydia always spoke unceremoniously of the nether parts: it made her feel aristocratic. 'Of course to look at your file. And then perhaps . . .'

'It's not as simple as all that.'

'I know it's not. That's *why*,' she said emphatically, as though Florence were the simpleton, 'I asked him to have a look. I think the hospital have treated you dreadfully, absolutely dreadfully. Apart from anything else, I can't see that it's very tactful of them to start poking around a woman who might be miscarrying with an operation through the *navel*, of all places. And now your arm as well! I think that if we can get one of their own onside to agree . . .'

'Listen to me, Mum!' Florence whispered urgently.

'Whatever is the matter with you today?' Lydia sounded surprised.

'I love Robert.'

'Of course you do. What's that got to do with anything?'

Florence paused. Was she really going to tell her mother about Thomas? In the circumstances there didn't seem to be any other choice.

'And I love Thomas,' Florence added quietly. 'Professor Marvelle.'

At this Lydia's eyes widened in horror and her green eyeshadow appeared to deepen. For some moments she seemed too shocked to speak.

'You don't mean you've . . . you haven't actually . . . ?'

'Yes.'

Again Lydia said nothing. Florence waited and watched as her mother took a seat.

'But . . . but this is dreadful,' Lydia protested, bewildered. 'And I

86

thought you and Robert were so happy! And he's so *nice*! How can you possibly . . . ?'

'Well, we are. And he is.'

'Well, then how . . . ?' Lydia sighed deeply and searched for an explanation. This was all wrong. 'No, you just haven't met the right man yet.'

'But that's what I'm trying to tell you – they're *both* the right man. It's possible to love two men at the same time.'

Florence had rehearsed this speech to imaginary audiences so many times that she could have given a complete abstract with bullet points.

'And the second thing is: I don't think there's any wrong in it. It's just that the world *thinks* it's wrong. For thousands or millions of years, everyone's thought it's wrong for the same reason that women are attracted to men who are strong and tall and good-looking.'

'Well, that's because they're the attractive ones,' Lydia objected, forgetting for a moment the immediate circumstances.

'*No!* Well, yes. But they're attractive to us because – you know about evolutionary biology, right?'

Lydia nodded doubtfully. Unlike Florence, the first in the family to go to university, her parents were uneducated. Florence remembered, however, the resistance she had encountered when she once tried to have the same discussion with Thomas. *Christ, this is a fun conversation,* he'd said, burying his head comically under a pillow. *Yes I always prefer algebra to sex myself.*

'It all goes back to when we lived in caves. We needed men to be strong so they could protect our babies from the other cave men with the clubs. And if they were tall and good-looking they were more likely to pass on healthy genes to our children. It's the same deal now. That's why we think they're attractive.'

'If you say so, my dear. But surely we think they're attractive because *they're attractive*.'

Lydia sat back with satisfaction at this triumph of irrefutable logic and touched her hairdo.

'All right,' Florence said, 'let's not get sidetracked. Point is: there's an evolutionary reason. It's not about right and wrong. It's about genes. And the same goes for prohibitions on adultery. Why does practically every society prohibit adultery?'

'Because it's *wrong*?'

'*No!* Because if we have sex with more than one man then we may fall pregnant by the wrong man and pass on the wrong genes.'

'Oh, my dear!' Lydia dropped to a whisper and, although there was still no one to hear, stood up and drew the curtain around the bed with elaborate care. It was a full minute before she spoke again. 'You don't mean . . . ?'

'Yes, exactly,' Florence replied. 'So he mustn't see my file.'

'No, he mustn't,' Lydia agreed, although she wasn't exactly clear why.

'Genes don't want that,' Florence said, resuming her explanation. 'And society doesn't want that. It wants to know that the landed estates are being passed on to the rightful heirs.'

'Nonsense,' Lydia said pleasantly, beginning to see advantages in her daughter's unexpected confession. To think that *her daughter* had actually seen a famous man *naked*! 'Who's got a landed estate?'

The future grandmother clasped her hands, warming romantically to the idea of dandling the great man's love child. 'And who minds when it's the son of the Professor? Or the daughter – just think of that!'

'What you've got to remember,' Florence continued, ignoring this interruption, 'is that the reasons why adultery is banned are not really moral ones. They're quite selfish, actually. It's all about paternity and property. And even if it wasn't about that, all morality is relativistic anyway.'

'Well, now,' Lydia replied, forgetting the Professor and, for a second, his appearance in the paper as well as on the radio, 'I don't think *that's* true either. You can't blame your relatives for *everything*, you know. It's true that I had two boyfriends, once, when I was about fifteen, but I can't say that I *loved* them both at the same time, or whatever it is you say you're managing to do. Hard enough to love *one* of the blighters at a time. Still, if it's the Professor we're talking about, then I can quite see . . . Yes. He *is* tall, isn't he?' Lydia mused. 'You're so right about that. But poor Robert,' she added insincerely.

Twelve

Half an hour later, Thomas Marvelle tip-tapped lightly up the remaining steps and emerged from the station onto the main road. He took a left towards the recording studio at Radio House. Several passers-by noticed the Professor, who was, indeed, well over six feet tall with cheeks in full bloom, and he smiled back warmly. Spotting a new mother in the crowd with a baby girl strapped to her chest – flowerpot pink sunhat, bare juicy legs dangling – he was reminded of the plight of poor Florence and felt a pang of anxious love. It was not in Thomas's nature to fret in the absence of the facts, however, and he quickly steered his mind in the direction of Radio House. At the reception desk, where the time – 09:36 – was displayed in giant red digits like an oversized alarm clock, he took a visitor's label and waited for his escort.

'Great!' the producer greeted him. 'You're here! You got my email about the change of format? Of course you did.'

Thomas nodded. Originally he had agreed to an interview; the producer now wanted a debate.

'So we've got Rita Morgan!' the producer said with a grin. 'Well, not exactly *got* her. She's on the line from L.A.'

Thomas frowned. *Rita Morgan?* The radical feminist who had made her name with that ridiculous book *The Rape of the Patient: Or, How Medicine Murders*? A fellow ectogeneticist or respiratory paediatrician

90

would have been nice. Even a bioethicist, with a book addressing the enormous difficulty of making beginning-of-life decisions on behalf of premature babies who could not speak for themselves, and a conclusion that there was, well, enormous difficulty. But Rita Morgan! It was hard to think of anyone he would like to talk to *less*. Particularly on prime-time radio, when he was just about to explain the summit of his life's work. They had clashed savagely, many years before, over his bestseller *F*ck On*. It was *The Joy of Sex* for the scientifically minded and Rita Morgan had castigated him, in a long and unimaginative article entitled 'F*ck off, Professor Marvelle', for denying the existence of the G-spot. In response he had castigated her for denying what excited some women sexually – in particular, for demonizing fantasies of rape and brutality – and thereby depriving a whole generation of women of a harmless erotic resource. Then his lover of the time had actually read Rita Morgan's famous book and everything changed overnight. An entire imaginary world constructed of their whispers – an uncivilization, as it were – collapsed and vanished.

For once, Thomas could not see where it had gone wrong. His personality was so forceful that women generally loved him like disciples. Until they became someone else's. He had lost two lovers to the Moonies, and a third to *Tapping the Healer Within*. Now he would have to endure old Rita Morgan herself. A relic from the 1970s whose armpits stank of garlic (well, perhaps there were some benefits to transatlantic communication). A woman who thought that patriarchy had hardly changed from prehistory to the present, and that it was her job to alert women to its workings everywhere. Not least, he supposed, inside Wet Incubators.

'All right,' he said. 'I can do that. But can I give you a word of advice in future?'

'Of course,' she replied coolly.

'You don't always have to pick an extremist, you know, in order to get a debate. Why give airtime to loony tunes?'

'I wouldn't say she's an extremist.' The producer sounded slightly affronted. 'She's very popular and we're very lucky to have her on the programme. And you, of course. Now. Did you get your copy of Rita's new book all right? Had a flick through?'

Rita Morgan! And her bloody book too! Why had he not been told about this? He had been told about this. He vaguely remembered throwing out something that had arrived in a padded envelope with a rubber band around it.

Again he nodded and the producer said, 'Marvellous! Looking forward to it!'

The programme had begun with a long interview of Rita Morgan, so they were already on air when Thomas entered the studio. The radio presenter looked up from his monitor, grinned and then winked at the Professor as he took a seat at the round table. Thomas had known Peter Potter when he was just some little turd working for *The Daily Turd*, or whatever that paper was called.

He put on his headphones as Peter continued, 'just *full* of the most *fasc*inating insights.'

There was a copy of a book called *The Womb and the Tomb* on the table – a study, evidently, of the supposed evils of birth technologies throughout the ages. The Professor reached forward, opened a page at random and began to read: 'Tutankhamun was mummified with his penis erect, for an eternity of bliss. Also in the tomb were the remains of two foetuses conceived by his wife. These practices, which sound so remote and exotic, in fact take us to the heart of the social and political mechanisms still controlling female reproduction, particularly when it appears to go "wrong" . . .'

Christ Almighty.

'So that's *The Womb and the Tomb* by Rita Morgan, on sale in the UK from Monday, at a recommended purchase price of £17.99.'

Rita laughed appreciatively. 'Thanks, Peter!'

'Professor Marvelle, inventor of the Wet Incubator, we've just been talking to Dr Rita Morgan about her latest book, *The Womb and the Tomb*.'

'Hi, Rita,' Thomas said unenthusiastically.

'Hey, Peter,' Rita replied merrily to the presenter instead, 'do you think you could say that one more time? You know, my name? And the title of my book? And especially the part about my name?'

Everyone, even Thomas, laughed.

'Professor Marvelle, I want to begin by asking, well, what's in a name? The Wet Incubator is called that because, unlike a normal incubator, it's filled with liquid, right?'

'It's an artificial amniotic fluid that we've found to be very successful. The basic principle of WI – of Wet Incubation – is that the foetus continues to gestate in fluid while its lungs mature. And that means that we will now be able to save the lives of younger babies than ever before. With Anna—'

'The first human patient ever to be Wet Incubated,' Peter interrupted for the benefit of listeners. 'Anna Mirabel, as her parents have named her, who came out of the incubator earlier today after fourteen weeks of additional "gestation" . . .'

'Yes. And for that to happen successfully, the foetal body has to be tricked, as it were, into believing that it hasn't been born and doesn't need, therefore, to do any of the things that would occur at a normal delivery.'

'And they would be . . . ?'

'Well, things like taking a breath in response to the high

intrathoracic pressure, or absorbing liquid from the lungs into the lymphatics, or the foetus changing how it circulates the blood around its heart. Closing the *ductus arteriosus* – that kind of thing. Because, of course, the foetus doesn't need to make the adaptation to extra-uterine life yet. Most of this part of the process,' the Professor continued more simply, realizing from Peter Potter's frown that he was in danger of losing his audience, 'is managed chemically, although a caesarean delivery also makes a physical difference to the behaviour of the lungs. Then after delivery the baby is placed straight into the WI, before its lungs have become operational or try to become operational . . .'

'You've only got a tiny window of opportunity, right?' Peter asked. 'To get the baby in there?'

'That's right. With Anna we did the transfer within seconds. If the foetal lungs have started to develop, then it's very important that they don't actually attempt to breathe. So that's why we suppress the instinct to breathe chemically. In most cases, though, the lungs will be far too primitive to inflate anyway. But for all kinds of reasons it's imperative to transfer the foetus as rapidly as possible from the mother to the Wet Incubator and that's why we prefer to use it in conjunction with a C-section, when we can exactly decide the moment of delivery.'

'So the baby's delivered, it's immediately placed in the Wet Incubator, and then what?'

'Well, basically, from that point on, the foetus experiences a new phase of uterine existence. Effectively, the Wet Incubator becomes its placenta.'

'Yes, I was wondering what happens to the real placenta?'

'It's removed manually after the delivery of the baby. The important thing, what makes the survival of the foetus possible, is that the Wet Incubator assumes the dual functions of the placenta: the removal of waste products and the supply of oxygen as well as nutrition.'

Thomas paused. The functions of the placenta: how easy it was to say and how hard it had been to do! Previous experimenters had not even been able to get the tubes connecting to the diminutive umbilicus to stay in place. As for the mimicry of pregnancy hormones, that was a recipe of daunting complexity. It made the formulation of Total Parenteral Nutrition – intravenous feeding developed for neonates in the 1960s – look like child's play. For unless everything was absolutely right, the vital thing would not happen and the newborns did not thrive. In Japan, foetal lambs dunked in a tank of amniotic fluid all died (Thomas was not surprised) within hours of their emergence. In California, a team of researchers had brought test-tube mice to term. However, the animals were all grotesque as well as terminal. But a prototype of WI had gestated seventeen still-living mice who were extraordinary for being so ordinary. In fact, it was only the chemistry of maternal emotions communicating themselves to the foetus that Thomas and his team had left alone.

'Can any baby go in the Wet Incubator?'

'No, it's specifically intended for foetuses of around twenty to twenty-three weeks who would otherwise be highly unlikely to survive due to insufficiently developed lungs.'

'And will it ever be used for younger foetuses?'

'In due course, we think so, yes.'

'In that case, Professor, I was wondering whether it wouldn't be more accurate, especially in the light of Rita's study, not to mention more *exciting*,' Peter Potter's voice dropped silkily, 'for our listeners at home, if you were to call the Wet Incubator . . . an Artificial Womb? Because that's basically what it is, isn't it?'

'No, it would be more accurate to call it what I've called it.'

And so it had begun. The perverse misinterpreters of his work were back in business, and now *his* medical breakthrough was being saddled to *her* pile of horseshit. He had paused only fractionally but already the interviewer was prompting, 'Rita?'

Hang on! Thomas thought. She doesn't know anything about it.

'Yes, Peter, you're absolutely right about this. The instruments of reproductive control typically disguise themselves as women's helpers. I think the really operative word in everything the Professor has said is "tricked". He talks about tricking the foetal body and that is what reproductive medicine always does. The names of these technologies and procedures sound so innocuous but they are in fact . . .'

Rita had her serious gushy voice on now. And it was true, Thomas reflected, that he had quite consciously decided to call his invention an incubator because the term was sanctioned by long usage in neonatology. But it was more than a matter of semantics: the technology was not designed to take on test-tube babies but specifically to facilitate lung development in mid-term prems. It was not and never would be an Artificial Womb. The bad press on those stretched back, as Rita was now busy explaining, to the most ancient myths. Jove impregnated Semele. It was not a rape – for once. But then she made a fatal request: to see him in his heavenly glory as if he were making love to his wife, the goddess Juno. The vision was literally blazing and Semele fried instantly. The foetus, however, survived – snatched from the flames and implanted in the artificial womb of Jove's thigh, like some huge supernumerary scrotal sack.

'So if we will only listen to our literature,' Rita concluded, 'we will learn why the new phallocratic birth technologies are to be feared. Personally, whenever I think of the word "medi*cine*", all I notice is the *sin*.'

'With respect, Dr Morgan,' Peter Potter intervened lightly, 'do you think you might just need to learn how to *spell*?'

Rita laughed good-naturedly and Thomas remembered that this was radio. It was meant to sound like a good time, with the presenter taking a wicked pop at you every so often and otherwise egging you on to the jovial murder of your debating opponent. This lethal joshing. Voices full of politician smiles. A mask of conviviality and a competition in ironic self-deprecation. He also remembered now the title of Rita's 1982 book: *The Feminist Osteopath*. No, *The Feminist Homeopath*. Her doctorate must be in homeopathy or psychology or some godforsaken discipline of that sort.

'All right, Professor,' Peter cued him, 'who put the sin in medicine? Is all this criticism justified?'

'Peter, you have to remember that I'm only a lowly person, without a *single – recognized – qualification* in . . . homeopathy, to my name.'

'Not like that big shot Rita Morgan, huh?' Rita Morgan joked amiably.

'Exactly. But insofar as I understand Rita's position, and she can correct me if I'm wrong . . .'

Rita Morgan argued that all conventional doctors were rapists. But some doctors were more rapist than others.

'Artificial Insemination, for instance, Rita will tell you, is rape in fancy dress, passing itself off as medical practice. Obs and Gynae are there to disempower women because a pack of nineteenth-century doctors got terrified of their awesome reproductive powers. And SCBUs exist, not to save the lives of babies, but to usurp the functions of the womb with gadgetry that's—'

Rita interrupted. 'As Professor Marvelle knows, it's a well-documented fact that the first AI *was* a rape. 1884. The patient was chloroformed and then syringed with a medical student's sperm. They never *asked*. They never even told her afterwards.'

'Thing is, Reet, I'm noticing a bit of a pattern here. Tutankhamun. Jove. 1884. If a technology can be associated with some unsavoury episode in the far distant past, then your argument seems to be that we should reject it now and for evermore. No doubt—'

'No, what I'm—'

'Just let me finish please. No doubt the next thing you're going to tell us is that in the nineteenth century the first dry incubators were displayed at world fairs so paying visitors could peer at the prems, along with all the other curiosities like dwarves and the dysmorphic. *Ergo*, all incubators are evil and we shouldn't be using them now. Everything forever tainted by its origins. A sort of bastardy of technology, if you like. Which is curious, not to mention confusing, because I know you've argued on many occasions that bastardy is a harmful social construct, an invention of men which says that women can't legitimize their own children. Right? But that's by the by. Let's go back a few years further. 1799. The French scientist Étienne Geoffroy Saint-Hilaire is in Egypt. He takes a look at what ordinary farmers are doing on the Nile – incubating chicken eggs in pots over slow-burning dung – and experiments with what happens if you shake them around a bit. Or pierce the shells. Or overheat them. The chicks don't do so well. They die. They come out deformed. So, what, let's abandon modern thermal warmer units, shall we? Now we know where they *came* from, now they're disgraced, let's wheel them out of SCBUs and NICUs the world over.'

'Dr Rita Morgan: is that what you're saying?' Peter Potter asked.

'That is not what I'm saying. The history of reproductive

interventions is alarming, yes, but sadly it is *not just* long-dead history. We find just the same atrocities practised in the present day. Women as the lab rats of medical experiment. Invasion of the body. The elimination of women's rights to control the reproductive functions of their own bodies. Overtreatment and medicalization of the natural processes of birth – all in the name of helpful healing, of course, but really all in the service of—'

'As a physician I can tell you that Nature is overrated. Try telling a hyena about the virtues of a natural birth. Am I allowed to say . . . ?' Spotted hyenas gave birth through the clitoris. 'Never mind. Let's just say that they give birth through a tract so narrow that two-thirds of their firstborn die before they can take a breath. So it's a mistake to get all sentimental about Mother Nature. Who has root canal treatment the "natural" way, without anaesthetic? Do *you*?'

'It's typical of doctors who want to experiment on women to claim that their technologies exist purely to help patients and alleviate their pain.'

'Of *course* the WI exists to help women!' Thomas was finding it difficult to hold back his fury now. '*And* their babies. Right now it is the very best form of medical intervention that can be offered to a woman who goes into an unstoppable preterm labour at less than twenty-three weeks.'

'Does that happen often?' Peter Potter asked mildly.

'No. I should emphasize that this is quite a rare medical event. So the technology has a very particular application. Which means that the fears of feminists, and the scaremongering of newspapers, who say that eventually there will mass ectogenesis for women with entirely healthy pregnancies – I just don't see that happening. The enormous cost, apart from anything, would be prohibitive. I remember Rita herself predicted that by the year 2000 all embryos would be routinely extracted from their mother's wombs and checked for genetic defects before reimplantation would be permitted. A wholly unfounded fantasy. The idea that foetal medicine is some kind of vast conspiracy against women that doctors, whether we realize it or not, are all implicated in, is simply – ' Thomas gave a short laugh – '*lu*dicrous. Whether or not we even use WI – the Wet Incubator – in the case of an extremely premature baby is entirely the mother's decision.'

'And there's a special legal reason for that too, isn't there?' Peter Potter said.

'Yes. Foetuses of less than twenty-four weeks are not recognized as persons in UK law, so any treatment decisions must defer to the mother's wishes.'

'And laws can change in *five* minutes!' Rita retorted. 'There doesn't *need* to be mass ectogenesis for that to happen. Once the technology is demonstrated to work in just a *single* case—'

'As, indeed, it now has,' Peter interjected.

Rita continued. 'Yes exactly and when you've got men like Randall Harrison and Al Johnson-Smith Junior going around saying – ' here she adopted a deep Southern accent – '"we can support prenatal life in the second trimester now", then changes to the law on both sides of the Atlantic are inevitably going to follow. Legal abortion will start to be withdrawn and all this talk of women's decisions and the mother's wishes is just a whitewash . . .'

'A *whitewash*! Look, it's a tendency of Rita's – of feminists and ideologists more generally, in fact – to clump everything together. To blackwash, if you like. And really it's an abdication of the responsibility to think hard about anything any more. Once you decide that it's all bad, that it's all corrupt, then you never have to think carefully about the individual cases and the particular circumstances – which is exactly what we have to do in medicine every day. Beginning- and end-of-life decisions, in particular, are highly situational. But if you just read everything through the lens of feminism, then all actions become equally significant – or insignificant. If I "save" a life, then I am merely supplying society with another patriarch or victim – right?'

'We come back to our starting point. "By a *commodius vicus* of recirculation—"'

'I'm not sure that quoting *Finnegans Wake* casts all that much light,' Thomas interrupted sarcastically.

'Look at the language, is what I mean. *Supplying*, the Professor says. Supply and demand. Economics, in other words. Why is it really called an incubator? Successful established businesses "incubate" new ones during the start-up period so they can become profitable more quickly. For the same reason we talk of sperm *banks*. So when I say whitewash, it *is* just a whitewash, trying to disguise the fact that women only have the "choices" – in inverted commas – that a male-dominated capitalist society allows them.'

'And some of our listeners,' Peter Potter responded drily, 'may well be wondering what choices are open to fathers and *their* unborn. So let's hear from them. Our first caller today is Jenny from Hampstead. Hello, Jenny! Who is your question for and what did you want to ask?'

There was a crackle and then a slightly embarrassed young woman began to speak. 'My question is for the Professor and I'd like to ask him: what does the Wet Incubator look like?'

'Oh.' The very simplicity and non-adversarial nature of the question took the Professor by surprise. 'Well, it's smaller than a conventional incubator, for starters, and rather elegant too, I think, a lovely egg shape, although I have seen some quite swish-looking dry incubators.'

The fundamental technological design of ordinary 'dry' incubators had changed relatively little since the 1920s. New products were therefore marketed either for their cosmetic attractions or greater cost-effectiveness. He remembered encountering some rather stylish, oval-shaped 'life pods' in a NICU (Neonatal Intensive Care Unit) in Norway, inspired by the sleekness of contemporary bathroom design. At the other extreme, budget incubators manufactured from recycled car parts were now being tried in the Indian market. The technology of 'dry' incubation was relatively simple. It was mostly about keeping babies warm. It was the instinct of any nursing mother – any fellow human being, in fact – expressed in plastic form. So you could dress it up or down, it still did the same thing. The WI retained and improved that original protective thermal function, but technologically it was radically different from the 'dry' incubator. Enormously complex, in fact.

'The people who had the most to do with the appearance of the Wet Incubator were Phoenix Resources.'

Everyone at Phoenix, the medical tech design company Thomas had taken the project to, had been helpful but their contributions were, in the event, relatively trivial. A grooveless outer casing for ease of cleaning. A tailor-made blackout cloth – used almost continuously, he explained to the radio questioner, in order to mimic the darkness of the womb. And a couple of extra 'save' functions on the underwater cameras that allowed the team to watch and record the progress of the foetus. Everything that was difficult and really innovative about the WI was Thomas's triumph alone. Members of his research team had sometimes been good at tracking down filter coffee. More recently, he had been grateful that the manufacturers, Incu-Med in Bologna, had simply done exactly what they were asked.

'And the incubator rotates on its stand,' Thomas added, 'so that the foetus has the sensation of being inside a living person. For about eight hours at night the rotations decrease to almost nothing to correspond to a mother's sleep pattern.'

The second listener, a teenage boy, asked, 'What do you do if you've got two premature babies and only one Wet Incubator?'

Thomas replied, 'The principle is called triage. I have to decide, not which baby most needs the help of the WI, but which baby is most likely to survive healthily in the long term. Candidates for the WI have generally already had an anomaly scan, to check for abnormalities, or if not we can do one on the spot. This isn't to say, of course,' he added hastily, 'that the WI would never be used for a foetus with a disability. I don't mean that at all. But if, say, the foetus was anencephalic – and we therefore knew for certain that the baby would not live for more than a few days – then it would not be an appropriate use of the technology, particularly since we only have one incubator at the moment. But if, say, the choice was between a female and a male foetus and all other things were equal, we would select the female because for reasons unknown to us they thrive better than males.'

'It's called eugenics,' Rita said firmly. 'The selection and engineering of human babies who are deemed suitable "products", and the discarding of the supposedly defective ones. The survival of the foetus, as the Professor likes to call it, is the survival of the fittest and it depends on neglect of the weakest.'

Thomas sighed impatiently. 'You know, I think that if we could just, for a second – for a *fraction* of a second, a decimal place is all I'm asking – just look at this subject from *any other* point of view than the homeopathic-feminist one, then I could explain quite easily why it's not a short hop from the Wet Incubator to *The Matrix* or the Third Reich.'

Later that day, Thomas would pick up a copy of the *Evening News* with a lead article entitled, 'A Short Hop from Wet Inc to *The Matrix*?'

Thirteen

Side A of the neonatal intensive care unit resembled the Starship Enterprise on a good day. All systems humming with efficiency, automated glass doors swished instantly open or shut with a slight, satisfying push of large metal buttons. Slimline employees – well, mostly slimline, their colleague Sheryl wasn't – wore blue and white uniforms that matched the walls. Like the babies, everything was new.

Side A took in the most critically ill babies – whether due to their extreme prematurity or other complications. The Wet Incubator was housed in an adjacent corridor, and the patients who emerged from it would be brought here, to side A, before progressing, as was hoped, to the less intensive care regime of side B and then, finally, going home with their parents.

While Thomas was en-route back to the hospital following his media appearance, Helen sanitized her hands with an alcohol rub from the wall dispenser outside side A, then let herself in with the swipe card attached to the bottom of her royal blue blouson. She told herself she was not thinking about . . . Was Gloria Vine buried there too? . . . Gloria, an energetic sexagenarian who had worn regal winter coats and was seen around the hospital almost as often after her retirement as she had been before. Helen had never been close to her, but ever since Gloria had died unexpectedly in the same week as Helen's baby, she found herself thinking about her frequently. Sometimes she would see a stranger in the street, or an outpatient waiting in the hospital, and think: *Goodness me! That might be Gloria!* But as the stranger came closer, Gloria Vine would always vanish.

His small untouched bones . . . No, she had left the cemetery behind her this morning and then Joseph had kissed her cheek and now she was busy and thinking only of the tasks ahead.

In a small bright room to the left she opened the fridge. Phalanxes of Sterifeed milk bottles stoutly confronted her. She took out the highest tray, placed it on the Formica worktop, and checked that the contents corresponded, in amount and type, to a list held in the top drawer that she'd prepared the day before. It gave her a simple satisfaction to work down the list. To tick that Baby Anna Mirabel did indeed have six bottles of FM (type SMA) of 156ml each and that Emily Jane – although she had necrotizing entercoliticis, which meant that portions of her intestines were dead and had been surgically removed like so many coils of black pudding – nonetheless had the correct number of feeds today, comprising half BM, half FM, plus her antibiotics. Then Helen took out another tray and another, occasionally supplementing or substituting a feed, not because the technician had made any mistakes but because she was working to more recent information and, in one or two cases, having a brighter idea about the feeding regime. Finally all of the bottles were back in the fridge, waiting to be useful. An army of plastic lifesavers.

Crossing the hall, she used another alcohol rub, opened the door and then washed her hands in one of two large low rectangular basins that looked like gleaming pig troughs. The water drummed noisily on the metal in the near-silence of the unit. She dried her hands carefully and then set about applying alcohol rub from the next wall dispenser. At the reception desk she returned a series of telephone calls from parents who for one reason or another could not visit their babies in person. Trauma. Work commitments. Sometimes, she suspected, sheer laziness. There were mothers she privately regarded with contempt; others for whom she felt the deepest empathy. As there was nothing material to report in any of these cases, anxieties were alleviated and consciences were allayed all round. Three-quarters of an hour later she walked down the short corridor to the third and final room in the unit, where she was sharing the shift with Sheryl.

It was at this point that she realized she could hear the baby crying. It was faint but quite persistent. This was unusual. Only well babies cried. The sick ones here did not have the energy. And Edward Bailey, the child who had been born last Tuesday without eyes, simply could not cry. Outside the glass door she applied alcohol rub a fourth time, just as thoroughly, then pressed the lighted entry button. A second later the door closed automatically behind her.

All was silent – eerily so, she sometimes felt – and today she was especially afraid. Sheryl had her head bent over paperwork. The room was calm and still except for the low hum of the machines. None of the babies was crying. None of them, in fact, was awake, not even Anna Mirabel, whose parents stood silently beside her cot, holding hands. Helen hoped it was a baby upstairs, then, or out in the corridor, who was crying, and once the door had closed she was prevented from hearing it. She hoped – with a tremor of fear – that it was not an aural hallucination, something more than the thoughts that had disturbed her in the cemetery. She did not, however, hold out very much hope. The sound was clearly of a baby crying and there was some unreal quality to its projection that could only mean one thing.

There used to be a baby crying inside her head, but he had stopped some weeks ago. Or rather, she had, reluctantly, stopped herself. So reluctantly that she hardly trusted herself to decide whether he – or the sound – was back or not. She felt a moment of sick anxiety. Mercifully, there wasn't time to worry about it. Not with Anna Mirabel's parents here and the doctors due for rounds at any moment.

'You got kids?' the father asked politely as she approached them.

'Um – no,' Helen replied as the glass door swished open again and she watched Professor Marvelle arrive like a celebrity with his juniors in tow. 'No kids.'

Only at the bottom of the autopsy form. 'Relationship to child. Mother.'

They looked down at the sleeping Anna. She wore nothing but wires and a nappy, a special micro-size that Pampers made for hospitals. It was important not to let her overheat in the dry incubator. She had been transferred from the Wet Incubator Room just a few hours before. Helen was conscious of her investment in this baby. Everyone was interested in Anna, of course, as the first user of the Wet Incubator, but for Helen this tiny patient's progress was also uniquely significant. Silently she would evaluate other women's bumps in relation to the one she should have been carrying. These were her son's contemporaries – still gestating. Today the four months since her miscarriage had elapsed and those contemporaries were being born upstairs. Some had arrived earlier; within a couple of weeks there would be none left. The last would be induced a fortnight after the due date. But she could also make comparisons with the new arrivals in the SCBU. Anna was twenty weeks and a day when they placed her inside the Wet Incubator. The size and the age that Helen's son should have been at the time of her scan. One day the new technology might even be offered to a foetus of eighteen weeks and then there would be an exact correspondence. A point of resumption at last.

As he came into the room the Professor held up his hands and announced, in a mock-booming voice, 'It's all right! Don't panic! I'm here now.'

The first time Helen had heard this it had been moderately funny. Now it irritated her that everyone laughed enthusiastically, especially Sheryl, who was fat and frizzy and desperate to flirt. And hadn't anyone noticed there were parents here?

Helen opened the portal doors of the dry incubator while a junior doctor – still resistant to Thomas's teasing – in a bogey-green V-neck cashmere sweater, check shirt and floppy bow tie, began to summarize.

'This is Anna Mirabel on her first day on side A, her ninety-eighth day in all. Anna—'

'And this is Mummy and Daddy,' Helen interrupted.

She beamed rather too hard and indicated in the direction of the baby's parents. So what if she annoyed Thomas Marvelle? Stephen and Sally had shrunk back in the direction of a dado rail, which ran the whole room, with sockets and plugs bearing electrical safety stickers. Thomas had already acknowledged the pair, in fact, with a brief nod.

'Hello, Mummy and Daddy,' everyone else said and smiled politely.

All eyes returned to the baby girl. Little Anna had begun to stir, her face wrinkling as though she was frowning, as though she understood that everyone around the bedside was counting on her to make medical history – as the first baby ever to be Wet Incubated and the youngest, therefore, to survive without any significant morbidity – when all she wanted to do was sleep. Warily she opened her eyes, but only a fraction before shutting them again, as though she would much rather that everyone went away. Thomas watched her with an attention that was more arresting than the baby herself. His face, concentrated with sympathy, read her body like some difficult but melodious inscription that had yet to communicate its secret. Then suddenly the baby made a movement that caught everyone's attention.

The four red twigs that were her arms and legs shot out like an alarmed starfish. Her eyes were wide open now and staring blindly. The telephone had started to ring.

'Moro,' Thomas whispered, thrilled for her. Two neurologists had told him that Anna had the moro reflex, exactly as a newborn should, but this was the first time he'd observed it for himself. 'It's all right, little one. It's only the telephone.'

Anna's limbs were so light she could suspend them indefinitely without apparent effort. They hung centimetres above the tiny mattress, as though racked, or paralysed in position. Gradually she relaxed, her eyes closed, and the limbs sank, then retracted foetally into her body. As the junior spoke of the baby's recent transferral to side A, her lowered ventilation requirement, and the general prognosis, a small bubble of spit formed at the bow of her mouth, then popped. Again Anna opened her eyes briefly. Then she slipped back into sleep.

'Good girl!' Thomas whispered and smiled. The parents felt proud and almost tearful. The young people stood around awkwardly and seemed embarrassed by the Professor's tenderness, his incredulous murmuring, but he didn't care.

'Observe!' Thomas said a moment later, flinging an arm in the direction of another baby, in the adjacent cot, who was due for discharge that afternoon.

The child reposed like a supermarket chicken. Thomas was fond of this baby too; the last to be born before the WI become operational, he seemed to represent every patient that the Professor had been unable to do enough for. Every imperfect intervention, every halfway technology designed by others. The child's tiny rear was slightly elevated.

'Observe the bum in the air! The bum in the air is also a very good sign. Forget *The Contented Little Baby* book. It's the contented little bum you're after.'

Sheryl giggled.

The telephone was still ringing softly as the team left the room. Thomas glanced at Helen as though to say: Don't you have a telephone to answer? A nappy to change? But she merely looked back at him and stood her ground.

Sheryl answered the telephone and turned to Helen. 'It's your husband.'

'Tell him I'll phone him in my next break,' Helen replied without moving.

Fourteen

It was lunchtime, in fact, before Helen could return Joseph's call. Turning right along a short corridor, she made for the stockroom. For a moment she stood there in the dark and strained for the sound of a baby crying, her lost little boy, not knowing what she wanted: to hear it or not to hear it. She felt her heart rate rising unsteadily and by habit took her own pulse. Breathing slowly she decided that she couldn't hear anything now. Whatever had happened earlier, wherever the strange noise of the crying baby had come from, it was over. Calming herself down with this thought, she felt relieved, on the whole, and only slightly regretful.

Shutting the door, leaving a fractional crack of light, she turned on her mobile. Then she lowered herself carefully into a broken rocking chair with a jade green padded seat cover that the administration had promised to have repaired two weeks before.

The stockroom was her responsibility and it had become her sanctuary. All of the neatly organized stocks, supplies, preparations, methods and protocols of her profession insulated its practitioners, to an extent, from all the shocks. The births of human monsters. The deaths of baby children. And all the daily disasters in between, the rather complicated states of disarray into which the body had fallen. Abnormality was a failure of organization – a result of cells not going where they ought and doing what they should. From the very inception of life we were required to organize ourselves. We turned ourselves from a ball of cells into a disc with a hole, 'the primitive streak', through which our cells streamed and arranged themselves in three layers. These streaming cells looked, Helen imagined, much like a computer-generated image of sand running to the corner of the screen – smoothly and slickly attracted in the right direction. Getting ourselves together was, then, our primitive streak. Sometimes, however, the primordial chaos remained fairly chaotic: many sick neonates had once been disorganized embryos. An element of personal blame seemed to attach to the embryos themselves if you thought of them as being well or badly organized. But Helen, who was unsparing of herself, did, in fact, think of anomalous embryos as being rather like teenage boys in the face of a command to tidy their bedrooms. Indeed, it was commonplace in the neonatal unit to urge the newborns, 'Come on! Show us what you're made of!'

Sometimes they were made of too much, though, and the results of disorganization were superfluities as well as omissions. Supernumerary ears dangling from necks like a sick joke from the men's toy shop. A frieze of hearts. On one occasion, parts for twenty-one foetuses were counted – by the legs remaining inside the brain of their sibling – like a hideous origami, or as though the whole stock cupboard had been taken to a single bedside and repeated its contents over the spread. Such births were highly confidential: intriguing tragedies, devastating curiosities, kept out of the papers if at all possible. And there would have been many more such births, of course, were it not for the natural filter of miscarriage. One in two hundred miscarried foetuses, for example, was cyclopic. In order to avoid such disasters, the embryo needed a lot of help to organize itself: signalling molecules urged cells this way and that. To go there or to become that – brain or bone. Theoretically, these original cells could become any part of the body and the signalling molecules were therefore competing for their attention. Become leg! No, lung! Everyone was pitching for their own corner.

'More knob, please!' Joseph had once shouted, immediately in role as noggin, when Helen explained this process to him. 'If you could all just make your way down there quickly and quietly, thank you!'

Helen had been aghast. She found this sort of joke distasteful as well as reductive. She'd said that if he wanted a truer analogy, the embryos who became neonatal patients faced a new set of 'noggins'. Doctors specializing in different areas of the human body stood over them and determined the relative priority of brain, heart, lungs and limbs, in what was to be done. Joseph waited for the punchline – there was none – then said, 'You're a funny girl, you know that.'

Now she dialled the home number. Joseph picked up almost immediately.

'I just wanted to check you were all right,' he said.

'I'm all right,' she said and sighed.

'It wasn't – isn't – easy for you, my love.'

'Or for you.'

'It's different for you.'

'Is it?' she asked more intensely. 'Don't you think about it?'

'Yes, I do.'

In the near-darkness, on the telephone, almost anonymous, it was easier to ask her urgent, held-back questions.

'What do you think? Tell me!'

'I think of,' Joseph sighed, thought, sighed, 'well, his indignity. When we saw him he was sort of caught out, naked, with his tiny pot belly, before he'd even had time to grow proper *skin*! It didn't look as though we should even be looking at him.'

'Yes,' Helen replied. 'I'm so used to seeing them small and red – whereas you . . .'

'It's all right, my love.'

They paused.

'Shall I pick you up? Five past eight?'

'All right.'

Emerging from the stock cupboard she heard laughter. It was Sheryl, who dragged her by the arm into the kitchenette opposite.

'Oh, it was so funny!' Sheryl said. 'Thomas was so cross, you should have *heard* him! He wanted to know what the terrible noise was but they were all too afraid to tell him!'

Sheryl wept with laughter and was obliged to sit down on the only stool. It took several minutes before Helen heard the whole story of the juniors' latest blunder – and discovered the source of the earlier 'crying'. Generally, silence reigned in the neonatal nurseries. Parents crept around, solemn and afraid, like visitors to Dachau; doctors and nurses worked quietly, even in urgent circumstances, because premature babies were known to be affected adversely by loud noises. But different rules applied in the nearby Wet Incubator Room: Sophie Rose, the new Wet Incubee, and only the second human patient to use the technology, was still gestating. So the idea was to replicate the uterine experience of the foetus, including external noise. The WI had a Speak mode. Most of Thomas's efforts in this area, however, had been in restraining the frivolous innovations of his underlings on the research team. Apparently they had put on some sort of crying baby CD, which Thomas hadn't heard before.

'So then he said to them, "Acclimatize the foetus to life on planet earth, huh! You Too Can Learn Crying In A Week?" Crying In A Week!' Sheryl repeated, shaking helplessly with laughter again. 'And he said, "That's not even how they cry, you great banana! What are you trying to turn the kid into – a fire engine?"' Sheryl wiped her eyes.

A Movement cycle was also left on for most of the day. This was designed to make the foetus feel that s/he had not just been left in a plastic box on some shelf in a laboratory, but was inside a walking, standing, bending, sitting woman who sometimes went up or down the stairs, took a lift or a bus – or, in one abandoned program, a hovercraft.

'A *hover*craft!' Sheryl shrieked. 'Can you just i*magine*! Oh, *come on*, girl, have a laugh will you!'

'I'm sorry,' Helen replied earnestly and tried to explain. 'I've never had much of a sense of humour. When I was a child I used to say that I couldn't see what function jokes served.'

'Yes, I can see that about you.'

At five past eight, Helen left the hospital alone. A heavily pregnant woman wearing a familiar, terrified look on her face hobbled past with the support of her partner. Helen took a left, in the direction of the student housing block – a surprisingly grand affair, at least from the outside, in a former manor house. Further down the slope she passed the new children's wing, which was clad in large squares of primary colour, as though everything could be as easily fixed as Lego. A minute later she stood waiting for Joseph by the staff car park and looked back at the old wing of the main hospital building. The central stairwell was like a lighthouse. But behind the huge 1960s windows, inside each cubicle inside each room inside each ward, there were people in pain. Women, mostly. Girls too. This was the discovery that she had made, four months ago and twenty-five years too late – how real pain was. How slow and how inescapable. Emotional pain especially. And not only her own pain, but everyone else's. It was not always the traumatic losses that troubled her. More generally she would find herself thinking of places she had once lived and men she had once loved and even of teachers she had once had. It was all so irrecoverably gone and she felt full of pain for its passing and anxiety for the people who had been part of those times. Where were they now?

But certainly it was the unhappier endings of pregnancy that dominated her mourning thoughts. She knew now what an abortion was. She had never wanted an abortion, of course, but inadvertently she had been through the same physical experience – the hospital used the same chemical evacuators – and it had broken her heart to think of all the others. Some of them younger. Less ready. And – worst of all, the part she had been spared – guilty of a decision. Joseph's words on the telephone had reminded her of an incident during her medical training when a midwife was administering an abortifacient to a teenager. The girl was told to come back in forty-eight hours.

Will it hurt when . . . ? the girl asked timidly.

When you come back? the midwife had replied euphemistically. Yes.

I can't lie to you. It *will* hurt a bit. But we can give you painkillers.

Will I see it?

If you want to, yes. You can see it when it's born. Or we can take it away and you can see it afterwards, when you're ready.

What will it – look like?

Very red. They're like – little aliens. My son has a toy, I always think they look like that. But you don't have to see it till you're ready.

But still the girl couldn't visualize how anything was going to happen. Will I have to push? she asked.

The midwife had raised her head sadly. No, she said. It's still very small. That makes it easier.

Easier. Helen looked up at Level 7, the top storey of the hospital, and stared. It had enormous wall-length windows, like a penthouse without the luxury. Neonatal nurses rarely if ever had reason to go to Level 7. No one born on Level 7 lived. Not for more than a few minutes, anyway. That was why they were all the way up on Level 7. Far from the operating theatres, the neonatal nurseries, and all the other sites of intervention. That was where the chemical abortions were done, mostly for reasons of convenience and youth, occasionally after a serious handicap had been detected by ultrasound or amniocentesis. Someone up there had a view of the late evening sunset, the lurid pink and orange abstract that God had been busy with. Someone else was looking at the blanket on the bed that had been made for them – the cellular, open-weave, crochet-effect white blanket that looked as if it belonged in a cot. And someone else was perhaps looking at the bin in the bathroom – the large yellow disposal sack on a metal frame with powerful jaws and a black cross above the words 'Human Waste'. She felt in pain for all of them. No longer merely observing the trauma of the world, but trying to feel what she imagined the others must be feeling. At times it was nearly too much for her. She remembered that her GP had been baffled when she said she was upset, as much as anything, by what happened to these other women.

'But yours was a miscarriage,' she recalled him objecting gently.

'Yes, but don't you see – I'm luckier than them.'

The doctor had replied sensibly. 'I don't think you've been lucky at all. And it's what they choose and the best thing in the circumstances.'

Then he'd signed her off work for another fortnight.

She continued to stare at the building, thinking of the new women behind those windows. Their turn today. And as she began to imagine, then actually to feel, the combination of those traumas once again devolving on her single person, to calculate and to stagger under that great multiplication of pain upon pain, her heart felt like a clenched fist.

Miscarriage. Abortion. Stillbirth. Women everywhere, grieving for someone they had barely known. Aching to hold someone who could not be held.

All this pain – it half-persuaded her that it had to have a meaning. There had to be some purpose, which she could not yet fathom, for which she had been made to suffer. Trying to breathe slowly and evenly, she vaguely recalled some lines from Wordsworth at school. The passage which eluded her went like this:

> How strange, that all
> The terrors, pains, and early miseries,
> Regrets, vexations, lassitudes interfused
> Within my mind, should e'er have borne a part,
> And that a needful part, in making up
> The calm existence that is mine when I
> Am worthy of myself! Praise to the end!
> Thanks to the means which Nature deigned to employ

She used to think that Wordsworth was merely soft-minded. Now she wasn't so sure. It was in our nature to look for meaning, to make meaning. Perhaps that was it: it was in her own power to make the most significant event of her life – for that was how it felt – mean something, after all. But what, exactly? And how?

She took another breath and looked further down the road, towards the mini-roundabout, for the approach of Joseph's car. Nothing – not even a taxi. The blood collection vehicles were all parked up for the night. The area was otherwise quiet. The wind stirred and flicked her fringe. She patted it back into place and tried to be calm. But then she thought of the male child who had been dry incubated in the early afternoon. Half an hour later he turned grey and died. His parents, his poor devastated parents, now she brought their terrible new pain into her heart too, had already named him Daniel Matthew. His eyes had not even needed closing. He would have been a candidate for Wet Incubation, but Sophie Rose was already using the only machine. No doubt the story would get to the papers, giving satisfaction to the more heartless among Thomas Marvelle's enemies. She wasn't one of them. Her heart was hurting more than ever.

A minute passed and then suddenly, dreadfully, the sound that she was afraid of hearing had come back again. Crying. And not strange crying like this morning. She had dismissed this morning, finally pushed this morning quite out of her mind, after Sheryl had reported the gossip about the Wet Incubator and she had passed a busy hour when two dozen bedding bales were changed and twenty-nine forms were filled out in not as many minutes.

She listened anxiously. The cry persisted. A second time on the very same day, in quite a different place, with no Wet Incubator to blame this time, the sound could not be dismissed. She *was* hallucinating. The realization, the certainty of it, filled her with fear.

Tensely she drew in breath, held very still, counted five pine trees on the outer perimeter of the hospital grounds, no six, and tried to make sense of the sound. She hadn't heard anything like this since the first few weeks after the baby's death. And yet, incredibly, it seemed that this was where she was again: back in bed, gripped by the imaginary cries that came from the corner of a far-off room. Here lies the baby no one will ever pick up. At first, in those early days, she had craved to go where that sound led. To turn up the volume. It would be easier. And it was the only way she had of joining her baby. But it was madness. Or would soon lead to madness. And so, although it had felt as if she was rejecting her own child in selfish preference for her own survival, she had decided firmly: to listen harder, to distinguish sounds, to recognize that it was not, that it could not be, the cry of her baby but that it might be, *must* be, the washing machine, the vacuum cleaner, the mower.

None of these solutions seemed likely in this spot by the staff car park, however, and she was terrified that a quick check would rule them all out. And what *then*?

Hesitating, wary, Helen inclined her head very slightly to the left, towards the sound of the crying, which seemed to be increasing – surely a bad sign. Indeed, it was more than crying now. It was an animal in his death throes, the hysteria of a pig to the slaughter, an SOS terrified by its own futility. And there, coming around the corner, she saw Joseph. He was struggling to hold their screaming, three-year-old nephew Jack. Kayleigh must have needed a babysitter. Helen began to walk towards them. Jack flailed and thrashed as though Joseph would surely drown him this time. For all this effort, however, he slipped rather slowly down his uncle's body, water with legs that could kick, in the process pulling up his own T-shirt and baring his belly and the top of Spiderman pants. At last Joseph was able to release the boy carefully to the ground where he lay supine. Helen watched, relieved. For a moment Jack seemed to calm down. But still he arched his back in rigid defiance and refused the dummy Joseph proffered, as if it were an insult. Legs in stirrup position, shunting himself backward, next he was aiming for something to hit his head against and thereby trigger a new reason for indignation and pain. When, after a few attempts, that failed – there were no obstacles, no useful walls behind – he simply lifted his skull and nutted it, though cautiously, on the pavement. At this latest injustice a great wail went up to heaven.

Helen exhaled and even smiled. She was not hallucinating. Perhaps she didn't need to be afraid of herself any more. Sometimes, if you were strong-minded as well as lucky, sanity was a choice, and she had made it.

'Kayleigh had to work late,' Joseph explained.

'Auntie Helen!' the small boy said brightly, to her surprise, and immediately sat up. He seemed to have forgotten his tantrum of a moment ago entirely. 'Uncle Joe isn't sharing,' he complained confidently. '*I* share. I sharing with my cousin and my – cousin. Where's my cousin in your tummy?' he demanded.

'*Jack*,' Joseph warned him gently.

'It's all right,' Helen said. 'He went away. Sometimes that happens.'

'Oh.' Jack thought for a moment. 'My daddy went away.' Then he repeated this insight in the form of a list. 'My daddy went away, my baby went away, my daddy . . . You want a cold compress?'

He touched her forehead briefly with his palm. 'That's a cold compress. Look!' He raised his T-shirt again and stuck out his belly. 'I've got gingerbread man in my tummy. Have you got gingerbread man in *your* tummy?'

'No, but I have got sandwiches in my tummy.'

'Have you got sandwiches in your tummy? *Look!*' he addressed a passer-by urgently. 'She's got sandwiches in her tummy!'

'Has she now,' the stranger replied pleasantly.

Fifteen

On Level 2, Lydia nodded wisely as her daughter said it was possible, even desirable, to love both a younger man and an older. Florence was aware of the dangers of paining Robert – or herself – but she had learned from Thomas to look past the dangers, most of the time at least. What was the point in being miserable? Let alone *worrying* about becoming miserable? And they didn't want Robert to be miserable either.

'For God's sake, don't deprive him,' Thomas had said to her, right at the beginning. 'I don't want the poor guy going crazy with frustration! Not to mention that you don't want him fucking someone else.'

'But *I* am!'

'Very hard, I think, for a marriage to survive infidelity on both sides. It's hard enough as it is.'

The case required no special pleading. Going to bed with Robert had become additionally exciting for Florence in ways that she could not possibly explain to her mother. *You are a whore*, she would think to herself. A thought which thrilled and tipped her over some of the most sublime precipices she had ever known. This erotically productive thought was not one, however, she held sincerely. She did not think of her behaviour as infidelity but as a species of love, a love that dared not speak its name, a love that had yet to be widely accepted and finally understood. Particularly by her husband.

'I'm sure,' Thomas had said to her once, 'that in the eyes of the world it's wrong. But it doesn't feel wrong to me.'

Florence agreed. Fact was, she kept two men sexually happy. It was the sort of thing you ought to be given a medal for – not criticized about or divorced over.

'I love a young man and an old one,' she said now to her mother.

'But especially the older one,' Lydia advised.

Just then they were interrupted by the approach of a nurse wearing thick maroon spectacle frames. 'Look, I'm going to get someone to come and talk to you about your stitches, okay? She's not going to be in tomorrow when you're getting discharged, so if you've got any questions . . . If you wouldn't mind,' she addressed Lydia now, 'waiting in the corridor, please?'

The nurse drew the curtain around and left Florence to wait.

'Hello!' Robert said a moment later, putting his head through the curtain.

'Oh, good,' Florence said. 'You're here. They're going to tell me about the stitches now.'

'So there are two kinds of stitches,' the new nurse said. 'Dissolvable and non-dissolvable.'

'And which have I got?' Florence asked.

The nurse inspected Florence's bared navel carefully. The whole area felt strangely stretched, and its appearance was altered beyond all recognition, like a cosmetic surgery she had never requested. Instead of the old familiar twist in the heart of her navel, there was now a bland flatland. She had already spent a considerable part of the day just watching it. She wondered what the nurse was thinking. Eventually the woman looked up.

'Your stitches are looking good. You should bathe or shower as usual.'

'Does that mean they're not dissolvable then?' Robert asked.

'If they dissolve after seven to ten days of normal bathing or showering, then they're dissolvable. If you find they're not dissolving after that point,' the nurse addressed Florence, 'then they're the other kind and you'll need to see your GP about getting them removed. Don't worry. It shouldn't be painful.'

'I think I'd rather they just dissolved,' Florence said.

The nurse smiled. 'Well, I'm sure you've got the dissolvable ones, then,' she replied, standing up to leave.

'How useless was that,' Robert commiserated. 'Shall I get you a Kit Kat?'

'Two,' Florence sighed. 'Chunky ones, if they have them. And a Twix.'

'It's *simple*, Mum!' Florence whispered while Robert went to raid the snack machines for her consolation. 'All you've got to say to Thomas – to Professor Marvelle – is, "We've changed our minds. We're sorry for troubling him." And then he won't look in the file. He won't want to press it in front of you, or do anything that might look odd. Let alone with Robert here.'

'So my line is, "We've changed our minds. We're sorry for troubling him."'

'Troubling *you*.'

'Troubling you.'

'Remember that he doesn't know that you know, so that means that . . .'

Lydia frowned. 'I think I'll just stick to my line.'

'Good. And can you put the file in the bedside cabinet please?'

Lydia moved it from the end of the bedrail. After these elaborate preparations, however, Thomas arrived at the most logical and least conspicuous time for a doctor whose mistress was a married woman

125

and whose family he would naturally prefer to avoid: after visiting hours, when Lydia and Robert had gone.

'Sweetheart!' Thomas said, when he was sure that Florence was awake. 'Are you all right?'

'I think so,' she said, liking how kindly he was looking at her. How parentally. A gentle concerned frown spread across his forehead and it was all for her.

'Well, let's have a look,' he said simply, drawing the curtains around them.

Florence pushed down the bedcovers and raised her pyjama top. 'Can you tell me if they're dissolvable or non-dissolvable?'

'Non-dissolvable,' he replied straightaway. 'I'll take them out for you in a few days, all right?'

Thomas's can-do nature was not the least of his attractions to Florence.

'That makes me feel better already,' she said.

'Good!' He stood up and rested a hand lightly on Florence's belly. 'They're only a couple of teeny-weeny ones, you know,' he said tenderly. 'Quite superficial.'

Not, then, the pillars of her well being that she had supposed.

'What about that?' she said, pointing to the small slug that seemed to have taken up residence in her navel – a black blob of dried blood.

'Absolutely nothing to worry about,' Thomas pronounced. 'In fact I'd kiss your belly button if I wasn't worried it was going to hurt you, it looks so sweet! And so do you, in your little jim-jams! Now. Where's your file?'

Florence hesitated. 'In the bedside cupboard,' she heard herself confessing.

'Well, what's it doing in there?'

'I just didn't feel like letting anyone have a look at it.'

'Sometimes,' Thomas replied, taking a step towards the cupboard, and then, thinking better of it, a seat instead, 'you are a very strange woman.'

Sixteen

'Auntie Helen,' Jack had said on the ride home. 'Are you my best friend?'

'Yes, if you like.'

'Auntie Helen,' he repeated, the enquiry now turning into a declaration, 'you are my best friend. And Uncle Joe is my best friend. And Mummy is my best friend. And Lisa May is my best friend. And David P is my best friend. Auntie Helen, are you having a birthday card?'

'On my birthday I expect I will.'

'Is there any cake?' he asked hopefully.

'We'll have to ask your mummy about that,' Helen replied as they turned into the driveway.

'But she said yes *already*!' Jack wailed indignantly.

Kayleigh came out to meet them, her peroxide blonde curls slightly bedraggled by the long shift at work. 'Has he been okay?' she asked tentatively, smiling at Jack through the car window.

'He's been absolutely fine,' Helen replied, while Joseph freed the small boy from the booster seat they had installed. 'Any time. We love having him.'

She hadn't told her sister the significance of the day. It was difficult enough to talk to Joseph about it, and he had been there.

'Now give your auntie a kiss goodbye,' Kayleigh instructed as Jack got out of the car.

Helen crouched so he could reach her.

'What, a kissy-kiss?' he asked and, without waiting for a reply, kissed Helen smack on the lips.

'Is that how you kiss the girls?' Helen smiled.

'No, like this,' he said, repeating the action more slowly.

Everyone laughed.

'Is that funny?' Jack asked, grinning.

'That's very funny,' Joseph replied.

'Is that *very* funny? That's very funny! It's very funny!'

'Sweet kid,' Joseph said as they got back into the car.

It was a ten-minute drive to the marital home, a tiny rented flat in a busy but expensive part of town. A once generously sized Victorian family home, it had been converted – rather ingeniously, in the view of the landlord – into slivers of living accommodation. The front door hung badly, so every time Helen put her key in the lock it burst open as though a couple of heavies were shouldering their way in behind her. The door could not, however, open fully in the minuscule hallway, which contained nothing but a coat rack with four pegs. All unusable, because the hallway then became impassable.

She did not lock the door. Joseph was parking the car and could only be a few paces behind. She made her way straight to the bedroom, opened the New England-style shutter door of the wardrobe, and squeezed in her fleece. Immediately she became aware of the people in the adjacent flat, doing it again. Groaning. Moaning. Making the bed creak. It was like her mother and her boyfriends – or the overacting in student productions she remembered from university. As though everyone was auditioning for children's television. Had they no shame? The only thing she knew about the couple downstairs was that a full can of Coke had once been lobbed like a brick into their front room from the street outside. She remembered the woman screaming inconsolably. The man trying to talk to her. Even Joseph went downstairs to talk to her but it did no good. She just kept going, for the rest of the evening, and everyone had felt nervous of burglars for a while. Now the couple adjacent had stopped. No, they were starting again.

Joseph was closing the front door. There was a twinkle in his eyes as he joined his wife in the bedroom and heard their eager neighbours; there was possibly – but surely not – an invitation. She concentrated on looking piously displeased, even when he said, 'Just taking a leaf out of Jack's book.' She would permit him to put his arms briefly around her. Except for kisses on the cheek at their daily parting, physical contact between them now rather surprised her. As though the perimeter of her personal space was a literal barrier and he had just walked through it, like Superman or a ghost. Then there were more excited yelps from the couple next door. She extracted herself from Joseph – by drawing her shoulders in and backing away – easily enough. It was the day of the birth that hadn't happened. If that made any sense. It made sense to her. She wanted to get out of the bedroom. To think about all the pain in the world, not the people who were joyously at it – they had got to the 'oh honey, oh honey, oh honey' stage – just the other side of the studwork.

The news would help.

'And a summary of tonight's headlines. A woman was on trial today at the Old Bailey for the kidnap of *two* of her sister's children. The Prime Minister has visited a bakery on his first day in Pakistan. And finally –'

Unfortunately there was now the beginning of a lilt in the broadcaster's voice, the same faintly incredulous and thrilled tone she reserved for a young British javelin thrower making it to the Olympic finals, or the successful copulation of pandas in Edinburgh Zoo.

' – the latest medical miracle: Wet Incubation. The world's youngest-ever surviving baby, Anna Mirabel, spent a total of ninety-*eight* days in the world's first Wet Incubator and is said to be thriving in the Special Care Baby Unit at the William and Mary Hospital. Later in the programme we will be speaking to her parents and showing an interview we recorded earlier with the doctor, writer, and inventor of the new technology, Professor Thomas J. Marvelle. But first, our weather.'

'It's going well, then?' Joseph said.

'What?'

'The incubator.'

'Yes.'

Helen replied unenthusiastically, as though she would prefer to end the conversation there, but Joseph persevered.

'Yeah, I was listening to him on the radio today. He was pretty good, I thought. And then when I was driving home they were talking about the technology going to America and what happened there, it was back in the eighties, with Baby Doe. I never knew that!'

Joseph's ability to take a purely recreational pleasure in other people's misery offended his wife. He watched the news as if it were a Hollywood disaster movie.

'Yeah, apparently these parents had said they didn't want their baby to have an operation to repair his bowel, I think it was, because he was born with Down's Syndrome. And the doctors agreed with them, and you'd have thought that would have been the end of it. But then this attorney – nothing to do with the parents or the hospital – actually sued them for prejudice against the disabled and the whole thing went crazy. The government got involved. Reagan. There were posters on the walls in every neonatal unit with an emergency phone line saying if you think a baby's not getting the treatment it should, you can rat on the doctors and the parents by ringing this number . . .'

'I know about Baby Doe,' Helen replied shortly.

After supper Joseph gave up and went to the pub. Helen lay in bed watching the small TV and listening to further speculation about the sanity of the female kidnapper. She had become hypervigilant about her own state of mind. Conscientiousness dictated that she would have to seek help for any serious psychotic symptoms and, if necessary, take further leave from work. In more paranoid moments she feared a diagnosis that would compromise her ability to work at all. Her initial Post-Traumatic Stress Disorder was nothing out of the ordinary, of course. Auditory hallucinations and even flashbacks for up to a month were perfectly normal – as the literature for patients liked to put it – and once she had put her mind to the problem, these bizarre symptoms had gone away rather quickly. What replaced the strange experiences, however, was something almost as bad: the constant dread of their return. It was true that she was the one who had, quite successfully, banished them. So she was unlikely ever to deliberately invite them back. To succumb to the temptation of those half-crazed states of mind in which she could have some contact with her child. The only place she could meet him safely now was in dreams and memories. She knew that. But there was more involved in the case.

Helen felt honour-bound, even if there was risk to herself, to keep the child alive in her own mind. She was the only person in the world, apart from Joseph, who could do it. No one else would ever know him. He might have grown up. He might well have lived until his eighty-ninth birthday. But instead, no one would even meet him now. No one would ever have a chance to love him. So keeping each

132

detail of each episode from four months before in the front of her mind was the very least she could do. It was also the only thing she could do.

Some good would come from it – she just didn't know what yet.

'Professor,' the newscaster was saying, 'a lot of people have been describing this as "a landmark moment" in medical science. What does the invention of Wet Incubation mean to you?'

'It means that a very premature baby who would otherwise have died has survived and will go on to lead, we have every reason to believe, a completely normal life.' Thomas spoke with a lamp and a vase of tulips perched either side of his head. 'The great problem that we have faced in treating foetuses at the limits of viability – and that we will continue to face until Wet Incubators are available in all neonatal units – is quality of life in the long term. It's always been our major dilemma – saving babies, some of whom then go on to suffer terribly. We have a tendency to err on the side of life, and sometimes the results . . . But what's different, *cru*cially different, about Wet Incubation is that it isn't a halfway technology.'

'A halfway technology?'

'In common parlance, a cure that's worse than the disease. Arguably worse, at least. Think of the iron lung. It was used to treat polio sufferers. But patients still had to live in an iron lung. Even its modern replacement – the biphasic cuirass – is hardly ideal. The Wet Incubator isn't like that. A baby who has been treated with WI isn't going to spend the rest of his or her life attached to a ventilator. The survival of the foetus, as I call it, should mean a long and healthy life.'

The survival of the fittest: Helen's mind began to drift. Darwin had borrowed the phrase from an economist. The resources of the natural world were finite. There was only so much food and soil to go around. Only the fittest, therefore, only those best adapted to their environment, could secure those resources and survive. The NHS was comparably overstretched, everyone knew that. She sank deeper into the pillows. She felt warm and tired but could not seem to turn her brain off. Yes: how could one justify the enormous hospital bills – occasionally they exceeded the million pound mark – of babies who had been kept alive but only to suffer, or to live, if it could be called living, brainless lives upstairs in paediatrics? Now she seemed to see herself in the hospital lift. The buttons blinked by. Level 3. Paediatrics. Inert toddlers still on ventilators. This was the survival of the weakest. *So many more people could have been helped,* someone said, *with the sums of money involved. But even if one ignored the financial cost,* someone else argued, *a medical misintervention of that magnitude was an act of human unkindness. I can tell you from experience that it's not neglect – far from it – but too much misguided attention which causes the greater suffering in such cases.*

On the other hand, the first speaker said sleepily, *neonatology makes a greater pay-off than any other branch of medicine. Save a baby's life and generally you are saving a very long life indeed.*

And women, she heard the Professor say, *who for all sorts of reasons can't sustain a pregnancy to term. If a diagnosis of imminent preterm delivery can be made, and the foetus is otherwise viable . . . But suppose that's not the case. I'm thinking now of a nurse who works in our unit. We couldn't save the baby. Of course we couldn't. I mean, she didn't even* notice *that the baby had died. And he was* inside *her. What did she think we* could do about it?

It was outrageous. They were talking about her! Even if it *was* all true and she deserved to be shamed. And there was Gloria Vine – laughing along with the rest of them before fading out in a stagey cloud of smoke.

Some time later she realized what had happened: she had dozed off. She woke abruptly with a wet neck and strange pools of water filling her ears. Tears, evidently shed in her sleep. Peering anxiously into the semi-darkness of the bedroom, which was now lit only by television flickers, she made sure that the dressing-table chair was indeed a chair, a process which she repeated for the rest of the furniture. Joseph wasn't back yet. She got up slowly, turned the television off – people were now laughing at an overweight comedian – and made her way to the bathroom. She glanced at the tub as she closed the door. The night before the birth they had taken one last bath – her and the baby. She remembered watching her hand lap the lukewarm water over the bump. In hope. Hopeless hope. Warmth revived – didn't it? Wouldn't it? Lapping the water, over and over again, to David Attenborough's grave tones: *The mother licks her dead young. She is puzzled, dismayed, anxious. She will do this for hours and then, finally . . .*

They would never have another bath together. She went and stood by the window. The pebbled glass caught a streetlamp and glowed. The wrought iron catch curled around like a handwritten flourish. She studied these items patiently. Then she looked down at herself in Joseph's shaving mirror as she drank water from the glass. Her hair was very short now – Joseph wanted her to grow it again – and the strangely light blue eyes appeared colourless. Her nose was tiny and coveted by friends. She had been beautiful. She wished she cared.

She knew what was coming next. She tried to drink the water slowly, purposefully, feeling it go coldly down her throat. As though that could ward off her fate. She steadied herself against the sink. But it would happen anyway.

It's happening. The worst of the flashbacks.

It's Level 7 time now and at the edge of her vision someone has come back into the room. The midwife. Helen sees herself lying on the bed the way the midwife has instructed: knickers off, legs drawn up, the blanket covering her from the waist down. So that pessaries to induce the labour can be inserted. A modesty pose – as though she somehow shan't notice that the only person in the room this screens her nakedness from is herself.

Now. 'Are you ready?'

The midwife pushes a pessary inside. Then another. Four times in all, each time saying, almost penitently, 'I'm so sorry.'

Sorry for the violation? Sorry that the baby is dead? It's like swallowing four aspirins on a dry throat, without a glass of water.

When she's finished the midwife suggests, 'You might feel a bit cold after a while.'

And this is where she is, this is where she always is: labouring on the toilet, sitting gripped, gripping the rim, looking to the royal-blue towel rail for guidance, living only for the moment when the pain will ebb away, certain to return.

Joseph's head appears in the doorway. Helen ignores it and he knows, by now, not to say anything. The moment, where is the moment . . .

How long until the moment, only the moment . . .

And then (astonishment!) a large jelly has shot through her cervix – with such ease that everything is, briefly, in the past tense already. The force of the waters breaking has shocked her, already, into standing. Knees slightly bent, she finds she's hopped forward fractionally – trying, in the alarm, to move away from herself.

She's definitely felt it happen.

And also: she wants to know if it's happened. So she starts to dip her head. However.

'Joe?' Helen calls into the other room. The midwife must have

136

gone and she daren't, not on her own, not even after all these hours. 'Is that – ?'

Joseph looks down sympathetically into the toilet pan, shaking his head. Helen is ashamed of herself. 'No, honey,' he says, 'there's only liquid.'

'But I felt it!' she protests.

'I'm sorry,' he says, trying to smile supportively.

So Helen crouches, opening her legs wider this time and, now it's safe, now there's definitely nothing there, peeks between them.

And hanging there, slowly spinning on the umbilical cord, is a smooth ellipsoid of flesh. A shiny guinea pig, perhaps. It is uniform or rather unformed – apart from one slight undulation where a neck should be – and doesn't appear to have a head. The lack of detail is horrifying. It's the baby you deliver in a dream. But this is not one of her dreams.

'No, no!' Helen shouts, 'that's *it*! That's, that's – the baby.'

Joseph realizes this is his moment and pulls the orange emergency cord.

'Sit down!' the midwife barks, a minute later. 'But well done.'

Helen obeys, taking the guinea pig down with her into the pan. Now that the midwife is here, Helen can look again. Hands and feet that were curled into the body spring out mechanically, prosthetically, as the liquid stirs an illusion of life, and she's transfixed. The limbs are still disproportionately small. Smaller, in fact, than anyone's in the Special Care Baby Unit at work. And unnaturally close to the body, *like a* – she's too late to stop the thought – *rodent's*. Helen is so determined not to be revolted that she doesn't notice she's delighted. There's a face!

'It always happens when I'm about to go home,' the midwife says as she severs them for ever.

In reply, Helen says what she doesn't mean: 'It's a miracle.' As if she's a neutral admirer of human reproduction, just happened to be passing . . . What she means is, 'I love this baby.' But the truth is that she's ashamed of loving, so hastily, so hopelessly, what is, clearly, a dead thing.

Whose legs are like – no, don't, *don't* – a frog's. That's what she notices when the midwife brings the baby back, she doesn't know how many minutes later, in a miniature Moses basket that would do for a bread roll. The midwife first insisted on cleaning her up (as if Helen cares), and lifting the baby out of the liquid. Then she injected Helen's leg – so she could 'spit it out', meaning the placenta.

He comes back repackaged, fun-size. He's only eighteen weeks. Most of him is covered by the corner of a handkerchief. Gradually the midwife pulls it back, shows them their own child. The fingernails and the penis are sketched the same way: as tiny flecks of white. Although no one can be sure it *is* a penis, not absolutely, because even at eighteen weeks a clitoris can be deceptively engorged. But that's how it looks to Helen. Like the teeniest white light bulb, for a doll's house chandelier. The autopsy will tell for certain. Right elbow kinked, an arm poses coolly across the belly, with the index finger pointing in advance of the others. The legs are slanted leftwards like a skier's, she now decides, more humanely. Inside them there's a delta of tiny crimson rivers, going nowhere. Momentarily she considers touching this Peter Pan, this Thomas Thumb, but he's so red, so unready, so strangely *shining*, although he's no longer wet, that she's afraid, irrationally afraid, that it might hurt him.

Too young to have grown skin, he looks like an internal organ.

Her heart.

She searches for evidence of how he died. The face is exhausted, resigned, the whole body a wound. She's afraid she's worn him out with her own misery. The nights she's spent crying, never thinking about him but only of herself, no wonder he decided not to bother, if it was going to be like that!

And then as she surveys the canary kettle in the room, bought for the canary cushions that were evidently bought for the canary curtains – the thing is, *forgive me*, she thinks, she's in pain. It's been an hour now, according to another midwife, who must be prettier, because Joseph scrambles to get his goofy woollen hat off. The pressure of the placenta is as relentless as anything that's come before. *Commonly,* she reminds herself, *a woman who cannot keep the foetus inside her womb cannot rid herself of the placenta.*

'Do you want more paracetamol?' the midwife asks.

Helen nods and two pills are served in a small paper dish crinkled like a miniature Camembert. She wants to kneel by the bed but *he's* there. She thinks his presence is distracting her from delivering the placenta. So she has him moved, ridiculously, to the top of the canary microwave. But he's still there. He's always there.

'Take it away,' she says, in the end.

Take it away. How long the words echo in her mind. Especially when – *forgive me* – it wasn't the placenta. A more efficient midwife burst the large blood clot on the cervix an hour later.

And – *forgive me* – when they asked her if she wanted him brought back, she said no anyway.

And – *forgive me* – when they asked her for a name, she only shook her head.

A day later she is leaving the hospital empty-handed. Empty-armed. The only woman coming out of Maternity without a baby. The darkest sunglasses shutter her face. Her perfect white cotton pyjama bottoms – the ones which raised the midwife's eyebrows but emerged, in the event, unscathed – are tucked into her rabbit-lined boots. No one can see anyway. Her winter coat is long and weighs on her strangely. Progress towards the door is painstaking for the brief time she is without Joseph's arm. He's paying for a parking ticket because they forgot her staff pass. It's been forty-eight hours. She rests her hands on the edge of the pamphlet table – 'Be Wise, Immunise' – and as it takes her weight she notices she is trembling. She remembers what they've said. That she can come back, any time in the next week, to see him, because 'sometimes women ring up and say they just have to'. She already knows that she is not going to come back again – not for that. But she wonders whether going into work, or even to the ordinary maternity ward, just to see some living babies, would relieve her lonely arms. It's only round the corner, two corridors away. *I could do that. I couldn't do that.* She's afraid the other nurses won't trust her motives. They'll think that all she wants to do is steal a patient. That's what people always believe. The worst.

So she turns, rather slowly and weakly, in Joseph's direction instead. And that's when she spots the buggy, propped against the ticket machine. Lightweight, muddy wheels in the air, a piece of wool tied around the handle like a luggage item someone wants to distinguish from the crowd. She's shocked – even while it's still happening – by what that mere sight does to her. There's barely time to touch her sunglasses and check that the world won't see her cry over a folded pushchair.

A few days later, she is sitting on the toilet when something substantial slips out of her again. In terror she tries to discover what it is. Certainly it is a perfectly formed example of whatever it is. The consistency of jelly. The moulded outline. Like a small raspberry-coloured crème caramel. In bewilderment she shows it to Joseph, who is at a loss and shows it to someone else, she never finds out who. Kayleigh? Kayleigh had never mentioned it. Joseph comes back to tell her that it is simply blood. She's been lying down for days and it must have congealed inside her in that shape. It is February when she gets dressed again.

And this is where she is every day, every night. With a shudder, love comes shooting through her cervix. But no matter how many times she gives birth to him, he never lives.

Not even once.

PART THREE

Human Intervention

Seventeen

In the longer term, the Wet Incubator was a disappointment to the British press. For a start, it actually worked. The first time it worked, and saved the life of Anna Mirabel, this was newsworthy. Even the second and the third time, when Sophie Rose and a little boy called Jacob were successfully de-incubated and the newspapers nicknamed the Wet Incubator the 'Born Again' Machine (or BAM! for short), there was a modest amount of coverage. The exact number of days and hours and even minutes the patients had spent in the Wet Incubator, the middle names their parents had chosen for them, the first clothes they had worn, were all points of media interest and national discussion, supplying conversation in supermarket queues, at doctors' surgeries, and across garden fences throughout the land for days at a time. Once it was apparent that the Wet Incubator worked, there was then a hope that it could be demonstrated *not* to work. But all of the patients who emerged from the small curvaceous fluid-filled machine simply failed to develop superfluous heads, or digits, or even asthma. New hopes that parents had been either coerced or deceived into participation in the clinical trial, that the true results had been hushed up, that babies who failed to thrive in the Wet Incubator were sometimes silently replaced in the depth of night by healthy orphans, were all dashed in their turn. Every parent interviewed was simply very happy.

The feminist reaction to the new technology was, in fact, the only promising lead for a long time. The difference between the invention of Wet Incubation, and the expulsion of women from the planet, was proving difficult to discern. 'Ectopia or dystopia?' one headline enquired. Captions proud of their wordplay announced 'One small step for man – one great fall for womankind.' And there were the inevitable limp jokes about Thomas's 'Marvellous Medicine' and 'Professor Marvel: the Oz connection'. Meantime the small print concentrated on misunderstanding the Professor's adaptation of the phrase 'the survival of the fittest'. Taking a lead from Rita Morgan's analysis of the hidden economics of the situation, opinion columnists were writing ardently in the cause of fantasy arguments: about the time when Wet Incubators would be monopolized by the spawn of the wealthy and well-connected. For many weeks there were debates in the Letters pages about the economic as well as ethical consequences of Wet Incubation. Pro-life religious groups were insisting that abortion be illegalized by next spring at the outside, now that the technology was up and running for supporting the survival of the foetus independent of the mother. Meantime, pro-choicers were extending their range of options to include working mothers who did not actually want to terminate the pregnancy but to delegate it to a machine. What the warring factions held in common was a belief in the machine as a solution – ignoring the fact that these were not the problems it had ever been intended to fix.

The pro-abortionists most alarmed by the new technology (in case it really should spell the end of abortion) were not, however, up in arms. Unlike the anti-abortion Christian activists, it was not in their nature to be militant. They wrote pamphlets like 'Ban Wet Incubation – Not Women's Choices' and even posted Thomas copies, but Professor Marvelle's life was never actually in danger.

For a while he felt slightly fearful of protesters of all persuasions but could discern no alteration in the behaviour of the only ones he saw regularly. These were not, in fact, pro-abortionists but rather the anti-abortion placard-holders ('Abortion stops a beating heart') from the local evangelical church who stood on a verge beside the zebra crossing outside the hospital. Logically the anti-abortionists ought to be on his side, insofar as he represented a side. He saved foetal lives, after all. But he didn't trust anyone who held up a piece of cardboard in the rain to be logical.

In the event, the abortion laws showed no sign of changing. Musings about the long-term health consequences of the new technology were revived instead. But since this 'human cost' could not yet be calculated, other questions began to be asked. The economic angle was back in favour – this time with a twist. Who had paid for the development of WI technology, and more importantly, *why*? There were the beginnings of a scandal when no grants from public funding bodies could be discovered. Thomas Marvelle was reluctant to identify where the money had come from. A junior health minister's job was at stake. In the circumstances the Professor explained that he had not applied for any external funding, preferring to use a considerable part of his personal fortune – largely inherited from his father – instead. This was what innovators did: self-invest.

'And if you want to know the truth,' he said to friends, then finally in a statement to the press, 'I couldn't be bothered to fill out the forms.'

This indeed had the ring of truth and at last the matter was left alone. The attention of the pack now turned to the law on euthanasia, which seemed more susceptible to change after several high-profile suicide pacts by elderly society couples. Thomas Marvelle could breathe again.

He had not forgotten, however, his run-in with Bob Goldman at the Californian conference. Goldman was his former mentor, a pioneer of American neonatology under whom he had trained. But the eminent Goldman had become disillusioned by neonatal intervention, by the emotional pain inflicted on the parents of babies who were going to die anyway, and by the suffering of the severely disabled survivors of the NICU. As a result Goldman had become the field's severest critic. He now taught bioethics with a specialism in extreme prematurity, and co-edited *The Lancet* for North America. From time to time he served as an expert witness in medical negligence lawsuits.

Phrases from the row kept going around Thomas's head, like an inescapable pop lyric.

'You wimped out, Bob, that's the truth, and now the view from your armchair—'

'Don't give me this "I'm saving lives while you're sitting around philosophizing" shit.'

'Well, aren't I?'

'No. You're saving lives while I'm – or rather we're – working out what life is, what exactly is being saved in these cases.'

'How profound.'

'Don't patronize me.'

'Don't patronize *me*. Don't you think I know what you say to people? "Yes, Marvelle, well he always *was* ambitious, even as a student. Especially as a student." *Ambitious!* Code for fucking "disastrous". And I'm not your fucking student any more.'

'You never were my student. You never listened to anything I said. You were just biding your time, serving out the apprenticeship, and now you're the one-man band you've always wanted to be. Employing PhDs by the bra size because the idea that one of them might actually have something to *contribute*—'

'Oh, come on! This is – this is—'

'That's right. This is not how neonatology works. It's not a one-man show. It never has been. It has no founder. No Louis Pasteur, no Marie Curie. It works collectively and no one individual can—'

'Well, I can see that's very convenient if you're a mediocrity. Sorry to disappoint. Sorry I'm not talentless enough for you, that I've spoiled the little picture of neonatal you've been trying to pass off as fact in your books . . .'

'And I thought you only read your own nowadays.'

'No, I read your books, Bob, because I know how damaging they are. The way they give the kids the impression that everything has been done here and now we can all sit back and become bioethicists instead.'

Goldman's most recent history of neonatology had defined three phases: 'the time of innovation' in the sixties and seventies, when the field expanded rapidly; 'the time of ignorance' in the eighties, when the limits of neonatology had first become painfully – and publicly – apparent, in a series of notoriously costly lawsuits; and the present time, when the field was supposedly in a stage of technical stagnation but ethical refinement. This meant there was widespread agreement on the basic ethical principles underlying the use of a limited number of well-established treatment procedures. Individual consciences could relax at last. Medical progress had been supplanted by moral progress. Until, that was, the Wet Incubator came along. The third edition of Goldman's book had been published two years before and now the morality of intervention was up for reconsideration again. Really Goldman ought to thank him, if anything, for giving him something new to say for the first time in a decade.

'Look, Tom,' Bob said, 'you ought to know that I've been offered a post at William and Mary.'

'What post?'

'The Professorship in Medical Ethics.'

'Oh, *that*.' It was a teaching post. 'It never occurred to me that *you* . . .' Thomas paused. So Goldman would be on all of the hospital ethics committees now. And the Hospital Board. Jesus Christ. 'You mean you're coming *because* of the Wet Incubator?'

'Yes.'

'Well, why didn't you say before I started shouting at you?!'

'I tried.'

'Hmm, I suppose you did.' Diplomatically Thomas laughed at himself. 'Well, as you know I've always been a model of tact and restraint.'

'You gotta expect a Baby Catherine,' Goldman had said later, over coffee.

Baby Catherine was the reason why Goldman had left neonatal in the end. She was the one he had done the most for – or to. The one who'd endured the longest, while he tried to prove that he could save her, only to discover that he couldn't.

'I'm not wishing it on you,' Goldman added. 'I'm just saying, wait and see how you feel then.'

'Yes, I'm sure the papers will have a fine time. But I'm afraid it won't make a jot of difference to me.'

In fact, by the time the first disaster with the Wet Incubator occurred, the world was not interested and it was not, in any case, a flaw in the technology. It was rather the flawlessness of the technology – his old problem of being too damn good at everything. And even the Professor's own attention was slightly diverted from the event by what had happened to Florence Brown.

Eighteen

For days after her operation, Florence simply rested in the lounge. She ate a lot of chocolate. She listened to a lot of speeches from Lydia.

'Florence dearest,' Lydia said on one of these occasions, 'I've been thinking. All this business about the cave men and the moral goodness of adultery and the patriarchal self-interest – is it? – of people who are against affairs. It's all very clever but this isn't one of your A levels.'

Florence had once written a defence of Iago for Mrs Padmore's class.

'I think you've just got to jolly well – ' a *jolly well* typically accompanied Lydia's exhortations, a piece of schoolmistressy rhetoric whose force she had long admired and whose efficacy she never doubted – 'to jolly well find out *whose* baby it is, exactly, if there *is* still a baby, and then *jolly well* stick with him, and only him. All right? Otherwise I'm afraid you're going to land up without either one of them and be completely miserable. You're going to get caught. A man just won't stand for this sort of thing. A woman may – but not a man. A man won't even *understand* what you're talking about.'

Florence half-listened, half-perused the exterior packaging of two identical bathroom mirrors propped against the coffee table. The room doubled up as storage room for MyBuild – or had, until Robert decided to fire them the day before. A steel bath and oval sinks now sat surreally next to the sofa. A large Victorian-style bath tap with white enamel fittings perched on the mantelpiece like a metal bird sculpture. Robert's bike – a new and expensive red contraption that she doubted he would use very much – lay on the floor. Its saddle had pleasingly sexual qualities. The pictures on the boxed mirrors showed that customers who used the product entered a state close to delirium. And in the inset illustration on the back of the box, they crooked their arms into Vs to demonstrate the ease with which the cord for the internal light switch could be pulled.

'*I'm* struggling to understand you, and I'm your mother. When is your appointment with Mr Harris?'

'Friday.'

'Friday.' Lydia seemed to think. 'Well why don't you watch some television and take your mind off things while I make dinner?'

So Florence watched television. For the rest of the week, in fact, she spent whole mornings and afternoons trying to be occupied by the fact that DFS had such a terrific range of sofas for the nation to choose between and then sit upon without even having to pay anything for the first year. She actually smiled encouragingly at the television set, as though it were new to the art of public speaking and could do with a little confidence boost.

Films featuring adulterous relationships, and programmes about property purchase and development, were quite absorbing – if alarming. They did more than confirm Lydia's warnings. As soon as a character so much as contemplated adultery, he or she was set on a path that would escalate to a certain and utter doom. One unhappily married man got no further than entering a cheap hotel room with the intention of committing the act with an equally unhappily married woman (an unhappiness which explained, though never justified, the proposed infidelity) before an attacker leapt out of the wardrobe. He beat the man unconscious and raped the woman. She fell pregnant and needed an abortion. Then the rapist blackmailed the woman, threatening to tell her husband of the 'affair'. Since she had no money, and the man who had been with her felt guilty about what she had suffered, he agreed to hand over tens of thousands of pounds that had been saved for his young daughter's life-saving leukaemia treatment. He would rather do this than tell his own wife about the 'affair'. Matters escalated to a point where the rapist was actually in his house, on a pretext, befriending his wife and daughter. And still the man found this preferable to telling his wife that he had been on the verge of – without actually ever committing – adultery.

Property investment was a gentler but equally cautionary tale. A presenter with pleasantly large and well-shaped breasts guided couples through such dilemmas as whether to buy in Venice or Bognor Regis. It was the new form of marriage guidance counselling, and couples were urged to 'compromise' and 'be flexible' whenever their dreams of a three-bedroom bungalow with views of the beach were translated into economic reality with a maisonette by the railway station.

Florence watched for hours, by turns pleased and anxious for the couples involved. Then on Friday they went to see Mr Harris.

Except it was not Mr Harris they saw. Nor was it the Chinese noodle or her emotional senior. Nor even the Kenyan surgeon they had met first of all. Florence lay down while Mr Harris's substitute Mr Harrington pressed hard on her stitches with the scan stick. It felt like having several sprigs of rosemary, or dried toenail, massaged into an open wound. Mr Harrington seemed oblivious. There was a moment so lacerating that Florence was all for saying that she didn't really need to know whether she was still pregnant or not, thank you very much. She would find out in a few months' time.

Remarkably, the embryo had survived. For a whole minute Florence was able to forget herself as she watched the heart beating on the monitor. Pulsing open and shut like a sea anemone, its entire being centred on the task, so small and certain in the blackness of the ocean. The embryo is all heart. We all begin as hearts. Everything else comes later. Thomas had told her that.

When Mr Harrington asked Florence whether she had any questions, any concerns, any worries whatsoever, she asked him – in a now-hopeless attempt to get back to the beginning of her story – how the misdiagnosis and the needless operation could have occurred in the first place. He replied that an ultrasound scan was like shining a torch into a dark cave and trying to interpret the shadows. *As sophisticated as that, huh!* she thought of saying. (Afterwards.) Gee *whizz*. Her stepfather George, of course, disagreed. George Morley's view was that if you took yourself off to the hospital and asked them to do something about you, then you could not very well complain about how it had turned out. It would be like presenting yourself for sectioning as a mental patient. Objecting afterwards was pointless.

'You *asked* for intervention, my girl,' George said when they dropped Florence back home.

He was looking suspiciously at all the books in Florence and Robert's living room, which were arranged neatly onto new shelves in the alcoves.

'You asked for it, and intervention is what you got! And if you weren't so bloody screwy about everything – ' he muttered as he went outside to wait in the car' – you'd understand that.'

With George gone, the women could resume telling each other everything that had happened.

'And that was when I knew that Sarah Jane was going to be just fine!' Lydia smiled.

'Sarah Jane?'

'Or Alexander Oliver, if things should turn out that way.'

'Mr Harrington said the embryo has had a growth spurt,' Florence panted in reply. 'That's why we couldn't see it properly before and why we can see it now. It was just too small before.'

'So you said to Mr Harrington, but couldn't it be a five-week-old embryo having an early growth spurt?'

'And that was when he said it couldn't be.'

Mr Harrington explained that such an early growth spurt simply wasn't possible: no embryo could possibly reach this developmental stage within a mere five weeks. It was a seven-weeker and therefore had to be Robert's baby.

'And when we were in the toilets you remember what I said to you?'

'Yes, Mum.'

'"So it's Robert you've got to *jolly well* stick to now." And "Mother Nature has chosen." All right, dear? Now promise me you're going to sever all ties with this Professor man.'

Florence promised. And it was true that after Lydia left, there was a wobbly moment when she thought that perhaps what she really wanted was to be with one man – and only one man – whatever her plans for initiating a new way of loving two men at a time might have been. But that man wasn't Robert, she realized. It was Thomas. It was just Sod's Law, of course: to realize this only now that she was pregnant with the other man's baby. But Sod's Law operated so comprehensively in Florence's life that it seemed to extend even to those areas, like who to love and how, where she might have reasonably expected to exert some sway in her own favour.

For the next few days, there were ever-shorter drafts of the longest love letter. It was now the first in the history of English letter-writing to be addressed to two men at once and then, in a wholly original swerve, become almost exclusively concerned with just one of them.

I love you and wish I could spend my life with you! she emailed Thomas urgently.

I love you and wish I could spend a week in California with you, he emailed straight back.

And the thing was, he meant it sincerely, he really did.

You would love it, he added.

She had chosen Thomas, but he had not chosen her. The next time they met he said – not actually in reference to Florence but a general philosophy of life – that he didn't believe it was *necessary* to choose. Butter and margarine, marmalade and strawberry jam – why, you just spread 'em both over your Marmite soldiers.

'I know it sounds an odd thing,' she said, even laughed, 'hoping a man will marry you because you're pregnant with someone else's baby. In the normal course of things, you get yourself pregnant with *his* baby and then you stand some sort of a chance.'

So Florence turned it into a joke and Thomas laughed too. That was how they got around it. Florence wanted Thomas to marry her – no, that laughter meant, she *had* wanted him to marry her, once, in the far-off time before the last few seconds. They laughed as much as to say that Florence was a funny woman who did funny sorts of things, not a painfully embarrassed one who was pregnant with the other guy's baby. And as time went on and her breasts began to exceed even the scope of the television presenter's, Florence remained aware of another possibility: perhaps, no matter what Mr Harrington said, she really was pregnant with Thomas's baby. It would not surprise her if his sperm had achieved seven weeks' work in the space of five. After all, she thought, this was Thomas Marvelle we were talking about.

Except it wasn't as though anyone *was* talking about it. She went back to work without saying anything to either Thomas or Robert about what she had consented to before the operation. It was marriage and adultery as usual. Robert played the happily expectant father and as for the question of the baby's real paternity, in her own mind it simply receded as the idea of the pregnancy grew on her – quite literally.

Nineteen

Six months later, outside the museum of the villages of Little and Greater Dillyford, there were rallying flags in lime and scarlet. Through the revolving doors a hexagonal donation box containing dollar bills and buttons had recently been repositioned to induce a greater amount of conscience in passers-by. It was half-day, however, and as Florence waited for Thomas to arrive, she passed an agreeable quarter of an hour drifting through suites of rooms where the plaster cornice was pretending to be marble frieze and the walls were painted the very shades of pigeon grey and pondweed least amenable to vision. She drifted and, like any woman nearing the end of her pregnancy, she dreamed.

In Florence's case, she dreamed of new displays, of transatlantic loans arranged with considerable difficulty but eventual success, and of culturally challenging exhibition titles like 'The Noble Adulteress', 'Adulterers and World Peace', and 'Adultery: The Road from Hollywood to Happiness' – all accompanied by well-respected Oxbridge monographs proving (no matter what Lydia might say) that capital A Adultery was in fact a surprising force for good in eradicating cholera, misery, illiteracy, Third World debt. And once the Dillyford exhibitions transferred to museums and galleries throughout the world, then the adultery revolution would come. Supported by new scientific research, issuing in headlines like 'Docs

Discover Gene for Two-Timing', 'Adulterers Not to Blame', 'Pope Confirms Seventh Commandment', ideally this change of moral attitude toward adultery would be (with the exception of the Pope) instant, permanent, and universal.

At the very minimum, she decided, seating herself on a sky-blue silk dais, she wanted to see more done for the adulterous. Or at least for the adulteress. She didn't mean people who were getting into bed with everyone regardless of their wedding ring. She meant people like her, who were quite serious about love but happened to feel it towards a couple of people at a time. There must be others out there – mustn't there? Accommodating female hearts who risked twice as much as everyone else, who were practically *firefighters* of the emotional life. Yes, the compatibility of loving two men at a time would be understood at last. In due course it would be recognized as an alternative lifestyle (The Two-Man Woman, perhaps) and there would be all sorts of radio advice on Overcoming the Mistaken Sense of Guilt, and Bigamy: Making the Decision. Tax relief, explained on Government Help Sheets, for those adulteresses who chose to stay in the marital home. And Health & Safety updates on 'What To Do When You Fall Pregnant', couriered to the door with complimentary mini-bottles of Nicolas Feuillante champagne and sachets of that pretzel and raisin mix she liked so much.

In the meantime, there was her 'Remains of Roman Britain in Dillyford' project to finalize. Footsteps and voices – of the last visitors to leave the museum – echoed underwater behind her. A whistle screeched blasphemously from the sole of someone wearing trainers. Then the receptionist said goodbye to her and all was still.

She was happy here.

It was less than half an hour before the lovers were lying sideways on three sofa cushions and a medium white towel that substituted for a sheet. One of the terrific things about Thomas, in Florence's view, was that he made time for love no matter what else was going on. Today he had arrived with a head full of a Hospital Board meeting and the 'ignorant pessimism' that was apparently evident in near enough everything everyone else had said on the occasion.

'I can't tell you how absolutely stupid it is.'

And when you looked at what Bob Goldman had written last week in *New Scientist* . . . Florence listened, or half-listened, respectfully, wondering how much longer it would be before she could get her knickers off. It seemed that the bearing of the Copenhagen polio epidemic of 1952 on the present situation was being explained to her in some detail. And then:

'You know what he said?'

Florence shook her head sympathetically.

'He said *every* – *single* – drug had been found via a screening programme, *or* by chance. Either by accident, or not by accident!'

Thomas paused and Florence tried to look as appreciative as she could of this impenetrable triumph. She remembered how patiently Thomas had reassured her, just a few weeks before, when she was worried about spotting. There were a couple of pinkish droplets when she wiped herself. On the internet it said this was nothing to be concerned about, 'unless accompanied by a sudden gush of clear or pink fluid'. And she thought there had been.

'That was just my spunk coming out of you,' Thomas had said, logically enough.

'That's what I thought at first. But it didn't look right. It wasn't thick. Or white. It was clear and thin.'

He could see how frightened she was. 'It changes in appearance after a few minutes.' She must know this – of course she must – but as there had never been any need to think about it before, somehow it didn't seem very convincing. 'Look, I can see you're not going to take my word for it, so I'm going to demonstrate for you.'

So he had, right there and then. A few minutes later they both watched as his dying emission turned clear and ran like water down the sides of his stomach. It was the simplest scientific demonstration he'd ever performed but one of the moments when she most thought he was a genius. A kind genius, that's what he was to her, and their lovemaking a sort of charitable form of depravity when he would take the time to tell her things, sometimes the most obscene and theoretically unpleasant things, when all of his inventiveness was channelled into helping her – for there was no question that he was helping her – travel along the dark path and arrive where she needed to be.

And here they were again, at last, with bubble-wrapped packages that she had not yet dealt with on a chipped Carrara marble table with gilded legs not far from their heads.

It was December but sunny, Thomas Marvelle whispered, and Florence Brown was swimming naked in a great blue pool where all the fish wanted to make love to her. The water was tactile and thick – a warm bath of semen. The seaweed pulled her legs pleasantly apart.

'Your swimming trunks are blue,' Florence replied, 'and, um, I think, that if I *wasn't* naked, my cozzy would have been white.'

Yes: pitiful. But she was only getting started. Thomas nodded absently. A moment afterward, as he thought of the next thing he wanted to say to her, there was a look of panic in his eyes and suddenly he opened his mouth like a cat and she could see the sharp little ends of his teeth shine. He drew in breath as though he'd burnt his tongue on the soup. He said *sshh* to himself and they exchanged The Anxious Glance, as Florence had come to think of it, whenever Thomas was warding off premature orgasm. Then, although his eyes did not actually move, Florence could see that his mind was, with great, *great* concentration, looking leftwards, past the dim brushland in which there dwelt two nuns, Nigella, Diana, donuts and sausages, Polo mints and snake pits, Diana again (in pearls of spunk), 64 The Private Shop, misshapen trussed-up breasts, Readers' Wives, black leather goods – and on to safely unsexy thoughts of Long Division and Richard Dawkins against the homeopaths.

Of course it was equally perilous to linger there, so a second later he looked down her body – now vast and veiny with the pregnancy – and then back into her eyes, his laughing with relief. Gauging her moment, she pushed him down with her hand, the way he liked. It shouldn't be hard and red for her, but it was hard and red for her, and she liked it when he told her things like that. *My dirty cock loves you. My spunk loves you.* Soon the film reels began to roll in their heads. All the love they'd made, all at once.

Their love life had developed rather slowly. This was, insofar as it could be, deliberate. They were frequent lovers and would go to bed every day if they could. Florence often marvelled that people could do this in the afternoon, legally and even for free. Just like the days when she discovered self-love, she marvelled even more that everyone was not doing it all of the time. Sometimes it *was* actually every day in the case of these lovers. So there was a sense of luxuriance and not needing to rush. They had spent about a year simply touching each other and it remained the preferred activity. There could be nothing more intimate than the kind of sex that you had with yourself. Nothing riskier to share.

Twenty minutes later, Florence levered herself slowly onto hands and knees and began to crawl backwards. Thomas lay still and looked at her so tenderly, like a bear with his cub, that she was afraid she might cry. If she cried he'd think there was something wrong. But all that was wrong was that she loved him. Putting her face right by his, she felt the nice familiar bristle against her cheek. And when they were like this, here, now, it was almost unbearable how much she loved him.

'Think your dirtiest thing,' Thomas suggested kindly as she looked down at him a moment later. 'Think what you have to think.'

So she did.

Afterwards, as Florence stood to dress, she was aware that a slight awkwardness had succeeded the earlier intimate abandon. She replaced tights, skirt, jumper, boots – all the same dark chocolate brown – and positioned black sunglasses in her blonde hair. She looked at Thomas and he smiled back. Retrospectively, she was almost baffled by the urgency of her feelings for him. She felt fond of him, of course, but no longer desperate to nail him to the floor. True, she was slightly sad that she felt this way. But it was not in her nature to pine. Instead the couple hunted about for friendly things to say to each other. Thomas told her how pretty her pregnant little belly looked now.

'Not so little, actually, any more!' he added with a laugh. 'The flourishing of Florence, hey?'

Florence smiled slightly, affecting a casual indifference to the compliment, while the great work in her body went forward in secret.

'And how's the house?' he asked politely. 'Plumbing sorted yet?'

'Oh God! Don't even ask!' she said, then kissed him spontaneously and out of simple affection.

They had new builders in – this time for the kitchen – but at the 'final' fix the day before, the two wall-mounted taps in the utility were loose and not equidistant from the spout. And there was a mix-up of the hot and cold water pipes. A great many more mistakes had been averted, however, by Florence's watchful, curator's eye:

really she knew more about what could go wrong with houses than could possibly be good for a person. Now Robert had insisted on converting the loft space, as well, before the baby arrived.

'Want a lift into town?' Thomas said, looking at his watch. 'I have to get back to the hospital soon. Before they totally fuck it up.'

'No, I think I'd better head home.'

So they kissed for the last time just behind the office door. Thomas waved from his car as Florence locked up the museum's front entrance. Not looking forward to what lay ahead at home, she decided on the longer route back. She felt like a whisky. But in consideration of the life of her unborn child, she'd confined herself that morning to a tin of coconut macaroons and two cups of chamomile tea.

She set off at a comfortably quick pace and it surprised her when, in the next street, there seemed to be nowhere for her lungs to exhale into and she was obliged to slow down. She stopped to allow the moment to pass. Bouts of sex combined with brisk walking in the eighth month of pregnancy was a mistake: one she'd made before. Then Florence took another two steps forward and there it was again – the constriction that seemed to mean she couldn't walk, or only very feebly, and was now seriously debating whether she would make it back home. Perhaps she could try someone's doorbell. Or perhaps she would be better off simply resting for a while on a garden wall. It was only a few steps to the nearest house and she tried to reassure herself with the observation that the road was more or less completely dry now after an earlier rain shower, which had been brief but surprisingly copious. On the pavement, only a few cartographic patches of damp – a Britain here, a couple of Frances there – remained. However, some other, invisible wall seemed to be holding her back. So she waited another second before she stumbled forward, failed to breathe, felt her legs give. Then everything in this world disappeared.

Twenty

The roses were red. The roses were blue. Just occasionally there were green ones too. Florence Brown was lying on a surprisingly comfortable bed, looking for the pattern. She recognized the material of the curtains – a thin white cotton slightly bobbled by washing, with a motif of clumpy, cabbage-like flowers – as the kind that Lydia might have chosen for her when she was a girl. Yes, it drifted fraily like a summer dress and the deep, unsubtle hem was ready for letting down next year. The colours of the flowers were improbable, she saw that. But now she was looking for the principle on which they were arranged: two separate strands of the same petals and stalks, somehow connected, like floral helixes, repeating themselves over and over again. It ought to be simple enough but every time she thought she had it, an anomaly would arise.

Similarly, there was no doubt some very obvious way of contacting Thomas. But whatever it was, it escaped her. Here she was, actually in his hospital, her face against a stiff cotton pillow in a widening pool of warm nap drool, and her Thomas didn't even know. Nor did Robert yet. Or Lydia. Or anyone else, in fact, she had known in her life so far. Florence would later look back on this as the time when the trouble really began. This was the point at which she began to lose the thread of her own story. Until now, having two men in her life had given her a stronger sense of self than ever before, a conviction that she had needs and rights which were all her own and that it was her chief business on this planet to obtain. Previously, everything important had been shared with Robert. In more recent times only she could piece her whole story together. But now! She would not, afterwards, remember anything of the ambulance or the paramedic who made mild jokes. She would, however, remember those curtains.

After the journey in the ambulance, they said she had been transferred from A & E to this Pregnancy Day Care Unit on Level 6. Then came the pillow. Soon, with some regret, she was even leaving that behind – sent to walk over to Cardiology, so they could perform an ECG test. Six white stickers with hard-core metal nipples were positioned around her left breast. Tiny metal clamps were now being applied to the metal nipples by a not unattractive woman – as though the warm whisper of fantasy, of Thomas talking intensely in her ear, had just turned into unappealing reality. A moment later, she watched as the printout came easily through the machine. This was reassuring and the result was, indeed, normal. The clamps were removed but the stickers were, without explanation, left in place. Then Florence was asked to wait.

The woman came back into the room with a mobile heart monitor which she said would record Florence's heart activity for the next twenty-four hours. Just in case Florence's heart was the reason why she had collapsed on her walk that afternoon. The woman impressed upon Florence the importance of returning the monitor promptly: it was impossible to redistribute them efficiently when they came back late, and sometimes they did not come back at all. The woman paused meaningfully and looked at Florence as though she did precious little these days but walk off with mobile heart monitors. Florence assured the woman that she would return the monitor without delay and then, having always believed in the pacifying effects of flattery, thanked the woman for her excellent work and added that she was looking forward to benefiting from the technological apparatus in question. Finally Florence was told to walk back to the Pregnancy Day Care Unit. It didn't seem to occur to anyone that she might collapse again.

Outdoors, between the two main buildings, the hospital grounds were busy with people walking around in their pyjamas. It looked like a community of the mad. Most inmates wore thick dressing gowns or winter coats over the top of their nightwear. In other cases, when the pyjamas were really scrubs, they wore stethoscopes – in a quite surprising range of colours, which was perhaps the medical equivalent of giving yourself a personality by writing in turquoise ink, or buying a laptop with a fuchsia lid. Outside the entrance to Maternity, two young postnatal women in fluffy white bathroom robes over tracksuit bottoms stood smoking. They looked like slightly grubby polar bears. Briefly Florence considered asking someone for directions to neonatology, but she remembered what Thomas had said about the high security measures and the impossibility of accessing the unit without authorization. It would be better to phone. The mobile in her pocket showed no signs of life, however, and her purse had disappeared.

In the circumstances, the Pregnancy Day Care Unit receptionist, whose ankles were elaborately bandaged with the thick cream straps of a new pair of mules, offered to let Florence make one free call. Feeling like an arrested suspect in a film, Florence elected to phone Robert.

'Sweetie,' he replied anxiously. 'I'm coming right away. You just hang on.'

She was relieved it was going to be Robert. She imagined that when she met Thomas he would say, 'Oh, you should have just *asked* for me! That would have been fine.' Or perhaps, with outraged concern for her, he would put it more hotly: 'Why *on earth* didn't you ask for me! You could have asked *anyone*. I could have come straightaway.'

But Robert wouldn't tell her off. All the same, Florence decided to get up and speak to the receptionist again.

'You shouldn't be out of bed,' the woman said, not unkindly.

'I was wondering if you could make an internal call for me, to Professor Marvelle. He works in neo—'

'Yes I know who he is. Is he your doctor?' she asked doubtfully.

'No, but – he's a friend.'

'I'll phone through a message to his NHS secretary, okay?' the receptionist offered.

Florence knew all about the NHS secretary Thomas shared with three other consultants. A young man innocent of spelling or notepaper or any enthusiasm for passing on messages, especially Thomas's. But she nodded meekly.

An hour and a half later, Florence Brown found herself watching rhomboids of light dancing on the wall. A young female doctor who could not remember the order of the questions she was supposed to ask a patient at this juncture had been all for sending her patient straight home. But someone else (Florence had lost track of exactly who) insisted on caution and once Robert arrived, he had fought for her rights too. His question, 'And you can absolutely *guarantee* that it's safe to send my wife home, can you?' had got results.

The hospital seemed like an extension of the building site their home had become – a nightmare of delay and incompetence. So here she was, dozing off, waiting to be scanned. Robert held her hand. She could feel the baby stirring. Early in the pregnancy – in fact, as early as the thirteenth week – she had first felt a small human hovercraft

168

powering through her liquid insides, the body itself too negligible to be felt yet, but the effects already apparent. At other times the suggestion of sleep would arrive infectiously in the middle of the morning, as though someone were not only yawning in the same room but actually yawning, irresistibly, inside her. And at night-time the baby conveyed to her, in vigorous speechless flurries, exactly where she could and could not lie. So she was not sure how to answer accurately when a tall, eager woman walked into the room, rousing her, and asked whether she could feel the baby kicking. 'Kick' did not really seem to cover the experience, and she was afraid that giving out the wrong information might lead to the wrong diagnosis again. The woman was wearing an impeccable linen blouse and skirt, like writing paper with a watermark. She looked reassuringly intelligent and turned out to be a cardiologist. A slight ironic smile was just waiting behind her lips.

'And what is this?' she asked, indicating the small digital device like a calculator that was clipped to Florence's cardigan.

'A heart monitor,' Florence said.

Glad to know something at last, Florence repeated confidently the information she had been given earlier.

'To record the activity for twenty-four hours. It tells you my pulse.'

'It tells me the time,' the woman replied drily.

Florence looked for the first time and it was true – the digits said 15.33.

'And have there been any problems in the pregnancy so far?'

Florence thought back. 'Well, at first they thought the pregnancy was ectopic, so I had to—'

'Yes, you had a laparoscopy,' the cardiologist interrupted. 'I read about that in your notes. Just a cyst on the ovary. And then?'

Florence explained about the visits to her GP and her midwife, both of them equally hopeless. She remembered the neon panic in the midwife's eyes when asked about the possibility of a home birth, and how that conversation ended: 'Shall we put you down for the hospital, then?' In charge of a birth? Florence wouldn't have put the woman in charge of a nappy. And when they discussed what had happened to Florence in hospital on the first occasion, the midwife had laughed: 'Dr Sharma is just obsessed with ectopic pregnancy,' she said. 'You're the fourth lady I know who he said was ectopic!'

'And were the other three ectopic pregnancies?'

'Oh, goodness me, yes.'

So this was Florence's midwife: the woman who couldn't tell the difference between an obsession and a diagnosis.

As for her date of birth, 22.03.77, that tricky fact, that complex data which no one seemed able to get their head around, Florence had simply given up trying to get it corrected on the NHS computer system. No matter whom she told, each new sheaf of stickers with her details still came out with a date in 1992 instead of 1977, filed ready for use – or misuse – at the back of the blue medical notes folder that she was obliged to carry everywhere until the birth. Each time she had an antenatal appointment at the hospital and biro-ed in a correction to the sticker on the front of the blue file, someone would simply slap a new one over it. As though her writing was some bizarre form of medical graffiti, and her folder some favoured patch for vandalism, which needed regular cleaning-up.

'The hospital admin do seem hopeless,' Robert confirmed.

'Right,' the woman said, her smile peeping out for certain now. 'I was thinking more of medical problems. Any shortness of breath? Pain?'

'A little when I'm walking.'

'And you feel the baby kicking?' the cardiologist asked finally, going back to her original question. 'Regularly, yes?'

'It's more like – fidgeting,' Florence replied carefully.

'Fidgeting,' the woman said, laughing. 'All right. Well, let's have a look at what this little fella's up to.'

Florence arranged herself on two thick pillows while the cardiologist applied jelly to her instruments and Robert smiled supportively. Florence had been scanned before, of course, but this time the scan stick behaved like an intelligent extension of the doctor's hand. It moved confidently, paused thoughtfully, and made some surprising but not uncomfortable about-turns. As if it were figure-skating on the ultrasound gel. Forty minutes later, there was a diagnosis.

As far as Florence could gather, one side of the baby's heart was barely working at all, while on the other side the blood was flowing backward. Surprisingly, this was not as lethal as it sounded. The cardiologist suspected a premature closure of the *ductus arteriosus*. Florence frowned, trying to remember if she had ever heard Thomas use this term.

'It's all right,' the cardiologist said, seeing her perplexity, 'I can explain. In fact I can even draw it for you.'

She took a pen out of the pocket of her blouse. Soon there was a cream page with lots of vigorous arrows in dark brown ink. When a baby was born, the cardiologist explained, the arterial duct of the heart was supposed to close to allow blood and oxygen to circulate properly. But this baby's duct was almost closed already and he was still *in utero*. It was such a rare event that the cardiologist had seen only one previous case in the whole of her career. Florence looked up into her kind, faintly amused eyes and tried to work out exactly how old she was: forty-five? Fifty?

'The trouble is,' the cardiologist admitted, pointing to the volcanic flashes of blue and red activity that denoted blood flow on the Doppler scan monitor, 'once you think you're spotting a pattern, it's hard to be sure that you're really seeing it and not just imagining it.'

Florence nodded gravely, thinking of the earlier curtains, which she had failed to master before they moved her on. What gave the cardiologist conviction in her diagnosis, however, was Florence's recent consumption of chamomile tea. Chamomile had anti-inflammatory properties which, like ibuprofen, could stimulate a premature closure of the duct. At least, the cardiologist thought that chamomile could. It was true that no papers on the subject had actually been published. A whole year would pass, in fact, before Thomas would email Florence the first article on the role of maternal ingestion of polyphenol-rich foods – not just herbal tea, but dark chocolate, oranges, cranberries, strawberries, apples, olive oil, soya beans, peanuts, tomatoes – as a factor in foetal ductal constriction. Coconut macaroons, Kit Kats, Pretzels, *pains au chocolat* and various of Florence's other vices were not on the list, though whether because they were irrelevant or had not yet been investigated she did not know. But the one previous case the cardiologist had seen involved a pregnant woman who was addicted to chamomile.

She handed Florence two paper towels to wipe away the jelly. Florence was unnerved to think that so much rested on two cups of herbal tea: it was difficult to have confidence in the hospital's diagnostic powers after her previous experience of surgery here, and, as the cardiologist herself admitted, if the baby was later discovered to have some other heart condition, then delivering him now would only compound his problems. The suspected ductal closure, however, would not be fatal or even harmful if the foetus could be extracted from the womb in time. Perhaps, Florence thought a little desperately, everyone would forgive her everything once he was delivered safely. Unite around his incubator and agree on the moral soundness of adultery and covertly attempted abortion.

Or not.

'So this duct thing is meant to close?' Robert clarified.

'Yes. But only once a baby is born.'

The trouble with doing it too soon, the cardiologist explained, when you were still in the womb, was the lack of oxygen to breathe. The baby's lungs would fill with blood instead and once that happened, the woman added quietly as Florence handed the towels back to her, he would die. They were running out of time. She would be prepped for theatre immediately.

Twenty-one

Florence Brown was transferred to a delivery suite in the basement, where it was eventually discovered that her ECG result had been lost in transit. The team of three responsible for this discovery – a midwife, an obstetrician, and a nurse retraining as a midwife – debated for some time what was to be done about it. Florence tried to tell them that the result was, in any case, entirely normal, but they told her that she could not possibly be operated on unless the ECG result was in the right section of her blue medical notes folder. A machine would have to be found.

Not long afterward, they trolleyed one into the room. It was clear, however, from the conversation that Florence overheard, and in particular one alarming exchange – 'so that connects to the heart wire, does it?' 'I *think* so' – that not one of the trio knew how it worked. Florence explained that she would rather not have machines attached to her heart, or even her breast, by people who had never used them before. If only the cardiologist were here. She seemed to know what she was about. But of course it was against the hospital rules for the same person ever to stay with you for very long.

'Sometimes,' the trainee midwife replied, 'we just have to get stuck in or things would never get done round here.'

'Well that's the thing – I'd rather you didn't just get "stuck in" to *me*.'

But all the protests of Florence Brown were to no avail. The six white stickers around her left breast were reattached to the machine, anyway, by three people who had never applied the tiny metal prongs in the vicinity of naked flesh before. Florence winced when they pressed the button and especially when the beep sounded, although actually she felt nothing. Then a thick white band of material was Velcroed successfully enough around her belly.

'And what did you say is wrong with the baby?' the obstetrician asked again.

'A premature closure of the *ductus arteriosus*.'

No one had ever heard of it. From now on, in fact, members of the hospital staff would regularly ask her about prematurely closing arterial ducts, as though she had been living with the condition all her life and had not just been introduced to it in the course of the afternoon.

'No,' she found herself explaining to the obstetrician, 'a patent arterial duct is exactly the *opposite* condition. That's when the duct doesn't close at all. But,' she added politely, 'I suppose they are easily confused.'

Florence sighed.

'Are you worried?' the midwife asked.

'Yes,' Florence verified. 'I'm worried.' Strangely enough, however, she had a feeling that the real disaster was still looming and that it would have nothing to do with a prematurely closing duct or even the paternity of the baby. There wasn't time to consider what this other catastrophe might be, however, not with the present crisis right upon her.

'Well you don't need to worry, okay,' the midwife replied, 'because I'm going to be with you the whole time. Right through the whole surgery, okay?'

In the meantime, this woman, with whom Florence would prefer not to share a railway platform, left the room to fetch a razor. Florence was put into a gown with a yellow trim and a printed pattern that issued its warning – 'hospital use only hospital use only hospital use only' – umpteen times and in at least four different unattractive colours. Her hair was tied back with an elastic band and she could feel it pulling on the strands. Her left hand was as good as useless now. A cannula dug into the back of it. Her index finger was inserted into a small grey box attached to a heart monitor with yellow and green crescent-shaped buttons. And the masking tape around her wedding ring stuck unintentionally to the other pieces of tape used to secure the first two items in place. The midwife and the trainee midwife chatted between her legs as they took turns at shaving her pubic hair. They struggled, however, with her surgical stockings, leaving Robert to complete the task instead.

When Lydia turned up with George, he told her she had 'nowt to fear, child'. Then Florence agreed to smile so that Robert could take a photo. Now that the C-section was imminent, he was so eager for the impending birth of his child, so optimistic that all would be well, that she couldn't refuse him.

'It's going to be okay, honey,' he kept repeating.

'And you know that because . . . ?' Florence replied impatiently.

'With a team like this,' he whispered jokingly in her ear, 'what could possibly go wrong?'

'That isn't even funny,' she said, laughing anyway. 'You know that isn't funny. I knew someone who never walked again after an epidural.'

'Paralysis? I wouldn't worry about that. Far too common. No, it's only the really, *really* rare things that happen to you, my sweet. If I were you, I'd start worrying about giving birth to a television set.'

Finally, a man in a McDonald's-type hat but with very good glasses asked Florence Brown if she was ready yet.

'Are you my surgeon?' she said.

'No, I'm your porter.'

The operating theatre looked like an engine room, but a surreally clean one. There were dials with large clock-like faces, and great crisscross levers, and the controls for some sort of industrial-sized oven all down one wall.

'Hi, I'm your anaesthetist,' a man said as he began to spray water from an aerosol can in large swathes across her lower body.

'You feel that?'

'Yes.'

'Well, I want you to remember that, okay?'

'Okay.'

Then Florence was asked to crouch on the trolley – foetal position, crash landing position, Ron Mueck's 'Boy' position – so the anaesthetist could inject her spine. The useless midwife stood in front with a colleague. In her restricted line of vision Florence could see their thighs and dangling hands.

'I want you to try and be as still as you possibly can, okay?' the anaesthetist asked.

'Okay,' Florence replied with difficulty, trying not even to move her lips, as she was uncertain whether he had started injecting. She meant what she'd said to Robert (where *was* Robert?): there was a woman at work who'd never walked again after an epidural because she had not stayed still enough during the spinal injection. So Florence was concentrating on staying very still. The trouble was, the crash landing position was pushing the baby right up into her lungs, and she was struggling to breathe again. She was anxious to ask exactly how long she would have to stay like this, but that would involve moving – if only her lips and chest. Then she heard quick light steps behind her – perhaps the anaesthetist returning with the syringe – which would mean he hadn't even started yet! Surely *someone* knew she needed to be talked through what was happening and exactly how much longer it would take?

'Blackpool,' Florence's midwife replied. 'The only thing was, we couldn't check into our hotel till three in the afternoon, so we went to a couple of places we wanted to see first, but you don't want to do *everything* on the first afternoon, do you, you're sort of thinking, I want to leave *something* to do on the other days, we'd booked three nights in total you see, so we went to the hotel at two and said look, would you mind if we had our rooms now, and they said yes we could have them, so we got them then.'

'Gosh – she is staying awfully still, isn't she?' the other midwife remarked. 'I don't think I've ever seen anyone stay quite so still before.'

'Well, that's because she's not in labour, is she,' Florence's midwife said with a laugh, 'so it's much easier for her. It always makes me laugh when they're having the most terrible contractions and then the anaesthetist tells them they have to stay absolutely still. Like how are they supposed to do that?'

I can feel my toes, Florence thought gloomily. And if she could still feel those, then it mustn't have worked properly.

The anaesthetist neatly pulled out the guide thread and took away the thin sheet of rectangular plastic he had placed over Florence's back.

'But Blackpool was a break from the pace, anyway?' the other midwife asked.

'Definitely,' Florence's midwife replied. 'Although, to be honest, I'd be bored doing the regular stuff. You know, up on Level 5.'

Her colleague was from Level 5, and Florence's midwife was keen to descry – far, far, on the horizon – her own position on the frontline of midwifery.

'I know you love it, of course you do, and it must be lovely, all those straightforward births and healthy babies, and the patients in and out like a shot, but the thing about me is, I need a challenge. I don't like it to be predictable.' She nodded towards the statuesque Florence. 'Like this one's got something I've never even *heard* of. But it's because she drank a lot of chamomile tea in the pregnancy. An awful lot of it, I heard.'

'But chamomile tea is safe, isn't it?'

'I've always advised my ladies against it.'

'*Have* you? Goodness!'

'You are allowed to move again, you know!' the midwife told Florence with a laugh. 'You can still speak, can't you?!'

'Has it worked?' Florence asked, deciding to maintain her pose until the anaesthetist himself said otherwise and only just moving her mouth, as though she'd had a face lift instead. 'Because I can still feel my toes.'

'It doesn't take immediate effect everywhere at once,' the anaesthetist replied. 'The toes are last.' Several pairs of hands helped Florence to lie back on the operating table. 'But you remember how you felt the water spray on your skin earlier?'

'Yes.'

The anaesthetist held up the aerosol can for Florence to see. 'Watch,' he instructed as he began spraying her again, from the waist downward. 'Do you feel that?'

She shook her head.

'What about that?'

Again she shook her head.

'That?'

'Slightly I do.'

The anaesthetist waited half a minute and tried again. 'Now?'

'Now I don't.'

'And what about that?'

'No, nothing.'

'Those are your toes and you can't feel them now, can you?'

'No, you're right, I can't,' she said, relieved by how patient and clear he was.

A minute later Robert was in the room, surreal in surgicals, sitting beside her head. She felt like a small wounded animal and only now, with Robert there, was it possible to cry at last.

'Oh, honey,' he said, troubled.

'Where were you?' she heard herself ask.

'They wouldn't let me in till the epidural was done.'

And then he started telling her how well she was doing, which seemed not to make sense, because never had she felt so incapable of doing a thing. No, now it was all being done *to* her: the blue tent was being constructed over her body regardless, the plastic sheet unfolded. The surgeons were coming in with their crooked arms strangely raised and making their introductions anyway. And she, Florence Brown, whoever that was, had no choice in the affair. And so, oddly, or perhaps not oddly, after a while she felt more connected to the anaesthetist, a good angel on one side of her head, than to Robert on the other. Quiet, watchful, empathetic, he was, after all, keeping her alive.

Twenty-two

It was a little after seven when Florence's good angel warned her that she would soon feel some pressure, though no pain, in her abdomen. It was going to be neatly squeezed from top to bottom, like a tube of double concentrate tomato paste, to eject the foetus. He was right. It was her shoulder that hurt.

'That's just referred pain,' the anaesthetist explained.

Just!

'The surgeons are asking if you want to see.'

Florence looked vaguely in the direction of the lowered tent as the pale turquoise alien was held up, like a sacrificial victim to Moloch, by men with headlamps and neat white bows in their hair. She realized she was expecting to hear a clap of thunder. Instead, there were bright repetitions of 'Congratulations, you have a son!'

Fortunately, though, it didn't seem possible to tell who *else's* son he was.

'My shoulder!' she said. The small person wrapped like a Russian doll was brought close to her face for just a moment, before they hurried him out of the room. She felt strangely detached from the whole business, as though she had not given birth to a baby at all.

'If it's really bad, I can give you something for it,' the anaesthetist replied.

Half an hour later, Florence Brown lay alone and still in pain, curiously unpregnant after the past eight months. Robert had been reluctant to leave her – but also eager, naturally enough, to see the baby in the neonatal ward, so she had told him it was fine to go. The baby needed him more than she did. She would not be able to visit the ward herself until she was mobile, or at least able to sit in a wheelchair. Things seemed less than promising at present. An attempt to slip fractionally down the pillows ended in an agony that was as vast as the distance travelled was tiny. It was not just her shoulder now: the cut of pain in her abdomen was equally lacerating. Alarmed, she held rigid. Was this the beginning of the real disaster, the one that had always been waiting for her, she asked herself superstitiously? The painkillers must have worn off – or perhaps it would be more accurate to say that they had never really worn *on* – and it seemed inadvisable to move either forward or backward or in any direction at all. Alas, maintaining her new position on the pillows was even less (considerably less) comfortable than before.

Miserably, Florence reviewed her options:

(1) To move ever again. (Out of the question. Not an option. Delete from List of Options.)

New List.

(1) Call the nurse and explain the difficulty.

But Florence had seen the nurse. In police constable shoes she was walking slowly towards a woman in the right-hand corner bed who moaned shamelessly, 'Oh oh oh!' Then Florence heard the nurse say that the woman couldn't have any more paracetamol.

'You've already had the maximum dose.' The nurse tutted and spoke wearily, for she was weary of all this pain. 'Painkillers are very powerful, you know.'

'But I'm still in pain!' the woman shouted.

Because that is the thing about paracetamol. Nowhere on the back of a packet of paracetamol will you read the words: 'suitable for the effects of major abdominal surgery.'

'Well, you can have more in – ' she consulted a clipboard, she peered at her wrist – 'an hour and forty minutes. All right? But really it's time to think about getting off them.'

When the patient did not reply the nurse bent down and inspected the catheter tucked over the bed rail. Satisfied, the doughty champion stood, turned, and began advancing directly towards Florence. What does she want with *me*? poor Florence thought. I didn't call her! (Did I?) But of course Florence knew very well what: guilty of the crimes of extinguishing the bedside lamp and asking Robert, before he left, to do what he could to block out the light falling in from the corridor. Whisking the cubicle curtain back, the nurse snapped the bedside light on with a resolute thumb.

'It was just,' Florence offered weakly, 'because of the light—'

'This is an observation bed,' the nurse observed. 'I cannot observe you if I cannot see you. Call me if you need anything else.'

A guidebook to Observation Ward etiquette, perhaps. On sale to all interested parties in a hospital gift shop like the one in the museum.

Please be assured that we will do all we can to make your stay comfortable in the post-op gynae observation ward. Very occasionally, a patient who is in a considerable amount of pain may find it difficult to sleep bolt upright with the lights shining in her face. Additionally, in rare cases, the regular stream of corridor traffic banging the double doors and staring at patients as they pass may be discomfiting. In these circumstances we would ask patients to be, as the name historically suggests, patient.

Then the nurse turned back. 'You are quite comfortable, aren't you?'

Florence nodded as deceptively as she could manage – imperative not to show any sign of weakness. Darkly she foresaw the nurse's regulation thumb on the Descend button of the bed controls. A brisk ZZmmm . . . all the way down all at once with no mercy. Then the final tearing jolt.

Again, not an option. Which left only:

New List.

(1) Stay like this all night, for ever if need be.

Right, then: that was settled. Florence shut her eyes and willed sleep and the unstirring depths of ebony night upon herself. Two minutes later, however, a biddy in the bed opposite, who had evidently not just given birth but perhaps been operated on for ovarian cancer, disturbed everyone by calling the nurse over. And quite voluntarily, so far as Florence could judge with her eyes still closed.

'I dreamt I was trapped – ooh – behind the cooker I was,' the biddy said chirpily. 'Funny things we dream about, aren't they?'

With half a fucking chance – Florence thought – *if you'd shut your big fucking pill hole*.

'But I can't really sleep. All this lying about in bed – ' the crone sighed industriously – 'it's not for me.'

It's the middle of the fucking night, woman, Florence added. (It was eight-thirty.) *Lying about in bed is where it's AT*.

Then she felt herself nodding like the prow of a vast ship. Dipping, drifting, nodding again, she began to dream of Thomas. They were only drinking chamomile tea but people could tell, just from the way they held their cups, that they loved each other. At St Andrews they couldn't find a room for her. There was too much building work going on. A disaster looming. Some time later she was woken up. A new nurse with a hostess trolley was serving an array of pills. Florence's eyes felt gritty but thank God for this new nurse who was pushing codeine and kinder advice.

'But the other nurse . . .' Florence objected, as the nurse approached her bedside smiling brightly.

Florence hardly knew why she should, at the very moment that things were looking slightly perky again, start fucking things up for herself.

'The other nurse,' she continued miserably anyway, 'said that painkillers are very powerful and we should all be getting off them.'

'Getting off them! You've only just had surgery today! No, it's very important to *stay on top of the pain*.'

Thank God: the new nurse would not let her fuck things up for herself anyway. And if pain was anything like adultery, then on top of it definitely sounded like the place to be.

'Is that your baby?' the nurse enquired fondly.

There was a Polaroid Florence didn't recognize propped on the cabinet beside the bed. Robert must have left it there. The nurse passed it across to her. It didn't look like Robert. But then, nor did it look like Thomas. Or even Florence. Reluctantly the new mother admitted responsibility with a nod. The baby looked more like something belonging to the other, grim nurse, than to Florence Brown. A miniature of her middle-aged son, perhaps, slumped pink and greasy after nine San Miguels and three packets of mature cheese and onion crisps from the English caff in Torremolinos.

'Well, I expect you'll be able to visit him in skaboo tomorrow,' the nurse said kindly.

'Skaboo?' It sounded like another planet.

'SCBU – the Special Care Baby Unit.'

Twenty-three

Eight hours later and five miles away, Helen Donald woke up with a jolt. Wet and cold and aware that she had had a shock. Her T-shirt clung to her back and her hair was dirty with sweat. She did not remember her dream – the worst one, in which she knew she was trapped inside a dream, where anything could happen to her, and she screamed desperately to wake up, but could not wake up. Joseph was lying beside her. She did not want to wake him too. There was no need or, at least, no point. There was even the risk of his mistaking it for a sexual advance. Instead she lay back, for a long time thinking of nothing. Then it came to her. It was him in the dream!

Remembering her child now reverted to a conscious act of will. In fact she was just about to light the first candle in her memory – to remember each thing that had happened until the moment he came through her body – when something she'd heard Professor Goldman say recently stopped her.

'We have to think of these babies as rational adults.'

Goldman was running free ethics classes for the staff of the neonatal wards, and she had gone along. She knew, of course, what he meant. A commonplace of neonatal bioethics, this notion was the ultimate basis for all medical decision-making on behalf of premature babies. Since prems could not speak for themselves, could not choose between treatment options or give informed consent, doctors had to postulate the wishes of the grown-up person the baby would become – or, in the case of terminally sick infants, should have become. They always imagined a rational adult and the decision was therefore usually obvious: one could reasonably assume, for example, that the adult incarnation of the baby would want the fairly simple operation that would allow him to grow up without heart troubles.

But sometimes, in cases of risky medical procedure and terminal illness, it was not so obvious. Then it was not a matter of using tried-and-tested procedures on obviously viable infants, but of applying the cutting edge of Thomas Marvelle's ingenuity to the smallest children in the world. Look at Simon Long, the latest graduate of the Wet Incubator, who had suffered a massive intercranial bleed three days later. She had watched as life leaked from him. Now his situation was hopeless.

Suddenly, however, Helen saw something new in the familiar idea: its application to her own particular case.

She got up and into the shower, where she clarified her thoughts. The water burst onto the shower curtain with a scratchy sound. Assorted mini-bottles of shower gel – part of an old wedding anniversary present from Kayleigh that had never been used – took up most of the soap tray. The soap bar was new and she liked its chalky dryness in her hand and the clean inscription of the product name. She held it under the spray as she pursued her idea. If she appealed to the only moral authority on the topic she could accept – her dead son – if she thought of him as a grown-up rational person and imagined asking him what he would have wanted from his mother, then it was surely not this suffering. No doubt he would be glad that she cared so much for him, that she thought of him so often, but he would not want her to torment herself pointlessly like this for ever. The soap bar slipped and knocked loudly on the shower tray floor. She bent to retrieve it. No, of course he would not want that, because only a monster would want that. And her son would not have been a monster. He would have been like her little nephew Jack. Or like Joseph. He had my legs, Joseph had said to her once. She twisted the shower off, watching it slow and gather in a tail like long wet hair and then begin, patiently, to drip. She put her finger to the point in the shower head where the drip was coming from, but the water just grew around her finger instead. A moment later she got out and reached for a towel.

'I've decided to cheer up,' she said over breakfast.

'Well, thank God for that!' Joseph replied lightly. Then he dipped the paper and looked at his wife more carefully.

'No, it's all right,' she said, reading what was in his face, 'I'm not going mad.'

'Well, thank God for that too. Toast?'

She nodded. Her nights had become particularly hellish. 'It's got to stop somewhere, right?'

Joseph put down the paper. 'Of course it has, my love,' he said kindly.

Helen replied with the pleasure of someone who knows they are pleasing the other person. 'I think it could have stopped sooner, actually, if I'd just listened to you.'

'It's okay, my love.'

'And I think they should have listened to me. The hospital. When I said I wanted a surgical delivery. Because then . . .'

Everything was clear to her now. Had they listened to her in the first place, then she would not have been tormented by the experience of giving death instead of birth. There would have been fewer complications. True, gynae surgery always brought with it a very small risk of affecting the woman's subsequent fertility. But what were the physical risks of surgery in a case like hers compared to the mental effects of *not* having it? The long hours it took, the sheer physical detail embedded in her consciousness, the feeling of abandonment to terrible forces beyond her control – when it might have been a quiet gap under general anaesthetic instead. Or at least something less traumatic than what had actually passed. In the SCBU, the world she was used to, everything was so carefully measured and monitored. But up there on Level 7, it was savage. If only she had been permitted an operation – was it really too much to grant patients' wishes in such circumstances? The system was surely wrong. And she was part of the system, of course. Give parents what they ask for, would be her motto from now on. They knew, better than anyone, what they could cope with. And, more importantly, what they could not.

Joseph nodded vigorously. Now that the subject had become a debate, he knew where he was and how to get involved.

'It's all fiscal,' said Joseph, who manned a customer helpline at NatWest. 'You look at the cuts they're making. Why did they want to close the Dove unit? Because that unit looks after women with problems in the later stages of pregnancy and no one will say it, but the more pregnancies they save, then the more neonatal patients they're going to end up with in the long run, and the more cost it is all round. It's horrible to say it, but miscarriages save money. Particularly when the hospital is as cheapie-choo as they were with you.'

'I just want people to have more of a choice. You can throw all the money in the world at a problem and that can turn out badly too.'

'You mean with the incubator? Helen, no one's throwing any money away. It'll be just the same as the race to the moon and someone will be making a fortune out of the new Teflon. Professor

Marvelle is probably selling the patent for a new kind of fish tank as we speak.'

'Well, anyway,' she said earnestly, picking up the breakfast plates, 'from now on I'm going to be cheerful and rational.'

'Okay, Nurse Spock,' Joseph agreed, kissing her forehead.

Calmly she returned to the bedroom to collect her things for work. Then a thought occurred to her – the photograph of the baby in the secret jewellery drawer that she had never seen. She could leave it till this evening, but it would be a test of her new strength to look at it now. There was time and, besides, she was eager to meet her son in this mood of resolved happiness. In fact, she soon began to feel excited. The sage-green cardboard file was easily found among the drawer's collection of old bank statements, ring boxes, paste pearl necklaces, passports and building society passbooks. Someone had placed a piece of masking tape along each of the three edges that opened. Immediately she perceived the thoughtfulness of this act: it was impossible to open the file without meaning to. Someone had wanted to save her – or anyone else – from being accidentally distressed by its contents. At the same time, the masking tape was not difficult to loosen and the process did not damage the folder – just grazed the surface.

Now she began to slide the sheet of photographic paper out very slowly, taking care to touch only the very edge and not leave any fingerprints. As she caught a first blur of burgundy, there was a moment of anxious anticipation. What if that was all there was – a blur? What if – her old fear arose – there was no face, either because the photograph had been poorly taken, or because there had been none in the first place?

In fact, she was not disappointed. There were four photographs on the sheet, each with a face. This was a superabundance she had not expected. The photographs were not identical, either, and she tried to deduce the rationale that lay behind the photographer's decisions. Was the one that showed only the baby's head, with the cream blanket drawn up modestly as far as the shoulders, meant for sharing with relatives? What parental needs – for she now perceived the photographs in this light too – were these images trying to fill?

All of the images were shot against the backdrop of a thick cream sheet. The baby always lay slightly off-centre. In three of the photographs, he was uncovered. Two were horizontal and almost identical, one marginally closer to the baby than the other. Perhaps this was so that one could be used, or even given away to a grandparent, while the other was preserved safely in the file. He was a much darker red than she remembered. Where the blood had collected internally, at his sides and the very tip of his head, he looked black. Where the camera flash reflected on his body, he was glazed like a pot.

In the last image, a vertical one and immediately her favourite, his eyes appeared to look at her. In fact, a tiny black line sealed each of them, but these seals were turned in the direction of the viewer and an impression of communication was created. A few straggles of white tissue, like cirrus clouds on the deep red body, made for eyebrows and even hair. What surprised her was how much like a living foetus he looked, and how little like a dead body. He was caught, like a sculpture, in mid-action: his left hand rested on his belly, holding the end of the umbilical cord like a plaything, a comforter, while his right palm was held up to his ear as though the world were just too noisy. She was familiar with these gestures from the SCBU and especially the new Wet Incubator. She saw babies doing this every day. To see her own son now doing it too was simply enchanting. He was almost brought to life.

As she put the file carefully away, she thought of the photographer, like the masking tape, with gratitude. To discern what parents really needed – no matter how unorthodox – was a true work. This was the meaning of her suffering, this was what she had been meant to do.

And to think that her little boy had been here, all this while, patiently waiting for her.

O my little car crash.

Twenty-four

It wasn't long before her moment arrived. Later that day she was on side B of the neonatal unit, where the least intensive levels of care were provided. Unlike side A, where everyone was fighting for their life, on side B the inequality of the world resumed. These babies were either thriving and about to go home – 'pit-stop' babies. Or they were chronic cases who, while their prospects were poor, no longer required mechanical assistance in order to breathe. There ought to be a separate ward for the incurable and the terminal – but there was not. The parents of Simon Long, the baby who had haemorrhaged after leaving the Wet Incubator, were standing by his cot. Sheryl gestured manically with her eyes to Helen that they were in need of some attention.

Helen approached the pair cautiously. Simon's mother was a thin woman who always dressed in black and, lost in her universe of grief, never met anyone's eye. Most afternoons Helen would pass her in the corridor. Then she spent at least an hour with her dying son – placing him on her chest, where he would lie, while she leaned back into the chair and said nothing. The only time Helen saw her talk to anyone with enthusiasm was when the priest came, in black and purple, to hold the child too. As if *that* was going to do any good, Helen thought sceptically. Mrs Long had been away for three days, however, to see her mother, who was also very ill. Today she kept on her winter coat

– a big Cardinal Wolsey number – as though it might protect her. The father had his head down. The baby was awake but not moving inside a cotton sleepsuit, with a black-and-white Dalmatian print, that had been donated or left behind some months before. The hand-knitted powder-blue nightcap was incongruous.

'You've made him look like – like a homeless person,' the mother said angrily.

Helen looked and saw that she was right. The thin green gavage tube trailing from the baby's nose added to the effect, like some kind of extreme nasal piercing. He might have been a miniature rapper. The mother opened the cupboard below the cot, where two small glass bottles of sterile water and a tube of zinc ointment were stored on a grey cardboard tray with an indented logo. *Bodyguard*. What did that mean?

'Where are his clothes?' she asked Helen accusingly.

'I'm sorry?' Helen replied.

'I bought plenty of them.' The mother spoke sharply but it was almost refreshing. 'Why on earth have you dressed him up like this?'

'I will get the clothes,' Helen replied softly.

As Helen laid the clothes, which she had been keeping for them to take home, on the cot blanket, the impossibility of Simon Long ever wearing them now was clear. Within days he had shrunk to the tiniest old age pensioner. His thumbs were hugged inside his fingers – a symptom of brain damage, Helen explained gently, when the father, in hope, asked what it meant.

'Shall I get him out for you to hold him?'

So Helen laid Simon Long in the crook of his mother's coat sleeve, then walked carefully away, as though someone's life depended on it.

She took a seat beside Sheryl at the desk and continued with her share of the paperwork. From time to time she looked up at Simon

Long's parents. She had been there, had felt something just like they did now. Their hopelessness seemed to reconfigure the room. Not for the first time, Helen looked down the length of the ward and saw it as a kind of funeral parlour for babies. Or a multiple burial ceremony. Three small open caskets on either side. Teddies and flowers. A central aisle. And at the other end of the room, directly opposite her, a modest altar – bookcase, computer screen, heating controls.

The next day, the couple were back. The mother seemed nervous now, the father surprisingly purposeful as he tightened his arm around his wife.

'Could we have a word?' he asked Helen.

'Of course,' she replied. 'In private?'

Again there was no one in the unit but herself and Sheryl. This was common. New parents were often too daunted by the place. Helen took the Longs into the parents' room anyway. It was a small space dominated by the enormous window, which gave a view of identical windows in the block opposite, as though they were really looking at themselves through the wrong end of the binoculars.

'Coffee?' she asked. 'Tea?'

They both shook their heads. Someone had left the middle seat of the sofa – a fluffy flowery peach affair – in the recliner mode. Helen bent to tuck it away. Mrs Long took the matching rocking chair. Mr Long remained standing and looked out of the window. It was slightly ajar, tilting away from him at the bottom – the handle angled into the breeze outside. The purple curtain stirred. In the block opposite, identical curtains were sucked towards the window, and then let go again. Mechanically ventilated by the wind. Mr Long turned around as Helen closed the door.

'We're very grateful for everything you've done,' he began. The words were evidently well prepared. 'But we've made a decision. We think – ' he looked at his wife, who put her hand to her mouth as though the tears were coming from there – 'enough is enough. All these weeks, we've been coming in here. And now . . . My wife's talked to her priest and he says that "extraordinary efforts to preserve life" aren't necessary. Ordinary ones are "all that is required of us". So . . . We would like you to turn off the machines. We just – she just – needs a bit of closure, you know?'

'I can understand that,' Helen replied.

It was worse than she thought. They didn't understand their son's situation at all. Either it had not been explained to them properly, or, more probably, they had failed to grasp it, which was understandable in the circumstances. She glanced at the metal bit of the window lever. The curtains exhaled again.

'And there are two things you need to know,' she continued, taking care to look at Mr and Mrs Long equally. 'The first,' she said to Mrs Long, 'is that any major treatment decisions have to be discussed with Simon's doctors.'

'But *you're* the one who's looking after him!' Mr Long paused. 'Sorry.'

'It's okay.'

He was right. She had a responsibility here.

'The second and main thing,' she continued, 'is that the machines aren't keeping Simon alive. Simon is keeping Simon alive.'

'But there's so many of them!' Mr Long protested.

'I know it looks that way. In fact they're mostly monitors. So that we know what his heart rate is, and his blood pressure, and so on. The only thing we're actually doing to support his life is feeding him and keeping him hydrated. And we have to do that. It wouldn't be a kindness to withdraw palliative care.'

'No,' he agreed.

'It wouldn't be legal either. So it's a case of waiting. I'm very sorry. It may take . . . a while. But if it's too painful for you, then you might want to consider visiting a little less frequently. Or, or, if you wanted to,' Helen suggested carefully, not wanting to cause offence, 'you could stop visiting. We could keep you updated by telephone if you like. No one would blame you. It's what a lot of parents do.'

Mrs Long gasped. 'I can't abandon him.'

'Well, you wouldn't be abandoning him. He's being looked after.'

'She can't do that,' Mr Long said. 'She feels she's got to see him until . . .'

'I understand. And in that case, what we can do is let the doctors know that you don't want any heroic measures taken when we get to the later stages. We can ask for a No Code.'

She paused and saw Mr Long registering the meaning of 'later stages'. So there was further to go. Perhaps much further. It might be many weeks, or months, as they had been warned in the first place. It would take several days even to get a No Code officially endorsed. A 'period of reflection' was the protocol in end-of-life decisions. This orthodoxy seemed dubiously useful to Helen now. Extended periods of reflection had not changed her own view of how the hospital should have handled her miscarriage. She could see that all of Mr Long's purposefulness had vanished. Miserably he looked at his wife, then out of the window again.

'But,' Helen said, making her decision now, 'but on the other hand, it may not be too long. To be frank with you, I've seen, well, a change in him in the past few hours and in my view . . .'

She saw them listening intently to every word and knew it was the right decision. Here was something she could do. Something she *must* do. She had been in their dark place, with no one to help her out of it, and she could not bear that they should have to suffer any more than was strictly necessary as well. If they noticed that she was veering from her professional remit, they did not comment.

'. . . it is likely that his end will now be quick. And painless. Think of his haemorrhage.' She found the words were coming to her easily and took this as a confirming sign that she was doing right. 'His haemorrhage was sudden and unexpected too. I should think – about a week. Ten days at the very most.'

The euthanasia plan she was privately formulating would be more likely to succeed if she waited until the No Code was in place.

'So if anything should happen while you're out of the unit . . .'

'You'll tell us,' the father said with relief. 'She'll tell us,' he said to his wife, as though Simon were already resting in peace.

'Thank God.'

The three returned to the room where Simon lay asleep.

Twenty-five

Minutes later Helen was in the corner of the Hot Room, head bent over the new arrival. The baby, wrapped in tinfoil like a turkey, had just been brought from theatre to be dry incubated. Everyone stood intently around the table. They worked at breast-height, joking tensely, reading the tiny body for evidence. Helen listened to the usual chatter.

'Umbilical a bit of a giveaway.' A rat's tail of malnutrition, in fact.

'Is that the technical? "Giveaway"?'

'No. Dirty shoelace is the technical.'

'Grey worm,' someone else suggested.

'Shall I add that to the birth details?'

'Just think: if the mother had eaten a few peas and carrots we could all be watching the footie now.'

'Careful,' Thomas Marvelle warned Richard Young, the new registrar.

'Ah, yep, I see . . . thanks.'

'Peas and carrots – steady on!' Thomas replied to the others. 'You'll put us out of business.'

It was perfectly true. The main cause of prematurity was low birth weight, and the main cause of low birth weight was poverty. But vast sums of money were spent on neonatal care instead. More lives could be saved for less money if the funds were diverted to better prenatal care, nutrition and education. Or so the argument went.

Helen looked at the gloved fingers of Richard Young, fiddling with the thin tube. *We are all seduced,* she thought. Nobody in this room wanted to get up in the morning for something as pedestrian as prevention. They wanted to work miracles instead. They were captivated and seduced by the power of intervention. The survival of the foetus. The youngest, the littlest, the least likely of all. The one who would, in due course, grow up into Mozart. This wasn't about giving parents what they wanted. It was about private ambitions. Young was the new registrar and Thomas Marvelle was busy quoting Milton, the poet of preference when things got tricky.

'"The earth was formed but in the womb as yet / Of waters, embryon immature, involved. Methought I saw . . ." Take it easy there, tiger, will you.'

Everyone tensed as the Professor took over the tracheal intubation himself.

'"Methought I saw . . ." something about a glorious shape . . .' he murmured thoughtfully. 'Shape still glorious? "Who stooping opened my left side and took / From thence a rib, with cordial spirits warm." There.' He spoke with satisfaction. 'Cordial spirits *warm*! Warm! I mean – fucking hell!'

The Professor looked up expectantly. Like everyone else, Helen had no idea if this was admiration or censure of the line of poetry in question. Or something else altogether.

'All right, people, I think we're done here. Tell the mother,' Thomas said to Richard. 'And someone answer that bloody telephone.'

The team pulled off their plastic gloves and aprons and binned them. Helen was the first to reach the phone. She listened, then cupped her hand over the receiver, and addressed Thomas.

'They want to know if we'll use the WI for an eighteen-weeker on Level 7.'

An eighteen-week-old candidate for the WI! Thomas took the phone.

'Termination or miscarriage?' he asked briskly. 'I see.'

Mothers and midwives could be distressed when aborted foetuses were born alive and left to die. He had no wish to get involved – even were it possible – in a case of that kind, where emotion would be obscuring the other factors. The midwife explained, however, that a twenty-six-year-old woman was miscarrying twins in the Lambeth Suite. One twin was dead *in utero* and had just been delivered. The birth of the surviving twin was expected to follow imminently. He or she might be a candidate for the Wet Incubator. It was unlikely, however, that there would be time to get the mother into theatre for a C-section. Was Thomas willing to bring the WI to Level 7?

'So the twins are monochorionic?' Thomas clarified. 'All right. We're coming.'

In the lift Helen selected Level 7 for the first time, she realized, since . . . But it was not about her any more. She studied Young, a Californian who was tipped to return to his home state and head up a new Wet Incubation centre being built in Los Angeles. It was not *how* to perform the mercy killing that gave her pause. That was easy: a cannula would be in place, and everything else she needed was in the stock cupboard. It was when to do it and who else would be on duty that concerned her.

'Level 3. Doors – opening,' an electronic voice said, very deliberately.

The doors opened with a ding! but no one came in. Thomas jabbed the Level 7 button impatiently and began to catechize the junior doctors.

'Why did I ask if the twins were monochorionic?'

'Twins who share a sac are more likely to present complications:

preterm labour, intrauterine growth restriction, twin-twin transfusion syndrome, congenital—'

'Share a sac and what else?'

There was a long silence. 'Level 4. Doors – opening.'

'For Christ's sake! What else can twins share?'

Level 5 had lit up before anyone spoke.

'Well, they *can* . . . share DNA,' Helen heard some poor junior suggest tentatively.

'Only when they're fucking blastocysts in the first week of the pregnancy! And if that had happened, there wouldn't *be* twins now. Only a singleton pregnancy would have developed. So if anyone would care to make a relevant answer,' Thomas demanded, 'they can share a sac and what else?'

'A placenta?' someone else asked in an embarrassed way.

'A placenta! Thank *you*!'

Intent on her own thoughts, Helen hardly listened. She wanted to act quickly, to give the maximum emotional pain relief, as it were, to the parents of Baby Long. However, she was aware of the danger of being, not only discovered, but subsequently overridden. Even with a No Code in place, what would occur in the event of Simon crashing might be affected by the ethics – or the ambition – of the Registrar in charge. Many had a 'no one dies on my watch' attitude. And once they rushed into the room, the act of euthanasia might turn into one of resurrection. She could try someone who might be old and wise enough to let things be. It seemed safer, however, to pick someone who could be trusted to be complacent. Or incompetent. Or preferably both.

They had reached Level 7. Thomas went first, the incubator last.

Except you couldn't even trust the complacent and the incompetent to be that. Sometimes they could disappoint you with terrific bouts of efficiency and innovation. And there was no room for the maverick here. Better someone rule-bound, someone who couldn't afford to screw up, someone who was hyperconscious of the consequences. She needed someone who would adhere to the letter of the law so she could get on with determining its spirit. The probational registrar from California would be perfect: predictably, neonatal care was an area of complex litigation in America. Doctors sued for intervening. Doctors sued for not intervening. Careers destroyed over one alleged mistake. Young would follow the No Code. And she would make sure there was nothing in the manner of Simon's death to otherwise raise his suspicion.

All this was decided by the time they had reached the door of their next patient. Helen met the gaze of the frightened woman who was now in the Lambeth Suite. She knew the royal-blue skirting board by heart. And recalled in an instant all the hours she had spent here herself. How she had been abandoned to give birth. How she had knelt, prayerlessly, beside the bed. There had been no talk of how many centimetres dilated she was. No estimates of how far there might be to go. No one to tell her anything, really. Dead babies were a waste of resources. There were barely enough for the straightforward live births downstairs as it was. Joseph was right.

The woman's name was Jacqueline. She had been brought to Level 7 shortly before because this was the only suite available. Her dead baby lay in the diminutive Moses basket on the bedspread. The image of Helen's child. The eyelids were fused and swollen like a beaten boxer. The woman's partner sat sulkily in the armchair at the other end of the room. Helen tuned into what Thomas Marvelle was saying.

'Miss Hart – Jacqueline – my name is Thomas,' he said gently. 'Is it all right if I talk to you for a little while?'

Jacqueline nodded in agony.

'Jacqueline, we don't have much time, so what I'm going to do is summarize what I understand to have happened here, and I want you to listen very carefully and to stop me and tell me if I've got anything wrong, okay?'

Jacqueline listened speechlessly as Thomas sped through the history of the past hour: beginning with that far-distant event, her admission for bleeding, and almost ending with the delivery, six minutes before, of a dead eighteen-week-old foetus of uncertain gender.

'And soon you are going to give birth,' Thomas smiled encouragingly, 'to another baby. So we have some important decisions to make about what should happen once your baby is born. I don't want to overwhelm you but I am obliged to warn you – warn you both –' he said, turning round to the seated man, who was evidently the father of the babies, then back to Jacqueline ' – that severely premature babies generally have very little chance of surviving. And even less chance of surviving without serious handicap.'

'What chance?' the man asked suspiciously, looking in Richard Young's direction.

'Actually, we don't even have the stats for babies this young,' Young replied. He spoke with a strong accent.

'Fat chance, then,' the man said, surprising everyone with his cockiness. Normally parents had to be persuaded that nothing more could be done – not that something could.

Jacqueline closed her eyes and voyaged solo into her pain.

'And that's why,' Thomas continued, 'doctors don't generally make attempts to save or prolong the lives of foetuses who are less than twenty-four weeks.'

'So why are you – can't you see she's in pain?' the man objected, pleased to feel that he was on the moral high ground. 'Anyway, I'm not looking after a handicap, all right. Before she went in for this, we talked about it, all the nomlees – ' he meant anomalies, routinely checked for on scans – 'like having no head and the four chambers and that, and we decided if there was anything like that, she'd get—'

Again Thomas continued as though the man had not spoken. 'But in this hospital, luckily there's a new treatment that's been developed specifically for extremely premature babies. Even babies as young as yours.'

Jacqueline opened her eyes, located Thomas in her field of vision, and stared right at him.

'That's right,' he said, coming closer.

'What treatment?' Jacqueline asked, almost inaudibly. 'I thought they couldn't survive this early?'

'They can in this hospital,' Thomas replied. 'We call it the Wet Incubator. If the baby does not have any major abnormalities – and there is no evidence that your baby does – then what your baby really needs is a chance to grow lungs. Now I realize this isn't nearly enough time for you to think it through and give informed consent. But if you can *assent*, at this point, then you can confirm your consent later on. Or withdraw it. It's up to you. Everything is up to you.'

'Like if there's something wrong with the baby?' the man asked.

'Yes.' Then Thomas added slyly, for the father's benefit, 'Of course, with the amount of media attention you'll be getting, it isn't for everyone.'

'TV and that?' the man wanted to know.

'TV,' Thomas confirmed.

'Have other babies been in it?' Jacqueline asked.

'Yes. Seven, so far.' The figure included patients from the trial that was now running in a Californian hospital close to where the new centre for Wet Incubation would open.

'And they lived and they're okay?'

'Yes. All except one of the seven, who suffered an intercranial bleed soon after he was taken out of the incubator. The bleed isn't thought to be connected to his incubation – it's a common hazard of prematurity, unfortunately. And like all of the others that baby's lungs had matured extremely well as a result of the period of incubation.'

'What do you say?' Jacqueline asked Helen. Thomas was irritated by this instinctive appeal to another woman, as though Helen could advise her better than he could.

'Me? It's not up to me.'

'But if you were me?'

'I can't say. It's not for me to say.'

'Please say.'

Helen didn't actually say anything. She just looked as though she was about to shake her head.

'What are you doing!' Thomas exploded in the laundry cupboard where they had gone to confer.

The door was partly obstructed by a mass of used hospital gowns in a large yellow bucket. Thomas shoved this aside with an impatient foot and let the door drop shut.

'That baby – ' he raised a finger back in the direction of the room they had just left – 'is going to die.'

'You think I don't know that?'

'Well then what?'

'Simon Long,' Helen replied.

She would have preferred not even to mention the dying boy, in case it drew attention to her peculiar interest in the case. In the new circumstances, however, it felt imperative. Jacqueline Hart's situation was just as desperate as the Longs'.

'What about him?' Thomas said.

'You know what about him,' she replied quietly. 'He was nineteen weeks and look how that turned out. This baby is only eighteen!'

'Eighteen weeks six days and the twin looked more like a nineteen-weeker to me.'

'It shouldn't be used for patients under twenty weeks.'

'Didn't know you were running the trial, Nurse Donald.'

'But Simon Long!'

'Simon Long is now fully self-ventilating.'

'That is an interesting way of describing the situation.'

'Simon Long is self-ventilating,' Thomas repeated.

'And that is a triumph, I suppose? For you, anyway?'

'No. That is a tragedy. His lungs now work so well that his parents will probably have a long wait before he dies. Believe me, I'm more conscious of that than anyone. It's my incubator.'

His candour and sincerity surprised her and for a moment she even wondered if she might make him part of her plans. She imagined he would tell her what she already knew – that it would have been lawful and compatible with the principle of non-maleficence to turn off a ventilator, with the intention of ending the premature baby's life passively. The recent Nuffield guidelines made that clear. Simon, however, wasn't on a ventilator. He could breathe: he just couldn't do much else. Expressed differently: Simon Long was his own ventilator now. And that was the tragedy of it.

But there isn't always a switch to turn off, he would say, *as you well know*.

And he would be right. She thought of Joshua Lanning, the baby who had been born with only a brainstem apparent and now occupied the cot next to Simon's. His head deflated a little more each day, like an old balloon. Joshua had never been Wet Incubated, of course: in his case, the neurologist had hopes that the draining of the excess fluid on his brain would reveal a cortex and cerebrum. So far, it had not. But Joshua could breathe. There was no plug to pull.

What, though, was the breath of life without the life? And what was the difference, morally, between passive and active euthanasia?

Cowardice. She had read the results of a survey in *New Scientist* which showed that the vast majority of people agreed it would be preferable to allow one person to die in order to save the lives of five others. But hardly anyone was willing to actually push this one person off the bridge.

Conscience does make cowards of us all. Who had said that? Some writer. She thought of Professor Goldman, too, who said that neonatal ethics was just as great an endeavour as neonatal technology and that the new Wet Incubator had turned anyone associated with it into a moral pioneer. But she suspected that, when it came to it, ethicists were all talk and no balls. They would need a committee to resolve the bridge dilemma, a committee which would decide that it was irresolvable.

'Yes, there are things worse than death,' she said at last.

'Yes, and a shot at a long and healthy life isn't one of them,' he replied sarcastically. 'The fact that Simon Long is successfully self-ventilating tells me—'

They were quarrelling again: she had been foolish to think she could involve him in what she was planning. Marvelle wasn't cautious like Goldman. But he could not be deterred from his own vision either.

'Ventilation,' Helen replied hotly, 'is not the issue for Simon Long, not any more.'

'But it's the issue *now*, for Jacqueline Hart's baby, and we're offering her the only thing we've got and it is a very, *very* good option indeed.'

'She doesn't know what she wants, and the father . . .'

'Well, *he's* a moron. I think we've safely established that. And if we didn't treat people just because their fathers were morons, three-quarters of the patients could go home right now. But the mother would have assented if you hadn't interfered.'

'She's in *shock*! She's traumatized. She hardly knows *what* she's saying.'

'Well, if that's your argument, then she's in no position to make a decision anyway.'

'There's really no arguing with you, is there?'

'Hang on!' Thomas replied. 'I'd have said that an argument is *exactly* what we're having. It's just that you're not winning it.'

Helen absorbed this. It looked as though she was simply going to walk away.

'By the way,' she said antagonistically, turning on her heel, 'Simon's parents want a No Code and they've already said they won't be consenting to a necropsy.'

'Another brilliant day's work from you, then.'

The nurse was becoming a pain. Always quietly campaigning away for something. Some re-diagnosis of the patient. Some greater or lesser degree of aggression in the decided course of treatment. Some sentimental refusal of autopsy. Or, like all that 'hello, Mummy and Daddy' shit she went around enforcing, even some change in the way that a Professor of Neonatology communicated a routine greeting to the parents of a premature infant. What the fuck did it matter? And why the fuck didn't she see what *did* matter? Her agendas were tiresome and endless. An innocent word rarely passed the nurse's lips. Everything was loaded.

It had been going on for months and it was not difficult to discover why. Back in the Hot Room, as they intubated another baby fresh from theatre, he remembered how she'd fallen pregnant and then, even worse, actually lost the baby. The usual thing happened. She got views where she'd never had any before. She made difficulties where there was none. Thank goodness that Florence, by contrast, had the sense to listen to him. But at work, suddenly his clinical practice was being subtly undermined – or in this case, not so subtly – by what had absolutely nothing to do with it: a nurse's private life. He wouldn't have minded so much had any of her objections been held in principle, in the abstract, intellectually.

'"For who would lose, though full of pain, this intellectual being?"' The Professor looked around the table for an answer.

'Book two . . .' Richard Young replied, 'line, um, one hundred and forty-six? One hundred and forty-seven?'

'*Very* good! I'm impressed.'

Yes. There was something pathetic about only knowing what you thought about a thing once it had actually happened to you. *Not* that it had happened to her anyway. Her baby had not been a candidate for respiratory treatment. Or anything else, for that matter, as far as he knew.

And it was ridiculous, too, he thought, the way she'd made such a fuss about everyone *not* making a fuss. The details were coming back to him now. She had actually sent an email to the Head of Neonatology, which was then forwarded to the rest of the department, to the effect that she wished no one to remark on the loss of the pregnancy once she returned to work. She had never announced her pregnancy. The Head of Neonatology, to whom she'd confided the news so that maternity cover could be planned, was, the email implied, responsible for that offence. Why she couldn't just accept her colleagues' genuine condolences but had to go around so grief-stricken, so female fucking Hamlet, was beyond him. There was never any easiness, any relaxation about her. It was all quiet agony and brightly forced smiles.

So even when things were going well in the unit, there was much fussing, smoothing, re-smoothing, checking of work that didn't need checking, plumping of pillows that had already been plumped. And even in the staff room you would come across her rearranging items like the kettle (the kettle!) and the mug tree and the teabags to what she considered better 'artistic' effect – an industrial restlessness that bordered, if you asked him, on Obsessive Compulsive.

Perhaps the most irritating thing about her, though, was the way she seemed to believe she could look into each person's soul and discover that what they needed was exactly what she could best provide: a cup of boiled water, perhaps, or a slice of one of the dreadful homemade cakes she sometimes attempted to share around. Wholesome, healthful affairs which tasted of carob and damp sweaters. And he disliked the way she went around like the proud beauty of yesteryear and seemed not to realize quite how long ago yesteryear was now.

As for the WI, it was always the same when you tried to do something new. Other people's objections were stupid and weak and made him feel impatient. He thought of Larry Curtiss, who'd collaborated with Hirschowitz on the world's first fibre-optic gastroscope. Everyone laughed at him and said it couldn't be done – until it had been done. He was sick of these pessimists in the profession and even when their objections were weighty, he still felt impatient. Now that Bob Goldman was in post, predictably he'd been on Thomas's case about Baby Long.

'What you may be discovering, of course,' Bob had drawled that morning on the phone, 'is that babies who spend prolonged periods of time in the WI are prone to haemorrhage following the de-inc.'

'Naturally that's a consideration. But actually I—'

'How many babies have been in the WI now?' Bob interrupted. 'Six?'

'Seven.'

'Suppose that, on average, one in seven survivors subsequently has a Grade IV.' This was the severest form of brain bleed. 'Or one in ten.'

'As we both know, even if they bleed for Britain it can have relatively minor *sequelae*. In any case, there's absolutely no evidence of a causal link.'

'You can *deny* the causal link, of course. But do you have a single scrap of evidence to *disprove* it?'

He didn't, and Goldman knew he didn't, and that frustrated him too. Until he knew more, it would be impossible to say whether there was an optimal amount of time for spending in the WI, or a point at which the risks began seriously to outweigh the benefits. However, there were no quick answers. The health outcomes for WI patients would take many years to document. And it was therefore unreasonable to expect him to provide quick answers: no one, for example, had yet worked out the optimal level of oxygenation for prems. And that had been in common use in neonatal units for decades.

'There's a feeling, Tom, that the trial should slow down.'

'A *feeling*?' Thomas replied incredulously. 'Bob, you know as well as I do that there is widespread support for this trial in the neonatal community. It's only the papers and the – ' he snorted – 'the *papists* who're upset.'

Thomas had heard a Catholic priest claim, on a Sunday morning television programme, that the Wet Incubator interfered with God's plan for mankind: some mothers were meant to miscarry.

Surely, if there was a God, he could get around a little incubator?

Surely, indeed, He had foreseen the incubator? And if not, then He wasn't much of an administrator.

Thomas continued, 'Even some of my enemies, frankly, who are just about the last people in the world to have a good thing to say about me, have admitted—'

'But there is going to be a whole lot less support for it in this hospital community if things continue to go wrong. And once the news gets out . . .'

'*Continue* to go wrong? We've had *one* unfortunate outcome, which very likely hasn't got a thing to do with the WI. Suppose Bob Edwards had slowed down. Or John Gibbon. Or Joseph Murray.'

These were the pioneers, respectively, of IVF, of open-heart surgery, and of kidney transplantation. They had kept going for years in the face of disappointment, disaster and professional opposition.

'Yes, suppose Bob Edwards,' Thomas continued, 'had been put off by one bad result. You know what happened the first time he and Steptoe actually managed to get an embryo to implant?'

'Of course I know.' In fact, Goldman had forgotten.

'The pregnancy turned out to be ectopic. Then they started treating Lesley Brown. The first pregnancy miscarried after amniocentesis. The second pregnancy was chromosomally abnormal and aborted spontaneously. Suppose the papers had got hold of *that*. Everyone would have believed that IVF *caused* chromosomal abnormality. Ergo, let's have no IVF. Well, I don't give a shit what everyone believes or what the papers print.'

'I'm quite sure you don't,' Goldman replied drily. 'But the Hospital Board *does*.'

'And frankly,' Thomas continued, ignoring the last comment, 'the UK trial could hardly *be* any slower. One machine, one patient, weeks and weeks of obs. What we actually *need* are more machines.'

'I'm just letting you know, Tom, what people are saying and what might be coming to Committee.'

Goldman's gravity was beginning to enrage him. All this man-to-man, 'Tom' business.

'I may as well tell you, Tom,' Goldman continued, 'I'm in favour of a rethink about the parameters of the study: for the next year – at least – use of WI to be restricted to foetuses of not less than twenty-two weeks and not more than twenty-three.'

'Well, I'm not. That might leave the WI empty for weeks at a time.'

No, the only way of knowing more was to introduce more (and preferably younger) foetuses to the trial. The existing parameters were just fine: use of WI in cases where the extremity of the foetus's prematurity meant no other treatment option was available. That was what WI was *for*. It wasn't as though he was asking – or not yet, anyway – for a trial comparing wet and dry incubation on foetuses past the established boundaries of viability.

But when Thomas had gone back to talk to the parents of the eighteen-weeker they refused assent. Without the Wet Incubator, their baby had lived for less than a minute. Another Level 7 case. However, there was no point, he decided finally, in taking Helen's intervention to an ethics committee: it would just be stacked full of feminists.

And Goldman.

Twenty-six

There was no point, she told Joseph afterwards, in taking it to an ethics committee: the old boys' network would always prevail. Their Publius Naso, and all that.

'Thomas Marvelle,' she said as she watched her husband washing the dishes, 'is in a state of total and utter self-deception. He thinks he's a saviour and he's just an experimenter. He has *no* idea what it is like for women.'

Buoyed by her own new achievements, feeling almost like a saviour herself now, Helen turned and hugged her husband impulsively. His wet hands were on her back – no matter. She even managed a sort of laugh. Then she tried to stand back, but Joseph seemed unwilling to let go of her. Ah. She had brought this on herself. Well, she would have to extricate herself. But tactfully. She lifted her face to his and let him kiss her. Then bounced away as politely as she could manage with a 'Must finish the washing up!'

A concession followed. 'Let's have wine,' she said.

A bottle was found in the cupboard under the sink.

'At least that's one thing I don't do,' she continued. 'I don't deceive myself. For God's sake, tell me if I ever start, will you!'

It was a throwaway remark and she smiled at him.

'I think,' Joseph replied slowly, perceiving an opening, 'I think you *are* deceiving yourself.'

'Oh?' she said, still confident. She took a long sip of the wine. The sink burped loudly as Joseph pressed the pin to release the plug. Perhaps it was another one of those joke things in the offing.

'Yes,' he replied seriously. 'Somehow you've persuaded yourself that it's, it's, *all right* for us not to have a sex life. And – ' he paused – 'it's not "all right". It's not "all right" at all.'

The turn in the conversation, like the explicitness of the accusation, surprised her. Not that she blamed Joseph. Or herself. She blamed the couple next door. They were still having sex rather loudly. On Saturday nights, anyway. They groaned so people could hear and this was the result. She put down her wine glass suddenly and the liquid tilted about.

'Well I . . . you know I don't – I thought we decided – I'm not going to get pregnant now.'

'I'm not even talking about children. I'm just talking about sex.'

Just! He sounded bitter and she tried for once to see it from his point of view. Well, hers first. She had never been very interested in sex and then, after the miscarriage, her suffering had seemed to earn her the right never to have it again. It was less the reason than the pious excuse. Today, however, she was determined to put everything right.

'Okay,' she agreed softly.

'Do you even know how long it's been?' he asked, as though newly appalled by the discovery that he no longer had a sex life.

'No,' she said quietly, feeling reproved.

She avoided his eyes by looking at a spillage of gravy on the worktop from the night before. Although it had dried completely, she judged that it could be got off with one of the non-scratch scouring pads.

'We may as well be flatmates. In fact, that's exactly what we are. Flatmates.'

Flatmates? She looked up, astonished and injured. How could he possibly describe their marriage in those terms?

'Well, I'm sorry you feel that way,' she said insincerely. Then, putting the onus back onto him, 'Why didn't you say something before?'

'Well, it isn't easy to say, is it? Talking about something like this, it's always bound to cause enormous hurt.'

These words brought her back to her purpose. Why must everything always involve enormous hurt? Surely it could be quite easily resolved. It was only sex they were talking about, after all. A relatively trivial thing.

'It's all right, Joseph,' she said. 'We can fix this.'

He looked doubtful. But she meant it – for those few vague seconds in which she failed to grasp that fixing this would necessarily entail the occurrence of sexual intercourse. And presumably more than once. How often, or rather how infrequently, would be acceptable to him? she wondered as she held his gaze. Surely it could still be avoided, at least for tonight, on the basis that this would just be 'for the sake of it' and therefore inappropriate. Perhaps they could continue talking, theoretically, about how to fix their sex life and then, in due course, perhaps one night next week, or on holiday – there was more time on holiday, it would be better – begin to kiss with their tongues again. But Joseph's face had already shifted into blind desire, one of those lightning changes that men were capable of and which reminded her why she felt so justified in refusing him sex in the first place. His transformation from a state of miserable deprivation to one of eager arousal was so discontinuous that it was hard for her to take either of them seriously. If he was truly miserable, then why wasn't he still miserable about it? And if he was so instantly aroused, then what was it but an automatic reflex, a physical requirement of his own? What had any of it got to do with her? she asked herself resentfully. What was *wrong* with men? Now he was even kissing her face – wetly, rather irritatingly in fact – and murmuring into her ear. How he loved her! he said. And if he really loved her, she thought, then why couldn't he show it and leave well alone?

'Sometimes, you know,' she said, 'less is more.'

'No,' he replied, laughing happily. 'Less is just less!'

'Well, what about the washing-up?' she asked in a last desperate attempt to forestall the inevitable.

'Fuck the washing-up,' he said playfully. 'I prefer it dirty.'

It was hopeless. In the bedroom she tried to remind herself of times (there must have been some, mustn't there?) when she had enjoyed sex, of why anyone *would* enjoy sex, of romantic films she had seen in which people appeared, despite all the well-documented downsides to the activity (cystitis, AIDS, child prostitution, unwanted pregnancy, more cystitis), to be doing just that. But the memories were distant and the whole business seemed deeply implausible. A passage in D.H. Lawrence confirming her suspicion sprang to mind instead. A woman was in bed with her lover, thinking how ridiculous his buttocks looked as he fucked her. Yes, she had read the whole of D.H. Lawrence and this was the part that had stayed with her. It helped, though only a little, when Joseph massaged her clitoris for some minutes with the tip of his cock. He knew what he was doing, there was no doubt about it, and the action even seemed familiar. Gradually she realized he was repeating all of the things he used to do to her. Her body had a memory even if she did not. But what little desire she managed, momentarily, to find, was killed off by his saying, desperately, 'The thing is, Helen, I *need* this . . .'

She felt rebuked all over again. Here she was, submitting willingly, or half-willingly anyway, and there he was, in a state of pleasure so anguished and private that it seemed a trespass for her to be present at all.

Ten minutes later he looked to her for guidance about what should happen next. Should he delay? Would she manage it? She knew it would take an effort that she could not be bothered even to begin to make. Not that she would ever admit that. Or could he tell? She had always been sexually lazy. Perfectly capable of orgasm, of course. It was just a case of summoning any enthusiasm. The contrary endeavours of men and women in bed – the one trying their hardest to come, while the other was doing their damnedest *not* to – seemed to express the impossibility of the sexes ever understanding one another. Particularly on the matter of sex. But now, at last, there was a way out. A quick exit.

'Come,' she instructed him, as though she were the generous one. She watched as his face was transfigured into a final ugliness.

PART FOUR

The Pseudo-Mother

Twenty-seven

Florence woke up with hostility towards the universe. At some point in the night – maybe it was three, when the woman in the corner of the ward began her wailing again, or four, when the council rubbish lorry arrived outside the window making an electronic safety announcement of 'Attention! this vehicle is reversing. Attention! this vehicle . . .', but certainly by five-fifteen, when the nurse woke Florence to take her blood pressure and said, 'Did I wake you? You just rest now' – Florence Brown lost her sense of humour. Not her temper, but her temperament. She didn't actually shout, but she felt ready to do so if the opportunity arose. What had seemed absurd, and therefore manageable before, had now got beyond a joke.

Her body felt all wrong. Devoid of the pregnancy functions it had been performing for so long, there was almost nothing left for it to do but drain excess fluid into her ankles and get her ready to breastfeed a baby who was nowhere to be seen. Her left nipple had been leaking colostrum sporadically since the sixteenth week of the pregnancy. Now both nipples did so copiously and she could feel sticky pools collecting under the fat folds of her breasts. She felt ashamed not to be wearing a bra or even a T-shirt or anything at all under her surgical gown that could help absorb the liquid. These feelings were soon overtaken, however, by worse. When she rolled onto her side in an attempt to sit, she had the frightening sensation of her belly sliding away from the rest of her body and actually reached out a hand to catch it. It did not feel as though she had given birth, rather that the pregnancy had simply been subtracted from her body. As though the abortion she had once effectively consented to had at last come off. There was no baby in a cot beside the bed. Nothing to replace her emptiness or even to verify the fact that she had once been pregnant. Only the unpleasant photograph she did not recognize, the one from last night, was leaning against the bedside lamp again. The flash of the camera made the baby's skin look cling-filmed. Where was her inner companion, the underwater champion of the past few months? She only knew, in a horribly approximate way, that he was somewhere in the Special Care Baby Unit, which was somewhere in this hospital. And not to know *exactly* where he was, after he had lived right inside her for the past eight months, seemed to transgress a law as immutable as gravity. The only comfort was that Thomas worked there and that Robert had been there last night too.

Now, however, Robert was going to use his fortnight of paternity leave to help finish off the house while the baby was in the SCBU. It wasn't suitable for habitation by a newborn yet and, since no one had expected the baby to arrive so many weeks early, the pressure was on. As a result Florence was on her own again – or at least, she would be until Lydia and George arrived – when she just wanted Thomas and Robert. She just wanted the future in which everything had worked out fine. So she waited.

And waited. While other patients debated whether it was cornflakes or Weetabix today. And if Weetabix, whether one or two. And if skimmed milk could be found instead of semi-skimmed? Alternatively, any form of omega-3-enhanced milk would 'do just fine'. She waited as an epidural was tried and failed on the new patient in the opposite bed, who was brought back from surgery with her husband cursing the doctors. She waited as a hush of voices gathered in the next cubicle to soothe a frightened woman. As her cry modulated from relief to shame, the stench began. An enema. Two windows were opened and a hardy fly flew in, then out. The room was still full of the woman's smell as her cubicle curtains were jingled briskly back along the rails. Then Florence waited as the nice drug-dealing nurse spoke clear, schoolgirl French to a foreign woman who beamed politely as though there was nowhere on earth she would rather be than half-sat up on a hospital trolley with a slice of cold toast. Finally, there was world enough and time to finish the longest love letter of them all.

I love you for loving the pleasures of the flesh.

All of them.

Once on a hot night I had thrush. You went into me like acid. Only your nob end. Broom end. The next night was even hotter and I thought the pessary from the doctor would melt too rapidly to work. It trickled out of me glorious as garlic butter. And the scouring pad, which a million million chain-labouring organisms had been applying assiduously to my tender places, was, ah! instantly lifted away.

These things don't come again.

Once there was a miracle. For weeks I was living underwater, my ears blocked by painful crystals of honey wax. All I heard was the percussion: the pointless ringing, the surprising pop and inrush of air when I turned my head on the pillow at night. It was capable of waking me. When the nurse hosed my ear and said that a large, longstanding piece of the wax had moulded itself to the form of my ear drum, I wondered whether I would be perverse enough to ask to see its glory. Before I could decide there was a tremendous rush and then – I heard. All the world had the acoustic of the swimming pool. The tiled changing area. I put the key in the front

door, again and again, and ran all the taps in the house and turned the
pages of books, just to hear their music.

There was time – but it was not the time. Nothing seemed real. Florence had a baby, apparently, but still felt quite childless. When the grim nurse asked if Florence would like to see her baby now, as though it were Florence herself who had been holding things up all morning, she nodded silently. The wheelchair took her as far as the entrance to the neonatal unit on side A. The top half of a stable-type door was open. She could see down the corridor. So this was where Thomas worked. Then the wheelchair assistant pressed the intercom.

'You may have to wait a bit,' she explained. 'They don't have a receptionist. Someone will let you in when they have time. And don't forget to use this!'

With the tip of a painted nail the assistant tapped an alcohol rub dispenser mounted next to the intercom. She waited for Florence to get out of the wheelchair and then she walked away.

Pressing the dispenser, which was a little stiff, required a surprising amount of effort from Florence's stomach muscles. With the forward movement she was aware of some of the liquid that had collected under her breasts proceeding down her stomach. Then one drop even plopped onto the floor. She had no tissue, however, or even, after the major abdominal surgery, any possible way of bending down to wipe up the mess. So she could only stand there miserably aware of her disgrace. She looked up hopefully as someone came down the corridor. Was it Thomas? It was not Thomas.

Then the person who had been coming down the corridor took a left halfway down, long before he reached her. Florence lifted her arm, pressed the buzzer with some pain, and again there was no answer. She felt weak on her feet and looked behind her – no chairs, alas. She turned back and now there was someone coming again, yes, but at the very last moment the woman smiled and veered right, turning into another doorway Florence had not noticed before. How she could come so far down the corridor and even smile and yet leave Florence standing there seemed curious and rude to Florence. She would just have to wait, she supposed, till someone actually wanted to exit the unit. Or enter it, perhaps.

The corridor was empty for a long time. Eventually one of the neonatal nurses spotted her from the other end and rushed down, producing a swipe card. So much speed after so much delay was almost unaccountable.

'I'm sorry we can't give out swipe cards to parents,' Helen continued, using hers to let Florence in. 'Have you been waiting long?'

'No, not long,' Florence replied, in an English way, noticing the woman who had not let her into the unit earlier now emerging silently, but with the same encouraging smile, from the doorway to the right.

In fact, almost everyone Florence encountered was silent and smiling like a lunatic. Her sense of unreality was increasing. There was no natural light. So the place had the quality of a television show with the sound off.

'Have you been here before?' Helen added.

'No.'

'I didn't think so. Well, let me show you.'

So Helen showed Florence how and where to wash and dry her hands, which seemed to be the chief thing round here – first in the trough, up to the elbows, then with the alcohol rub again (at least the stickiness evaporated with pleasing speed), then in the small silver sink, concentrating especially on the palms. Above the sink there was a long internal window, with squares of mesh like maths paper, giving onto a room with several dry incubators. The nurse advised on hand creams to combat the effects of the repeated alcohol applications. Florence saw the words 'Baby Brown – Helen' written together on a small whiteboard in the hallway.

'Yes, he's one of mine,' Helen said, noticing the direction of Florence's gaze.

The new mother felt infuriated, unreasonably perhaps (what did she mean, one of *hers*?), but commented, almost apologetically, 'We haven't named him yet.'

'That's all right. Do you want to go in?'

So after rubbing her hands for the umpteenth time – there was another alcohol rub dispenser just to the left – Florence entered the Hot Room. Another silent smiler – Richard Young – acknowledged her from the other side of a phototherapy machine. Her life was rolling on like the usual farce, but now it felt as though it had taken a strangely sinister swerve. She had lost control, as usual, but this time she had lost it to a stranger to whom she had taken an instant dislike. The woman who was now placing a folder so calmly on top of the incubator that contained, apparently, Florence's baby.

Yes, she was definitely not herself.

A phototherapy machine meant a baby with jaundice. The other babies, these tiny human spatchcocks, were all in dry incubators. Except it was not apparent, at first, that there *were* any babies in the room. The patients were obscured and obliterated by all the machinery and monitors, and the modesty screens for nursing mothers. Helen stood beside the second incubator on the right, where a spider plant of wires sprawled onto the floor. She replaced another folder on a shelf, and said brightly, 'Here he is!'

Florence approached uncertainly. The tall machine beside the incubator – a square head on a silver pole – looked almost robotic. It had red digits like a slot machine that Florence could not interpret. The nurse pulled back the fleece baby blanket covering the incubator. Now she saw that inside the plastic space shuttle a small human slumbered in a breaststroke. He lay prone. A white blanket was coiled around him in the shape of a horseshoe. Although he wore only a nappy, like some miniature sauna user, the cumbersome apparatus confused his appearance. She tried to find her child in this strange hybrid of human and machine. Thick white wires were attached to his ankles by what appeared to be small tennis sweat bands, white with a blue underside. A red LED light blinking by his finger gave the tiny child a likeness to E.T. There were pictures of baby animals on his plasters and the words 'Baby Brown' on a paper name card that was Sellotaped to his incubator. In the illustration a pale blue rabbit was making off with a carrot almost as large as himself. The vegetable was hoisted onto his shoulder and the rabbit's gaze was intent, almost hunted. Presumably these nursery decorations were designed to make parents feel better. Except she was the parent – wasn't she? – and she didn't feel any better. She noticed that the baby's arm was attached to a piece of stiff card like a surfboard. Suddenly his legs extended alarmingly, like a frog about to leap. They were much too thin for his skin, which hung strangely in folds. She could not actually hear him through the plastic enclosure, so despite their physical proximity she felt far away. It was like watching a baby on video. Several minutes passed and after the initial fascination she realized, with fear in her heart, that she couldn't see herself in him. Or Robert or Thomas – she didn't know who she was looking for. It was just like the Polaroid back in the Observation ward. She could feel sorry for him, in the abstract, as an especially small member of the human race. But that was about all.

How could she possibly know for sure that he was *her* baby? Yes, she saw the white plastic anklet the baby was wearing, with a name and identity barcode, and the blue ticket with spaces for the mother's surname, the date and time of delivery, birth weight, gestational age, and notes for the mother: 'vit K, temp' (whatever that meant). But how easy it would be to swap those. How much confidence could you really put in a barcode and a piece of blue cardboard? Perhaps the nurse was deranged – there was certainly *some*thing odd about her – and it was all some kind of hideous practical joke.

Silently Helen opened one of the incubator's portal doors. Gently sliding in a hand, she said very kindly, 'Ah, what a sweetie, he's starting to wake. It's okay – put your hand in and touch him.'

Florence told herself not to be deceived by this apparent kindness. Cautiously she tried to stroke the baby's head. He flinched and recoiled at her touch, and seemed unable to decide whether to open or shut his eyes. Distrustful of the light, longing for the dark warm world he had been dreaming of only a moment before, he seemed not to know Florence or her hand. He only knew that being touched meant pain. A tube stuffed down his throat, perhaps, or another jab in the leg. His body felt strangely free and floppy but the new possibilities of movement were more frightening than liberating and certainly not enough to compensate for the new cruelties. He wanted to go back.

'What about his heart?' Florence asked.

Yes, his heart was how she would know him. She remembered what they'd said: he had a rare defect that the birth was supposed to remedy.

'How did the birth affect . . . they were hoping that if . . .' She started again. 'Once he was born, they said, this premature closure of the *ductus* thing would resolve itself. Has it?'

Helen frowned in a way that revealed she had no idea what Florence was talking about. 'I'm afraid I've never heard of a premature *closure* of the *ductus arteriosus*. Do you mean a patent arterial duct?'

'No,' Florence replied, continuing to stare unhappily at the baby. How bad-tempered and peevish he was! How little he wanted her!

'Well, you'll have to ask his doctors about that,' Helen said.

'When can I talk to his doctors?'

'I'll try to arrange an appointment, maybe in a day or two, okay, when we know some more? But he's doing really well for now.'

Helen took down the folder from the incubator and began reading.

'"Cried at birth. Born in good condition. Active, normal tone, good spontaneous cry, pink." This is all very good, Mummy.'

It took Florence a while to realize that 'Mummy' was meant as a reference to her and not a sign that the nurse was definitely crazy. How alarming that this woman was in charge.

'"HR" – that's heart rate – "eighty to one hundred. Facial O two" – oxygen – "given. At two minutes of age, some signs of respiratory distress with subcostal recession and nasal flaring . . ." Don't worry about that, it's quite normal for a prem. "At seven minutes of age, transferred to SCBU." I spoke to the night nurse who was here when they incubated him and I've been here most of the time since then.'

So that was everything – but what did any of it mean? Florence looked again at the boy in the box who did not want her to touch him. What the nurse was talking about, however confidently, was merely how the baby was doing *now*. She didn't know his history, the events of the day before. She could only point to numbers on monitors and flashing squares of different colours.

'No, I'm sorry,' Florence said, shaking her head and beginning to back away from the incubator.

'It's all right to be upset,' Helen replied. 'That's usual too.'

'It's not because I'm upset,' Florence said, beginning to cry. 'I mean, I *am* upset, but it's not because of that.'

Helen spoke gently. 'What's not because of that?'

Florence wiped the tears away firmly with the bottom of her palms. 'Do you mind if I look around the unit? I just want to check he's not in one of the other incubators. This baby has jaundice, then?'

But as she started to move towards the phototherapy machine in the next bay, Helen put out a restraining arm. To the sleep-deprived Florence this action seemed suspicious.

'I'm sorry but I can't let you do that,' Helen said.

She had not forgotten her new motto: give parents what they want. There was a conflict, however, with the privacy that other parents expected and she must try to balance it as best she could.

Helen continued, 'Patient confidentiality. We're not even allowed to disclose the names of the other patients. And I can't talk about what is wrong with the other babies, although you're right, that machine is used to treat jaundice.'

'You're not serious?'

'Yes.'

'But all the mistakes?' Florence objected, with the idea that she was now arguing with real cogency and power, and having no notion of her actual exhaustion. 'The midwife didn't know about the ECG. She couldn't even put the stockings on! And they never told me how long to stay still.'

Helen nodded sympathetically, as though she were really following this baffling summary of events.

'So how would I know?' Florence demanded.

Helen began to talk about the obstacles to bonding when a baby was in the SCBU. The difficulty of reconciling the idea of a perfect baby with the reality of the machines and the wires and the fears.

But there were things that could help establish a bond. Skin-to-skin contact. Breastfeeding. Talking and singing.

How would she know? As she half-listened to Helen's further recommendations – nappy-changing, bathing the baby, bringing the grandparents along – all that was forming in Florence's mind were the words she had sometimes feared that Robert would say, if the baby turned out to look like Thomas after all.

'I want a DNA test,' Florence said out loud, surprising herself again.

'Come with me,' Helen replied quietly.

Twenty-eight

Four hours later, after a deep and satisfying nap, Florence opened her eyes and realized that her request had been a complete piece of craziness. The nurse had taken her to the parents' room and gently refused, explaining that it would be counter-productive because the test would only serve to place a psychological barrier between herself and the baby.

'No,' Florence had shouted, 'it would serve to put my bloody mind at rest!'

In the end, and much to the nurse's surprise, Professor Marvelle had condescended to get involved and said that the patient's wishes were to be respected. So the sample had been taken and duly gone off for analysis.

Now, though, the idea that the nurse was deranged appeared to Florence in its true light. It was mere sleep-deprived paranoia. The baby seemed well, in the circumstances, and what other unknown disaster awaited her? None, none! She could almost smile about it. But what must Thomas think of her?

It wasn't long before he was actually in the room. A private one, with a sink of its own. He maintained a discreet distance in case Robert (who was, in fact, busy painting the nursery at home) or anyone else turned up. He took a very upright chair and asked her how she was feeling. Everyone was treating her rather nicely now.

It was not difficult to guess that Helen was behind this. She must have passed on the word that Florence was beginning to reject the baby. Some guff, no doubt, about her inability to identify a sick baby with the slumbering infant of her fondest dreams. Well, it was *their* fault anyway. If they hadn't made so many mistakes and stopped her from sleeping all night, then she might not have flipped in the first place. Even the bed linen was noisy. Made of taffeta, by the sound of it.

In the fold of her elbow Florence could feel the plaster – really, just a bob of cotton wool and a little masking tape – where the nurse in Phlebotomy had taken the blood sample for the test. She sat up cautiously with help from Thomas. Her arm was already beginning to blacken from the nurse bruising the vein with the needle.

'Are needles thicker nowadays, or something?' she asked him.

'Actually, they're thinner. Some nurses just aren't very good at taking blood.'

'So the nurses are thicker nowadays? God! Why *are* all the staff in this hospital so useless? Present company excepted.'

'They're not,' Thomas replied. 'Only about fifty per cent of them are useless. And what you find is that there's a kind of natural law in operation. A natural cycle. Every twelve hours it's musical chairs again and someone better comes along and sorts things out. The hospital is like one of those clocks with rain and sunshine figures. One lot are useless, but on the other hand, the other half are just *amazing*. Look how brilliant Gillian was!'

Gillian was the clever cardiologist who had diagnosed Baby Brown's unusual heart condition. Thomas had spent half an hour talking to her about the case.

'And you're sure she knows which baby is the one with the duct? Because that nurse didn't seem to know anything.'

235

'Sweetheart, of course I'm sure! How many newborns with premature closures of the *ductus arteriosus* do you think we've got in this hospital? And how many girlfriends with babies in the SCBU do you think *I've* got?'

'Well, why didn't the nurse know about his heart?'

'It's not her job to know about his heart. Not in any detail, anyway. It's her job to check that it's still beating.'

'You're right,' Florence sighed. 'I was just being silly.'

'So stop being silly! You've probably earned yourself at least one unnecessary visit from Social Services at it is. I thought you'd never stop shouting if I didn't sign for that test.' Thomas paused and exhaled. When he spoke again, his voice was gentler. 'But how are you feeling, apart from the paranoid delusions and psychotic episodes, that is?' he teased.

'I'm fine. I even managed to go to the toilet.'

'*Did* you!' he said with genuine delight.

And that was the thing about Thomas. He was improbably interested in everything about her. Even when she had nothing much to say, which was most of the time. Thomas: five hundred and ninety-two words on Tchaikovsky. Florence: 'Oh right,' followed by something about wanting a wee.

'I had to ask for help getting my pyjama bottoms back on, though,' she added.

'Well, you old sexpot!'

But the merriment soon faded from his face and Florence wondered what was wrong. Had he discovered from her file what she had done all those months ago, the first time she was in hospital? Was he jealous because the baby wasn't his? Or preoccupied because it *was*? Did he know something she didn't?

'Christ!' Thomas said, as though he could read her thoughts.

In fact, he was thinking of recent events and especially his conversation with Helen Donald.

'Why does everyone think that everything is about *me*? It's not about me. It's like when I read in *Our Times* that the WI is "a highly personal technology". My "attempt to return to the womb after a series of early life traumas". "The birth of his younger sister and the sight of his mother breastfeeding no doubt exacerbated his separation anxiety as a toddler." Apparently I'm a misogynist – witness the fact that I've been married twice and now have three lovely daughters. Well, doesn't *that* all make a terrific amount of sense?'

Thomas distorted his face so that it looked pleasantly crazed. Florence laughed. But again Thomas's good humour faded quickly.

'I didn't like her,' Florence said, referring again to Helen.

'Well, I don't much like her either. I could have saved a baby – till she put the spoke in.'

'How'd you mean?'

'There's been a bit of a disaster with a WI baby. Brain bleed and then people start wondering, was it the WI?'

'Could it have been?'

'*No!*' Thomas replied furiously, as though she was his enemy now too. 'Of course, *anything's* possible.' He paused to think of some way of explaining it. 'Look, we've tried to avoid brain injury by not removing any babies from the WI till they're at least thirty-two weeks. The germinal matrix – an immature network of blood vessels in the baby's brain – has disappeared by then. Haemorrhage is uncommon after this point, but it's not impossible. And Simon Long haemorrhaged. But his lungs are excellent. If someone drove him home and they had a car accident, you couldn't blame that on the incubator, could you? The Wet Incubator doesn't inoculate against all future harm. It's not a fucking *mascot*. Anyway, it's not just her,

237

alas. Goldman's been giving these ethics classes to the nurses and then telling me they're upset. "So what?" I said to him. "The nurses are always upset about something. Maybe you should stop giving them ethics classes and they'd have less to worry about." He thinks I'm an incorrigible maverick. Well, I suppose I am. But what are we going to do? Abandon the trial because little Helen Donald is still weeping into her cornflakes?'

'I feel nervous thinking that she's there, looking after my baby, when I'm not.'

'Don't be silly. She's an excellent *nurse*, all right, just rather less excellent as a human being. Highly conscientious. Always double-checking her double-checking. A little *too* conscientious, if anything. And just because *I'm* at the end of my stethoscope with her, doesn't mean that *you* have to be.'

'She told me I couldn't look at the other babies.'

'Well, she was right. It's the protocol. And she's probably feeling a bit extra protective of the babies at the moment, because of Simon Long. Which means she'll be protective of *your* baby too.'

But Florence didn't much like the sound of that either.

Twenty-nine

Realizing the foolishness of her error Florence Brown returned as quickly as she could – in a manner of speaking – to the neonatal unit. There were new limits to her physical powers which still had to be learned. It was as though she had entered old age abruptly and the number of simple tasks she could not now accomplish without incurring considerable physical pain was astonishing. Indeed, previously she had hardly been aware of them *as* individual tasks – lifting the polystyrene cup, taking the sip. The movement from sitting position to standing seemed to involve several particularly onerous manoeuvres. Curiously, however, as she regained her breath and studied the noticeboard in her new room, she realized this powerlessness did not frustrate her. On the contrary, she felt acceptance wash over her almost like a physical sensation. Pinned to the board were more pictures of Baby Brown left by Robert. His cheeks appeared scalded, his misery complete. She would not protest any longer. She would allow it all to be done to her now. Her state of mind had fitted itself to the state of her body. Her request for the DNA test was the last of the fighting talk.

There was no one available to take her downstairs in a wheelchair and Florence could barely walk, let alone hold open the many sets of heavy double doors en route to the SCBU. So it was a matter of waiting till someone else wanted to go through them and then dodging at her snail's pace into the gap. There were lots of people in the hospital corridors and she remembered how once she had been in that world where you could laugh and chat and even drink coffee quite casually. There was an in/out register to be signed before she even left the ward. There was the inevitably long wait by the stable door entrance to the unit. But there was also a moment of triumph when she spotted someone's staff swipe card left lying on a radiator grille, and decided without much hesitation – perhaps she was not quite *all* passive acceptance now – to pocket it in her dressing gown for future use.

'Hello there,' a doctor said.

'Yes?' she replied guiltily.

'You're Florence Brown, right?'

'Yes.'

'I'm giving a presentation on your baby's case tomorrow morning and I was wondering if you could help me out. There's a rumour going around the hospital that you drank a lot of chamomile tea during the pregnancy. Is that true?'

The world's newest expert on factors of causation in foetal ductal constriction simply nodded. She walked the short distance to the sinks and set about the many washings of her hands. At last she was in the Hot Room. And here her fears were more than realized. The baby was gone.

In the bay where Baby Brown should have been, there wasn't even an incubator. And there were no staff in the room either. Why hadn't the doctor told her? As though she had known it all along, Florence Brown found she had explanations for everything: they had taken the incubator away for reasons of hygiene as well as tact. They thought it would be less distressing for her to see the empty bay first, and understand its meaning before they told her the truth. The staff were absent because they were busy preparing the body, or phoning her room with an urgent message for her to come down to the SCBU. Except she was already here. She caught a glimpse of another baby, in the first bay, who wore an oxygen mask. Several washing machine waste pipes appeared to be emerging from his abdomen. She looked away. This time she would not even attempt to find her son in the other bays: a mix-up, whether accidental or malicious, was not what had happened here. If only it were that. A kidnap. A mistake. But it was neither.

A few moments later, a nurse she did not know – Sheryl – put her head around the door. So now they would tell her. It was his heart. And they must have decided that the news would be better not coming from Helen Donald.

'Baby Brown's mum, right?'

Florence could only nod. Why was the woman so happy?

'He's in here,' she said.

Florence followed sickly. So they had laid him out already. Just as she'd thought. She imagined the wake as she was taken into a long narrow room behind the Hot Room.

'We've just transferred him from Intensive Care,' Sheryl explained. 'He only needs High Dependency now.'

He was alive! Better than ever, in fact. Florence made it onto a stool beside his incubator. The nurse donned a new plastic apron and gloves. Opening the cupboard below the incubator – 'Sorry,' she said, squeezing past Florence – she took out a Tupperware bowl with a Post-it note and another identical one containing cotton wool balls. Florence watched passively as these items were placed on top of the incubator, along with a paper bag, like an aeroplane sick bag, with a 'No Smoking' sign and a pattern of green clouds. Then the nurse filled the first bowl with water from the sink and opened the bag, which crackled with the promise of sweets or pastries. Finally she slid her hands into opposite portal doors at the lower end of the incubator.

The process of removing the tarry, seaweed-green poo from the baby's bottom was protracted and painstaking and enough to restore the new mother's calm. Many cotton wool balls were delicately dabbed in the water, then onto his skin, then moved fastidiously into the bag, as though the nurse were gently removing grime to reveal the oil painting underneath. And as though this process, and the materials used, would themselves be a matter of historical record and archival interest.

So this was changing a nappy. Florence almost expected to be offered the paper bag that had been filled so labour-intensively. It was, instead, sealed and dropped into a yellow steel bin. Then Sheryl disposed of the apron and washed her hands before putting on a new one.

Next Florence watched as donor breast milk – she was not yet lactating herself – descended the green gavage tube through the baby's nostril. This magnolia milk would – eventually, hopefully – enter his stomach. He was too weak to suck yet. Cloudy Sellotape stuck the tube to his cheek, and he reached up for it. The nurse prevented him.

'You want to try?' she asked, offering to let Florence hold the syringe.

'I don't know. I mean, I don't even know how . . .'

'It's easy,' Sheryl encouraged. 'And I wouldn't let you if it wasn't perfectly safe.'

Florence pondered it. The baby lay supine. She could see how hard his chest was working. His breath came in rapid pants, like a dog's, like one press-up after another, so that he was continually in a state of inflation or deflation. A human whoopee cushion. His whole body, in fact, seemed given over to the task of breathing. He still looked like a stranger, and not even like the photograph of the night before, but she felt pity for the little thing. There was a white plastic clip with tiny serrated teeth around his dying umbilical cord. His eyes were navy. Taking the syringe into her hands and carefully maintaining its vertical position, Florence tried to think of the least invasive way she might establish contact with him.

'Don't hold it too high,' Sheryl advised.

Without a plunger, the milk descended the syringe by simple gravity. A millimetre at a time. Five minutes later, as Florence's arm began to ache, she saw the point of the nurse's advice and propped the elbow on her other hand. She pondered the problem of touching Baby Brown. Earlier he had disliked it. She knew that babies had a grasping reflex – place anything in their palm and they would grab onto it. Holding hands was the universal language of trust.

Ten minutes later, as the nurse aspirated Baby Brown's stomach to check whether the milk had reached the right place (it had), Florence slid her thumb, which was bigger than all of his fingers put together, under his hand. At the same time she placed her index finger in his palm. And that was how they held hands for the first time.

Soon after she got back to her room a midwife brought in a small trolley tower. The woman looked up in some surprise at the top of the door, where Florence had got Robert to put her discarded hospital gown in an attempt to reduce light coming in at night. Florence thought she was in for another ticking off. Thankfully the woman said nothing. On the top shelf of the tower there was a cement-coloured object of industrial solidity that Florence could not place. On the bottom shelf there was a large lunchbox tub with a broken-hinged lid in cobalt blue. Also a saucer with a paper napkin and what looked like several strong mints. In the tub floated various plastic items including a small funnel. This was, it transpired, a breast pump system. It encouraged lactation so that she would be ready when the baby was.

'Always return the setting to zero. You don't want to wrench your nipple off.'

Quite.

Florence soon discovered that it was difficult to entrust her nipple to a machine. Any part of the unprotected breast would, she thought, be un-ideal, but the nipple particularly so. The nipple was like all extremities: sensitive, wary, no fool in short. It was true that there were penis pumps. But the desire for a larger penis was a special category of human endeavour.

'If you just remove the funnel for a moment,' the midwife said, grasping the end of Florence's left teat and pinching hard.

'Ow,' Florence said lamely.

'Sorry. I'm just trying to get things going. I thought that might . . .'

What? Kick-start milk production with the element of surprise? Now Florence's nipple felt pinched as well as useless.

'I wouldn't let her overdo that,' said George, who was getting very bored indeed by the second afternoon. Florence sat with her back to him, supported by Lydia, who was helping her use the breast pump. Robert was still working to finish the house and his visits were therefore much shorter than theirs.

'Whatever do you mean?' Lydia asked. '"Overdo"?'

'When Father would milk the cows, sometimes if he milked them too much, they got frisky.'

'*You*,' Lydia said firmly, 'be quiet.'

'I suppose,' he mused thoughtfully, 'they must do a pot of tea somewhere round here.'

Florence's stepfather had retired the previous year – from laying carpets and drinking tea – and it was firmly entrenched in his mind that the object of any activity, any visit, was the crowning cup of tea.

'I suppose I could ask . . .'

'Don't you go bothering any of the midwives,' Lydia warned. 'They've got better things to do. If you *have* to have a cup of tea—'

'A pot. *Has* to be a pot. And four lumps of sugar.'

'*I'm* not going to get it. If you have to have tea – in the desired receptacle,' Lydia mocked, 'with the requisite dose . . .'

'Is there any more yet?' Florence asked rather desperately, wishing they would both shut up. Lydia looked down and seemed to calculate for a moment. Even George was silent now.

Then Lydia said, 'No.'

'What – none *at all*?'

'None at all.'

'How can there be none at all?'

George sighed. Hadn't he told them not to go overdoing it? And where was his cup of tea?

'Listen to me,' Lydia said, leaning further forward and kissing Florence's cheek. 'It *will* come. Promise!' Lydia added cutely. 'Lots will come. Lots and lots! It just takes a bit of time, that's all. Go out to the lift—'

'I'm not doing *this* in the *lift*!'

'Not you, dear. Take the lift down to Level 2 I think it is, and follow the signs for the Legionnaires tea room.'

George stood slowly and set off, as though much against his will.

'What the hell is *that*?!' he asked as the hospital gown fluttered from the top of the doorway onto his head.

'Just leave it,' Lydia said grimly.

'Is this why you didn't breastfeed *me*?' Florence asked.

'No. It wasn't advised back then. But your milk will come very soon.'

However, when Florence's milk still did not come, she was referred to the hospital breastfeeding counsellor. To begin with, Florence thought that the woman was making incredibly long speeches. Then she realized that the woman had bad breath, so no matter how briefly she spoke – in fact, her conversational style was rather abbreviated – you were always dying for her to finish sooner. And like many people with bad breath, the breastfeeding counsellor was perfectly aware of her condition and therefore leaned closely towards her listeners, trying to discern whether, after swilling the double strength all-day fireguard mint mouthwash for the full ten minutes, things were getting any better.

'Can be difficult,' the breastfeeding counsellor said. 'Doing it for a machine . . . not the same.'

Florence had the impression that they were really talking about vibrators. Certainly the old breast pump huffed and puffed like an emphysemic trying to have sex. And that was off-putting.

'Photo of baby?' the woman asked.

Florence nodded to indicate that she had one in her possession.

'Try looking,' the woman suggested. 'May help milk come.'

'Drip!' Robert said joyfully, four hours later.

He was lying sideways on the bed, making a triangle of his left arm. Behind him the mobile table was laden with packets of juice and tissues. It was too painful for Florence to bend over and look into the Sterifeed bottle herself. It was also disheartening: more than once she had seen the bottle steam up slightly and misinterpreted the condensation for milk. So now Robert was announcing each drip on arrival.

'Drip, drip!' he said encouragingly, then, excitedly, 'Okay, this is more like a pour.'

'A pour?' she said, thrilled.

'It's a pour, honey. Oh, it's a pour all right!'

'It was more of a flood, actually,' Florence began to say to whoever would listen.

The triumphant new parents went straight down to the SCBU.

Thirty

Surely everyone in the hospital could see that Florence Brown now held in her hand a bottle that was almost a whole quarter full of yolk-coloured milk. Her joy, however, was diluted: as usual she was apprehensive that something might have gone wrong with the baby since her last visit to the unit. Robert put his arm around her and she leant into his body as she walked. Lydia offered to carry the bottle. Instead of pressing the buzzer to the unit, Florence checked left, then right, then left again and drew the stolen staff swipe card discreetly from her dressing-gown pocket. Satisfyingly, the stable door clicked open instantly. At the sinks on side B – where Baby Brown had been transferred – she was impatient to be done with all the pharisaical rituals of hand-washing and antiseptic-rubbing. She and Robert grinned wearily at each other.

'How bad are yours?' she asked, indicating her hands.

'Oh, not as bad as yours,' he replied as he pressed the door button.

Robert gestured for Lydia to go first, but Lydia gestured for Florence to go first, and before the situation turned into the deadlock of a mini-roundabout, with everyone too polite to move and an ensuing collision, the new mother walked through. As a result she was the first to see it. Baby Brown's bay looked quite different. *Was* something wrong, then? Why had nobody told her? Glancing down the room she saw Helen holding a syringe with no stopper aloft another of the tiny

248

patients. A thin tentacle of green wire spiralled downward. She must be feeding him. The nurse looked transfixed by her own thoughts and did not seem to notice their entrance. There was definitely something unnerving about that woman. Whenever you talked to her, she seemed to be thinking of something else. What went on in her head?

Florence swallowed and stepped up to the incubator. The baby! He was bathed in a strangely beautiful blue light, as though the atmosphere was different in there, and yet the lid had actually been removed from the incubator. Most disturbingly, he had been blindfolded. Not his heart, then, not this time. It took her a moment to realize that he was under a phototherapy machine now.

'A touch of jaundice,' Helen remarked mildly from the other side of the room. 'I'll be there in a minute.'

Florence peered at the underside of the phototherapy machine. A ceiling of disco lights. The squares of yellow and green were dazzling. With the blindfold on, the baby looked like the world's tiniest first class flyer. On his way to life or maybe death. No sooner at Arrivals than he was back at Departures. Florence watched as he put up his impossibly small red hand, blindly feeling for the white blindfold that was evidently protecting his eyes. His movements were all slow-motion, as though he were underwater, still moving against the maternal tide. She remembered how she had once seen a three-day-old elephant in Sri Lanka, sweetly unable to move his own trunk yet, an encumbrance which dangled and trailed in front of him. The blindfold encircled her baby's head like a soldier's bandage. The material bore a silver and green sticker, on which the words 'natural biliband PREM' – *natural!* – were surmounted by the outline of an improbable duck. His hand persisted.

'I think he's trying to take the blindfold off,' she said, worried about his eyes, to Helen.

'Don't worry, I'll put it back on when I come over,' the nurse replied.

Soon the corner of an eyelid appeared. Slowly the eye itself opened and blinked. Florence was captivated and moved. He frowned uncertainly. He repeated the blinking as though he was trying to commit the action to memory. The expression was half-cross, half-shy. With the blindfold skew-whiff, the appearance of the tiny exasperated human was comical. Florence began to relax.

When the portal doors were opened Baby Brown became aware of their presence and perked up rather as though he had been expecting her.

'It's like a baby from outer space,' Lydia said, admiring the machinery as much as anything, and taking out her video camera.

The entry of their adult hands in the portal doors gave the incubator a new octopus-like appearance. With great animation the baby began to chatter in a language all of his own and to point to his impediments and tug on them: the nasal tube was gone, but the wrist cannula, the plastic anklets, the heart monitor, the blindfold, and the Sellotape remained. It was like watching a foreigner earnestly asking the way, pointing to his map, frowning intently, politely hopeful. He seemed to realize that Florence was not one of the pokers or the prickers or the stuffers or the wipers. Not one of the forcers. She was one of the talkers and the strokers. And what he was asking needed no translation: *Hey, guys, can you do anything about ditching these wires, please?*

'Little man,' Lydia promised the tiny incarcerated human, 'you will get out of here.'

'Tomorrow, I should think,' Sheryl said behind them. Florence turned to smile at the nurse, hoping that they could deal with her instead of Helen. She stepped forward to readjust the baby's blindfold.

'So soon?' Florence was surprised.

'He'll have been able to feed on formula mix for forty-eight hours by then. I'm afraid we can't keep them any longer than that. His jaundice isn't anything serious – just stick him in the sunshine whenever you can. And you can always try the transition to the breast once you're home.'

'Or "Niagara" as some of us call it,' Robert whispered fondly into Florence's ear.

'That's wonderful,' Lydia said. 'You are doing so, *so* well,' she continued very softly. 'Everyone is *so* pleased with you. And you're so beautiful!'

It was true: amid the crisis, Florence simply hadn't noticed before. The baby was covered with a soft dark pelt of ravishing beauty. As his body retracted into itself, she could see how he must have been positioned inside her these last few weeks. Every square centimetre maximized: one thumb tucked into an eyelid recess, the other hand clamped monkey-ishly around his head. Yes, there was no question now: this was her son.

Eventually Helen approached them as well. Again the blindfold needed readjusting. He was, she confirmed, in very good shape. An ultrasound had shown that his heart had mended itself. No long-term *sequelae* were anticipated. There would be one or two routine follow-up appointments for his newborn jaundice and to monitor the left bicupsid valve, but that was all.

'The doctor will write everything down on his discharge sheet and explain it to you tomorrow, okay?'

'Okay,' Florence agreed.

Everyone watched as Helen set about 'bathing' the baby with a few drops of sterile water from a glass bottle. Then Florence remembered the milk bottle she had brought. Placing it on top of the incubator,

Florence Brown waited for the neonatal unit to sit up and take notice. It stood there for several minutes.

Nothing seemed to be happening.

'I've brought some milk,' Florence said.

'Yes,' Helen replied distractedly, as she finished her task.

But still nothing was done with the bottle. A few minutes later Helen left the room, then came back soon afterwards and conferred with Sheryl. Finally she said in an odd voice that she was 'very sorry' but visitors would have to leave the unit. A new admission was expected in the Hot Room and the doctors preferred to work without extras around.

'All the babies need to die right away.'

'*What?*' Florence said.

'All the parents need to leave right away, please,' Helen repeated.

There were no other parents, in fact. Sometimes Florence saw the Longs. Jacqueline Hart, the mother of the dead twin babies mentioned by Thomas, had not, of course, appeared.

'But Sheryl is going to take you for your Health & Safety With Baby training session now,' Helen added, addressing Florence and Robert.

'It's one of the perks of having a baby in the SCBU,' Sheryl explained. 'And I can show you the suite you'll be using tonight before we discharge him tomorrow. Shouldn't take me any more than half an hour,' she said, turning back to Helen.

Half an hour: it would take much less than that to euthanize Baby Long. Helen's hands shook involuntarily as she put on the first plastic glove – then pulled it off. She didn't need it.

Thirty-one

A few minutes later Florence and Robert found themselves standing inside an apartment that looked as if it belonged in a run-down hotel. It was a hospital flat used by parents of premature babies for a night or two before they took their children home for real. Baby Brown would be joining them later. In the meantime Sheryl had brought two baby dolls as props for the training session. A girl and a boy, one white and one black, both of them monsters at least twice the size of Florence's baby.

'This is Annie.' Sheryl indicated the girl doll, who looked as though she'd had a tracheotomy (or perhaps broken her neck) as well as two long surgical incisions, either side of her mouth, for a double cleft palate.

'Bit of a minger, isn't she?' Robert said.

Sheryl frowned disapprovingly while Florence endeavoured to stifle a giggle.

'She's going to choke on her lunch,' Sheryl added, as she forced a marble into the doll's windpipe with an industrial index finger and grinned.

'Crikey,' Robert said. 'Dead ugly *and* dead unlucky.'

'But we're going to save her.' Sheryl had pioneered this Health & Safety tutorial. 'And this is George. We'll find out what happens to him a little bit later, okay?' She spoke as though she were presenting television.

Robert winked at Florence, trying to make her laugh. Her eyes pleaded for mercy. Now that Baby Brown was going home, now that everything was going to be all right, it felt legitimate to have a sense of humour again.

'Now,' Sheryl said, a quarter of an hour later, after the marble had shot satisfyingly out of Annie's mouth but Florence had very nearly killed her, anyway, by puncturing straight through the ribs and squashing her heart.

'Now if you were to see your own baby – or let's say George, it's George we've got here – George lying on the floor looking as though he's unconscious and can't breathe, what do you think's the first thing you should do?'

'Try to resuscitate him?' Robert suggested.

Sheryl smiled sympathetically. 'But the *very* first thing – what would that be? What would come even before a resuscitation attempt? Florence?'

Florence reflected seriously on the question before she answered. 'Fear? Panic?'

Sheryl continued to smile patiently. 'All right, I'm going to tell you this one, okay? The very first thing you must do if you see a child lying unconscious on the floor is: *check the floor for obstacles*. Now why do you think that is?'

Five minutes later, as George lay inert on the floor, Sheryl talked to the new parents about how to attract attention in an emergency situation.

'Even a small child, if you have another child, may be able to help you.'

'We don't,' Robert pointed out.

'But if you did.'

And with that the nurse turned to the other doll.

'Annie!' she urged. 'Annie! Can you do something very, *VERY* important for Mummy, please?' Sheryl paused. 'Make sure,' she explained, 'that you really do have the child's attention. Then tell Annie that you want her to go to the window and shout "HELP!" as loudly as possible. Go on – tell her, Florence.'

'Annie, I would like you to go to the window and shout for help as loudly as possible.'

'And shout *HELP!*' Sheryl shrieked, 'as loudly as possible. Try again.'

'Me?' Florence asked.

Sheryl nodded.

'Annie, I would like you to go to the window and shout *HELP HELP HELP!*' – Robert snorted as Florence gave it some welly this time – 'as loudly as possible.'

'All right, not *that* loudly!' Sheryl giggled. 'You'll have half of A&E in here. Annie can also bang on the window.'

'Some talents, then,' Robert said.

'So,' Sheryl continued, ignoring him. 'To recap. The first thing you must do if you see George lying on the floor and think he isn't breathing *is . . . ?*'

'Check the floor for obstacles so I don't stumble walking across to him,' Florence replied, suddenly recognizing what this was: an examination, a memory test that bore no resemblance to real life.

'And then?'

'Walk quickly towards him, but not so quickly I'm likely to stumble anyway and um . . .'

'And crush him with the weight of your falling body,' Sheryl reminded her quickly. 'And what else do you do at the same time as that?' She turned fiercely to Robert for an answer.

'Call for help. Even if we're alone – I mean, even if I'm alone. Or

255

even if there is only a small child, if we ever have a small child, in the house. Someone in the street may hear us and get help.'

'Good. And don't forget to call out to George as well. *George! GEORGE!*' Sheryl remonstrated, as though he wasn't coming for his dinner or was at it again – foraging up his nose with a finger. 'You call out to George because it may be that he's just fallen asleep. Or, even if he has fallen unconscious, shouting may be enough to rouse him. But we're assuming that George doesn't respond to our shouting and doesn't wake up. So let's move on to the next part of the process: making the emergency telephone call. And then once we've practised everything, we'll take it again from the top, all right? So you'll know what to do if it ever happens to you. Now. If we—'

There was a high-pitched electronic noise. 'My bleeper,' Sheryl said, looking at it. 'Damn. I'll have to go back down. But I think you've got the essentials – and I'll give you a full set of instructions before you leave tomorrow.' She smiled.

She was barely out of the room before Florence and Robert exploded with laughter.

Thirty-two

Yes, it was finally true, Florence thought after Sheryl left and they settled down to nap in the double bed. Florence Brown, curator of the Dillyford villages museum, had a baby of her own now. There was no stopping her happiness, in fact.

A day later she was standing with Thomas in her new kitchen.

'There's only a *single* join and it's invisible!' she said, indicating the ice-white stone worktop. 'You can't see it, can you?'

Thomas shook his head in agreement.

'And how is Robert?' he asked politely.

'Very happy. Very tired.'

Baby Brown snuffled wetly in her nape while she took out tea cups.

'An ability to do things one-handedly seems to be *the main* parenting skill,' she said, laughing confidently and kissing the baby's head. 'And look how the drainage grooves are cut into the stone.' She ran her finger pleasurably along a smooth incline towards the sink.

'Yes: remarkable,' Thomas replied shortly.

There was clearly something wrong but she was doing her best to be bright.

'Look, I've got something to tell you,' he said.

'Oh?' She felt her heart falter.

'He's dead,' Thomas said solemnly. 'Simon Long. He's dead.'

It was almost a relief. Before she could reply, however, the doorbell rang. It was the scaffolder for the loft conversion.

'Can I just nip to the loo?' he asked.

'Of course,' Florence replied. 'But would you mind taking off your shoes?'

He seemed to resent the idea. 'You tiled that bathroom recently?' he asked as he came back down the stairs.

'Yes. Why?'

'Shouldn't have, my love, not before your loft conversion. Not with all the banging they have to do. It sends vibrations down. Those tiles'll be falling straight off the walls.'

His gruffness lent this statement authority. His head-shaking seemed a practised skill. Then he manoeuvred himself over-elaborately around their suitcases, which stood in the hallway ready for a temporary move to George and Lydia's while the loft conversion team went about their work. Despite Robert's best efforts, the house was still not really suitable for a newborn and there was a lot more messy work to come.

'You were saying . . . ?' Florence asked as she walked back into the kitchen.

'He's dead.'

'What, *already*?'

'Yes. Early this morning. Must have been before they discharged you.'

'But that's . . . that's good – right? In the circumstances?'

'It's good for *him*, and for his parents. But what I want to know is *why*.'

'I thought he was terminal.'

'Yes, yes!' Thomas replied impatiently. 'But why *now*. I need to know . . .' He started again. 'If there's something wrong with the WI, we need to fix it.'

He spoke matter-of-factly, as though the Wet Incubator were just another broken washing machine.

'I thought you said it wasn't the WI!'

'Well, that was before he died so suddenly. I want to know why he stopped breathing. I need to see his lungs. But the parents won't consent to an autopsy. What *is* all this sentimentality? He's dead now and—'

'Will you stop saying that?' Florence said, thinking of Simon Long's mother. No wonder she was always so unfriendly.

'Sorry. But the only way we're going to find out anything now is through the necropsy. Otherwise Goldman may get his way and my hands will be tied. I don't see that parents should have the right to withhold consent.'

Thomas started to pace the room and set out his arguments. Florence watched through the window as the scaffolder began attaching a long-legged, H.G. Wellsian monster around the house. Similar scaffolding belonging to another company was already in place on the house opposite. The apparatus looked so inert but might, she sometimes fancied, activate the houses' destruction – the grey metal poles suddenly revealing themselves as bloodsuckers and the screw-bolts as fully rotational missile heads.

(She had read a lot of John Wyndham as a child.)

'We have to think of these patients as rational adults,' Thomas was saying, 'and if *I'd* died, I know that I'd want to know as much about it as possible. In fact,' he said, turning around and looking into Florence's eyes, his own now sparkling with ingenuity, 'I've thought of a way.'

Florence waited.

'I'm going to get my autopsy. I *deserve* an autopsy. I will see his lungs. I'll call in the police if I have to.'

'The police?' Florence was puzzled. 'What's that got to do with it?'

'Sometimes nurses take things into their own hands.'

Florence thought of Sheryl's hands around plastic Annie's throat.

'Or,' Thomas continued, 'they help the parents. Or the parents may have acted alone, knowing that they would have the right to refuse the autopsy.'

'I think you're getting carried away.'

'I think I'm not. It looks like he just stopped breathing – but trust me, Simon Long could breathe for Britain.'

'You really think a nurse might have been involved?'

'It's entirely possible. Anyway, point is, I don't want *my* invention being blamed instead. Because that's what'll happen in the end. You just wait. Story of my life.'

PART FIVE

The Story of her Life

Thirty-three

In the small hours of Friday the fifteenth, Florence Brown was apprehended in connection with the murder of Simon Long, and the abduction and suspected intended murder of Baby Brown. The case against her was reported to be 'watertight' as well as 'compelling'. There was DNA evidence proving that she was not the mother of Baby Brown, a falsified set of medical notes, and a stolen security pass believed to have enabled the suspect to gain unauthorized access to the SCBU on the day of Simon Long's death. The papers learned that the rooms were often left unstaffed for brief periods when no visiting parents had been admitted. The fact that Florence lived in a village and even curated the local archives made the matter more shocking. It was as if she had single-handedly devastated the dream of rural England and its glorious historical past to boot.

Normally the death of a terminally ill and hospitalized infant aroused no suspicion and was not a matter for police investigation. In this case, however, after the Professor sounded the alert, the wishes of the parents were overruled and a necropsy was performed. The cause of death was discovered to be an intravenous administration of adrenalin leading to sudden heart failure. The method of death at first inclined the police to believe that medical personnel had been involved and that this was a case of mercy killing. Several prominent cases of mercy killing at the end-of-life had been reported in the papers in recent months and there was a disinclination to prosecute the medics involved. Comparisons were drawn to the Netherlands, where 'baby euthanasia' was unofficially tolerated just so long as the requirements of the Groningen protocol were met: (1) the presence of hopeless and unbearable suffering; (2) the consent of the parents to the termination of life; (3) prior medical consultation, and; (4) careful execution of the termination. This was no doubt a similar case, a rare act of human kindness, and it was 'not in the public interest' to interfere. In fact DI Weston was just about to back off and tell the Professor that nothing would be done when one of the neonatal nurses approached him in confidence.

Sheryl told Weston that she had just received a report from the hospital microbiology department, marked 'Highly Confidential', which she would be passing on to Social Services immediately. The report contained unexpected data about a patient, Baby Brown, who had been discharged soon after the time of Simon Long's death into the care of his mother Florence Brown. In fact, the report contained the results of a DNA test proving that she was *not* his mother. The matter should be kept quiet until the test could be repeated. If she was an impostor who had already abducted one baby from the unit, then it was conceivable that she had murdered another patient. Sheryl managed not to giggle once throughout this entire conversation.

When the tests indeed came back with the same negative result, and when the hospital file about the pregnancy and labour gave evidence of having been tampered with, in a suspicious if rather amateur way, the two members of the Dillyford police force brought Florence in for questioning and an identity parade. They searched her home and museum office, and stood by as Social Services took Baby Brown away, despite all the protests of Robert, who was promised a paternity test.

'And can you tell us how this came into your possession?' DI Weston asked.

He held up Florence's blue medical notes folder. Florence trembled, even though the question was easy. She felt a droplet of milk prick painfully through each nipple.

'They're my pregnancy notes,' she said. 'When you get to a certain stage of the pregnancy, I can't remember which week exactly, the midwife gives them to you and you're supposed to carry them around everywhere in case you go into labour.'

She paused to exhale, as if her lungs were putting down two especially large shopping bags. Passing on the simple information was making her feel more confident. She took a new breath.

'I haven't seen them since the birth,' she added.

'But they're not your notes, are they?'

'Of course they're my notes.'

'These are the pregnancy notes of a young woman of seventeen,' the policeman continued patiently. 'There's her date of birth – 22.03.92. You can just make it out beneath the handwritten alteration. This young woman had two surgeries – a laparoscopic examination when she was six-and-a-half weeks pregnant, and a caesarean section when she was thirty-five weeks pregnant. Then she disappears off the face of the earth and *you* turn up. When we put you in the line-up this morning, we asked three people who were present at the birth of Baby Brown if they could confirm your identity. And not *one* of them recognized you.'

'Surgeons don't remember faces,' Florence said, repeating something Thomas had once told her.

'They weren't surgeons. We asked the midwife and the nurse. Then we asked the porter.'

The policeman paused expectantly. Florence felt obliged to respond.

'I don't know what to say about that, I suppose they see a lot of people,' she offered weakly.

'Now someone has gone through the whole file of this young woman and altered all of the dates of birth by hand. I should warn you that we've already been able to cross-match samples from your handwriting with these alterations. So I'm going to ask you now: was it you who made the changes to the date of birth in the file?'

'Yes, because they kept getting it wrong. It's wrong on the system. I had to correct it by hand.'

'You admit it was you, then?'

'I admit I wrote on *my own file*.'

'You mean you stole the notes of a woman with the same surname.'

'No, I didn't.'

'And in a number of places you've added your own forename, "Florence", to the patient surname "Brown".' Weston pointed to an example on the first page. 'You agree that's your handwriting?'

Florence nodded reluctantly.

'The suspect is nodding,' he said to the recording device. 'When did you steal the notes?'

'I didn't steal them.'

'You stole the notes,' DI Weston said firmly, 'and then you stole the baby.'

'I haven't stolen anything! I don't *steal* things.'

'And I suppose you didn't steal this either?'

Now the policeman held up the authorized staff access swipe card that Florence had, indeed, stolen off a radiator grille in the SCBU a few days before.

'We found it in your handbag. We know it was how you accessed the unit.'

'All right, I borrowed that. They don't have a receptionist in the unit and it was taking ages to get in every time, so . . .'

'So you helped yourself. Just like you helped yourself to someone else's baby.'

The policeman spoke disgustedly, as though Florence was a glutton, on to the fourth slice of cheesecake, rather than a suspected kidnapper with a mania for infanticide.

'We want you to tell us what happened to the real mother,' he said.

'I am the real mother!'

'The real mother,' PC Patricia Jennings intervened gently, 'is young. Very young. And she was probably very frightened by all the responsibility facing her. And you thought you were helping her, didn't you? Has she seen a doctor since she left the hospital?'

'This is all . . .'

'All a lot to talk about at once,' she said sympathetically. 'I know it is. And we understand that you are a victim too.'

This was more like it.

'You were pregnant once, weren't you?' the policewoman asked softly. 'Maybe more than once?'

'No, just once.'

'But then you lost the baby.'

'Nearly. But he survived. He was in the SCBU for about a week and then I took him home.'

'It must be very painful, losing a baby.'

'Yes but—'

'But he didn't survive, did he, your baby? And he was taken away from you, wasn't he? Almost immediately, I'd guess?' she asked kindly.

267

'Yes but not—'

'And when that happens, then sometimes, even years afterwards, it can affect a woman very deeply. It's completely natural that you should want to hold a baby,' PC Jennings continued.

At this empathetic mention of a baby, Florence began to feel tearful. She sensed the end of her nose going red, and struggled not to cry.

'*Completely* natural,' PC Jennings said encouragingly. 'Anyone can understand that. So you started to go to places where you knew you would find babies. Very small babies. Just like yours was.'

'That's not . . .' Florence said desperately.

'Not quite how it was? Because you felt angry too, understandably angry . . .'

'*No!*' Florence shouted.

The policeman and woman were both momentarily silent, to give Florence the impression that she had somehow overstepped the bounds and disgraced herself.

'One baby has been abducted from the unit where you are known to have spent at least a week,' DI Weston said gravely. 'And another baby is dead who should not be dead. Why would someone do a thing like that?'

Florence could not speak. Instead she stood up and wretchedly exposed the evidence of her pregnancy.

'The suspect is standing and lowering the top of her jeans,' DI Weston said respectfully to the recording device.

Below the wide navy band at the top of Florence's Mothercare jeans, stretch marks the colour of henna flamed angrily across her belly. She lowered the jeans a little further.

'The suspect is showing us what looks like . . .'

'A very recent caesarean scar,' PC Jennings confirmed, in a tone that was almost apologetic.

Florence sat down.

'So you lost the baby quite recently,' DI Weston said. 'Now can you tell us where the surgery—?'

Florence cut across him with the most useful thing she could remember. 'I asked the hospital for a DNA test. I didn't get any result back, but if *you* ask them . . .'

'We know about the DNA test,' DI Weston replied. 'You're saying that *you* requested it?'

'Yes, and why on earth would I have done that if I really was an impostor?'

'You tell me. Why did you ask for one?'

'Because I'd been up all night! I was confused. My baby had been taken to the SCBU as soon as he was born, I was separated from him for the first time ever, and I felt I only had their word for it that he was the right baby. And then I thought, *of course* it's the right baby. Because each of the babies in there has a very specific set of medical problems, there's no chance of mistaking one baby for another, it's not like an ordinary maternity ward. But when I started to ask the nurse about his problems . . .'

'Who was this nurse?'

'Her name's Helen Donald. And she didn't seem to know anything about the heart problem he'd been born with.'

'Which was?'

'A premature closure of the *ductus arteriosus*. So I felt worried and wanted to check they hadn't made a mistake or something. I haven't done anything wrong, okay! Just think about it for three seconds, will you.'

There was a pause. DI Weston looked at PC Jennings. Jennings nodded slightly and soon afterward Florence was escorted from the room.

Florence was taken to Dillyford's only holding cell. It was already occupied by a middle-aged woman who had been charged, the day before, with multiple burglaries and GBH, and wanted to know what Florence had done. Florence watched miserably through the barred window as two finches sitting on a fence flew off abruptly in separate directions, then looped round and rejoined neatly on a chimney stack. She turned back into the room. How was she going to express her milk in here? There was a dark grey blanket on each of the low bunks. She sat down and rested her palm against the cloth, which reminded her of Thomas's most handsome coat. She tried not to look in the direction of the other woman, who repeated her question.

'I haven't done anything wrong!' Florence replied angrily, after a pause.

'Save it for the jury,' the woman replied in a friendly way. 'Oh come on, don't be such a bore! What did you do?'

'I didn't do anything. Unless,' Florence said sardonically, 'you're counting my adultery.'

'*Adultery?*' To Florence's surprise, the woman sounded genuinely shocked. 'You mean you're *a cheater*?'

'I wouldn't put it like that.'

'They never do,' the woman replied grimly. 'Adultery!' she repeated.

Florence regretted having said anything now. 'And what about you?'

'*Me?* Look, I might smash someone's face in, from time to time, and nick a few things they don't need anyway, but I'd never rip the living heart out of a man like that. That's just plain *wrong*.'

'Hear, hear!' said the cleaner who was mopping the corridor.

'My crimes are external,' said the woman, who seemed unusually philosophical for a burglar. 'Professional, impersonal. There's a code of behaviour and I'm consistent. But this kind of internal, personal, *private* betrayal that you're talking about – this kind of *et tu, Brute?* situation – that's just *heinous*. That's what severs the bonds of human society. That's what cuts at the very fabric of what we are. Jesus was right. *Stone her.*'

Thankfully, Florence did not have to stay in the cell for very long. There was a scraping of padlocks and the door opened. PC Jennings walked Florence down the corridor, not in the direction of the interview room this time but some kind of small lounge with two sofas facing each other. The policewoman gestured – 'please' – and Florence sat. Her breasts now felt like swimming bands, and she wondered whether they would allow her to express the milk somewhere tranquil and private like this.

'Florence,' the policewoman said gently, 'I believe everything you told us earlier. But I'm afraid that means we have some rather bad news for you.'

She paused, just long enough for Florence to wonder why people always thought bad news was best delivered in slow motion.

'Not – my baby?'

PC Jennings smiled, kindly but sadly. 'He's fine, absolutely fine, please be assured about that. The bad news is the . . . well, the result of the test. It's been done three times now and what it proves, I'm afraid . . .' Another pause. Then PC Jennings said it all at once. 'The test proves that you can't be the mother. Not of this baby.'

'I thought you said you believed me!'

'I do believe you, Florence. And I also believe there has been a hospital error. Somehow your baby has been mixed up with someone else's baby, and you've been looking after each other's babies. I realize –'

PC Jennings had recently read a case of two women with the same surname who attended the same American fertility clinic and were mistakenly impregnated with each other's embryos. Florence began to cry and this time she could not stop.

' – I realize this must be enormously distressing for you. And we'll be doing everything we can to help find your baby. But before we release you, would you mind telling us if you found the neonatal unit in any way unprofessional? It may be that you will need to bring charges against the hospital and anything you can remember . . .'

Florence thought of Thomas and loyally shook her head.

Thirty-four

The tabloids went into overdrive. Or underdrive. Facts which had taken no more than half an hour to establish in conversation at the Dillyford police station, took several days to emerge in print. Headlines advanced gleefully from 'Wet Incubator Baby Dies' to 'Wet Incubator Baby Terminated' and from 'Baby Kidnapped on Marvelle's Watch' to 'Hospital Babies Switched and Murdered'. According to the earliest reports, a psychotic impostor, aged thirty-one, was believed to have spent nearly ten days in the British neonatal unit that housed the world's first Wet Incubator. After it was revealed that police had 'raided' Florence's desk at the museum for samples of her handwriting, visitors doubled over the whole weekend and sales of cream tea went up by more than fifteen per cent. In the lull between sittings for afternoon tea and early supper, people roamed the galleries and discerned the hand of Florence Brown in the arrangement of Iron Age pickaxes, an eighteenth-century hangman's rope and a replica of the lantern carried by Guy Fawkes. A modest Anglo-Saxon burial hoard gained a certain sinister fascination, especially by night, while the forthcoming exhibition, 'Remains of Roman Britain', was the first sell-out in the museum's entire history.

Then the conflicting information, the facts supporting Florence's innocence, began to emerge. There were a few nuts who tried to deal with this cognitive dissonance by maintaining that Florence Brown was surely guilty. Any difficulties – like exactly how an untrained person could have administered the fatal dose to Simon Long, like the fact that Florence did have a recent caesearean scar – were just explained away. Since a cannula had been left in place in Simon's hand, in order to provide pain relief, it was said to be 'only' a matter of employing a syringe. And didn't Florence Brown hold a St John's certificate in First Aid because she worked in a public building? Not to mention the fact that she had been seen, on several occasions, using a syringe on Baby Brown in conjunction with a gavage feeding tube. As for her stitches, they proved only that she'd recently undergone abdominal surgery, possibly abroad, judging by the handiwork, while the suitcases found in the hallway of her Dillyford home suggested an intention to escape the country for good. Yes, the police had had their woman and then unaccountably let her go. Since no one had ever come forward to identify herself as the 'real' mother of Baby Brown, and particularly since someone now seemed to remember a teenager in a dressing gown being bundled into the back of a van near the hospital, fears for the young woman's safety were confirmed. The real mother was missing, suspected dead, the conspiracy theorists said. 'That poor girl. And that poor bairn.' The midwife present at the birth of Baby Brown was quoted as saying that she 'always remembered her ladies' and that she had no recollection of Florence Brown. The contrary testimonials of the hospital staff who did indeed remember Florence – the cardiologist Gillian Ray, and the kindly anaesthetist in attendance at the caesarean birth – were not, at first, quoted by the papers. Then they were disregarded by those readers who were still determined to find Florence Brown guilty. And anything else that did not quite fit the picture in a logical way – like why an impostor would have agreed to, let alone *requested*, a DNA test, not to mention a loft conversion – was equally explicable. When one was dealing with a dangerous psychotic, they said, logical consistency was not to be expected. Florence Brown was a mass murderer – any fool, any drunk in a pub, could tell you that.

Public opinion turned unanimously in Florence's favour, however, after a new study revealed that one in three patients was the victim of some kind of hospital error, ninety per cent of which went unreported. How the first statistic could have been discovered, if the second was true, was never explained. But now everyone had a story – a pair of spectacles discovered inside their abdomen after surgery, an inaccurate dose of what was the wrong medication anyway, or at the very least an excessive number of bed sores – and Florence Brown was understood to be another victim of hospital error. Her baby must have been mixed up with somebody else's. Nobody believed that the gentle curator from Dillyford was guilty of kidnap, let alone murder, and what was more, they said, they never had.

'No,' George Morley said and went around shaking his head. 'No, even Florence isn't screwy enough for anything like that.'

'She isn't a bit screwy,' Lydia replied furiously. 'It's the system that's all screwed up. And it's all very well the papers changing their minds about her, but we still don't know *where* on earth her poor mite is, and as for the little fellow that we spent a week getting to know – well I feel sorry for him and his mother, whoever she is, too. The whole thing is just *awful*. *Every*one up that hospital should be sacked. Or shot. If you ask me, this is all Marvelle's fault.'

'She said he's doing more tests on her.'

'How many more *can* they do?'

'I don't know, I suppose they've got to try and match her with a lot of other babies.'

'She told me not all of the parents are allowing it.'

'Where is she, anyway?'

'Upstairs. Crying. I think she was expecting to hear something by now.' She pursued George into the kitchen. 'You know when they took her in for questioning I went to see him.'

'I know you did, my love.'

Lydia had told George about her encounter with Professor Marvelle at least seventeen times.

'And I told him that if this was all some plot of his and he'd had our little Florence spirited in there just because he was jealous and bitter after she broke it off with him all those months ago, then he could just forget about it. And you know what he tried to say?'

'And what did he try to say, my love?' George asked, as he took out a pint of milk, though he knew very well by now.

'He tried to say he had *no idea* what I was talking about! "What break-up!" he said. And then I said to him, "Don't play the innocent with me. You must be ninety if you're a day." "Fifty-four," he said. "Not a lot in it," I said. And I don't think he liked that.'

Lydia had in fact said, 'Fifty-four! You *jolly well* ought to be ashamed of yourself,' and Thomas had in fact replied, 'Listen, I'm not going to be hypocritical about this. Men have always desired younger women. And just because I'm now an old crust myself – ' he had grinned impishly – 'doesn't mean I've resigned myself to the mildewed offerings of the bingo hall.'

'He doesn't look fifty-four, I'll give him that,' George said. 'Not when you see him on the telly.'

'But that's only because he's still got all his hair and he's tall and slim and probably exercises quite a lot,' Lydia objected. 'And there's make-up.'

There was, in fact, another television interview later that day.

'Things aren't exactly going well for you, are they, Professor?'

Jeremy Paxman asked scornfully as Thomas Marvelle's face appeared on the video link.

'On the contrary, Jeremy, Wet Incubation has now saved the lives of six babies. That might not seem very many to you, but I can tell you that their parents—'

'Come on, Professor! One baby in your unit was recently killed by lethal injection and now it emerges that other babies are being mixed up at birth!' Paxman spoke with derisive incredulity. 'And is it true that one of the mothers concerned is a personal friend of yours?'

'That part is correct. But it was *not* a mix-up.'

'What do you mean, *not a mix-up*? There's DNA evidence, for goodness' sake, isn't there? You're surely not going to try to deny *that*, are you, Professor?'

'If you would just *listen*, Jeremy.'

'I'm all ears,' Paxman said and crossed his arms sceptically.

'There is a reason why the DNA tests appeared to show that Florence Brown was not the mother of her baby . . .'

Embarking on his explanation, Thomas realized it was like talking about the Wet Incubator – what had taken so long, painstakingly, to discover, could be rattled off so fast it sounded like science fiction. He carried on.

'Florence Brown is what we call a chimera. This means that she has two sets of DNA. The original tests sampled genetic material from the blood in her arms – DNA that does not correlate with Baby Brown's DNA. But we found that if you take sample material from Mrs Brown's ovaries or kidneys, for example, then her DNA corresponds to Baby Brown's DNA in exactly the way we would expect of a mother–child relationship.'

'Are you saying that DNA tests are unreliable and should be scrapped, then?' Paxman enquired.

'*No*,' Thomas replied, trying not to get impatient. 'No, I'm saying that in this specific case the initial results were misinterpreted. Understandably misinterpreted. Chimerism presents a problem in standard tests. But in the case of Robert Brown, the baby's father, a straightforward paternity test worked perfectly well. Just before we came on air, I received a telephone call from the microbiologist who has been working on the case to say that the results of both tests have now been conclusively verified. I understand that Social Services have been contacted with a view to ensuring that the baby is returned to his mother and father as soon as—'

'So mothers needn't worry that their babies are going to be mixed up at birth in your unit, just administered fatal shots of adrenalin, then!' Paxman scoffed.

He turned to his other interviewee, Rita Morgan, who perched on a uterus-shaped red-cloth sofa in her Californian home.

'Dr Rita Morgan, you were the first person to speak out publicly against the Wet Incubator. Do you feel justified now?'

'Taking credit hardly seems appropriate,' Rita replied. 'But yes.'

'And can you tell us how locals are reacting to the new centre for Wet Incubation that opened last week in Los Angeles?'

In Stipton, where George and Lydia lived, the locals were watching on the small set angled on a bracket above the bar. The landlord banged it at intervals while the wizened regulars sent sympathetic nods across the bar towards George. A great cheer had gone up at the news that Baby Brown would soon be returned to Florence. The only abstainer was one-eyed Tim, who'd always had a thing for Lydia and had been bitter ever since she said no to his caravan with the original protective plastic covering on the seats, and yes to George just because he had a bungalow and a Ford Mondeo in metallic silver.

'Drinks all round on me!' George shouted. He felt exhilarated for about the first time in a decade. 'I knew that Professor fella would sort her out. Lydia's met him actually.'

One-eyed Tim leaned proprietorially forward. '*Has* she?'

'She has, as a matter of fact. You hear that?' George said, turning to the barman. 'My stepdaughter's got *two* sets of DNA. That's why the tests kept showing she weren't the mother. But the Prof's found the right DNA somewhere else in her body. Sshhh – he's back on.'

'So you're saying that chimerism only occurs when a woman conceives twins?' Paxman asked the Professor.

'Yes,' Thomas replied. 'In this case, for instance, it would have been the *mother* of Florence Brown who conceived the twins. At a very early stage of a chimerical pregnancy, however, the twins fuse. The surviving embryo is a chimera – one person with the genetic material of two.'

'And are there many of these "chimeras", as you call them?'

This enquiry was even more withering than its predecessors, as though the Professor was a particularly unpleasant taste in Paxman's mouth. Thomas hesitated.

'You don't mean to say there's a question *you can't answer*, do you, Professor?'

'I expect the Professor—' Rita began.

'Actually,' Thomas spoke over her, '*no one* knows. The well-known fact is that many more twins are conceived than born. It's quite possible that lots of people are chimeras. Perhaps *you're* a chimera, Jeremy. But I don't think Rita is a chimera. She's more like a hydra. Or a pandemic. Now goodnight and fu-BLEEEEE! to the pair of you.'

The Professor had walked away from the camera. Paxman looked astonished and aghast. The alcoholics of Stipton cheered again.

'But Florence hasn't even got a twin!' Tim objected after the whoops died down.

'I know she hasn't got a twin. But when Lydia—'

'Lost all sense and shagged you!' someone shouted across the bar.

'Got knocked up,' George's friend said politely.

'When Lydia fell pregnant,' George continued, 'it must have been twins. Then one of the twins copped it in the very early stages and the one that survived – Florence – got some of her twin's DNA as well as her own. You heard the man: apparently it's very common.'

Tim raised a sceptical eyebrow.

'Just that most people never find out,' George continued. 'Some of them probably look a bit strange. Eyes of different colours and that. But most of them don't.'

'You hear that, Tim: *you're* definitely not a chimera, then!' the rude man shouted and half the bar sniggered.

'Has she got eyes of different colours then?' one-eyed Tim asked, determinedly ignoring them.

'No. They're both blue.'

There was an uncomfortable pause. George's friend tried to offer something encouraging. 'My uncle had a sheepdog like that. One blue, one brown. Or it might have been two green. I don't exactly remember.'

'You know what the Prof said when Lydia went to see him?'

'No?'

'"We have a saying in medicine," he says. "A diagnostic rule. *When you hear the sound of hooves, think of horses, not zebras.* But when the police took Florence in for questions and started accusing her, they were thinking of unicorns."'

'They were just thinking of unicorns,' George's companion echoed with agreeable exasperation and as though this were a commonly recognized failing of the British police force.

'And Paxman's right, you know. It's going to bugger up the whole of the legal system, pretty much, I should think, once it gets out that people can have more than one DNA. You just think of all the hundreds and millions of people who must have been cleared of crimes because they couldn't find the right DNA at the scene. When their *other* DNA might have been there the whole time! No, if they want to do it right, they'll probably have to start testing people all over their body to see if they've got the other DNA somewhere else.'

'Blimey,' someone said.

'I'm not having that,' someone else said.

George's mobile rang. It was Florence.

'Yes, love! I did.' George listened quietly for some time, then finally said, 'I know, love, it's wonderful. Why don't you come up the pub and celebrate? All right, my love. Of course you are.'

'What did she say?' George's friend asked.

George frowned. 'You know how she's always been a bit screwy, right?'

'All women are a bit screwy,' Tim said.

'Just because they won't screw *you*!' the rude man shouted.

'Oh, bugger off, will you,' George said. 'We're trying to have a sensible conversation here.' He turned back to his drinking companion. 'Well, it's a bit screwy but she said she thinks that having two sets of DNA explains everything. Not just that she's the mother. But everything about herself.'

'How does it do that, then?' George's friend enquired doubtfully.

'I don't know. It's "a poetic truth", she said. Like there's "shapes in the clouds of her life". Like "a method in the madness" of everything what's happened to her since she was a girl way back in the juniors.'

Poetry? George's friend looked blank.

George continued, 'But what's the bleedin' "poetic truth of life", I'd like to know, when it's at home?'

'What indeed?' his friend sympathized. 'Still, if Florence is a chimera, it still doesn't explain how the Long boy died, does it?'

'It's just a disgrace, going around killing babies,' the landlord observed quietly.

'Something ought to be done about it,' Tim agreed.

'Something ought to be done about *you*.'

A moment later, a buxom weather girl appeared on the set and all heads swivelled in that direction.

Thirty-five

Eyes closed and smiling to herself, Florence Brown knew what she had to do. There was practically scientific proof in its favour now. She was meant to love two men, just as she was meant to love this baby. It had all been demonstrated. As the sucking slackened, she pushed a finger gently inside the baby's mouth – just the way she had practised in the SCBU – in order to detach him from the larger of her breasts. Finished, he looked slightly stunned and gazed up wonderingly at the source of his well-being, not quite able to see her, as if she were a goddess. Now that he had put on some weight, she could see that the baby resembled Robert to an extraordinary – almost hilarious – degree, and it seemed incredible that she could ever have doubted it. It was like having a miniature Robert left on the pillow beside her. And as for Robert himself, whose natural forte was kindness, it was clear that he would make a wonderful father.

'Robert?' she called, removing the nipple shield, a tiny plastic sombrero that she dropped into a pot of Milton sterilizing fluid. 'Robert? Can I talk to you for a minute?'

'Hang on,' he said, and then, 'Hello!' in his friendliest voice as he opened the front door.

'I won't stay long,' she heard Thomas reply. *Thomas!* 'I just came to check that everything was all right.'

'Of course,' Robert said. 'Come in. They brought him back about an hour ago. Florence is, just, well, you can imagine, in a state of delirium. *Flo!*' he called up the stairs. 'You've got a visitor!'

Florence advanced slowly down towards them, the baby nestled against her in a jersey sling. Robert was right: she looked so shiny with happiness that Thomas almost forgot himself and kissed her.

'Thomas!' she said.

Both men smiled at her.

'Doesn't it all make sense?' she said, grinning confidently and looking from Robert to Thomas. 'We belong together, don't you think?'

'Of course you do!' Thomas replied, feigning to misunderstand her. 'You're a family once you've got a baby.'

'Would you like a glass of champagne?' Robert asked politely.

Thomas nodded. 'I would, actually.'

Robert went in the direction of the cellar.

'You can't do this to him, honey,' Thomas said in a low voice. 'You'll only hurt him.' He paused.

'But he'll be grateful to you now,' Florence whispered. 'Won't he?'

'No. No one is grateful to you for fucking his wife.'

Florence pondered this for a moment, and was about to object, when Thomas stopped her.

'Florence,' he said, very carefully. 'Florence: I'm going away for a bit.'

'Going away where?'

'To California.'

'But you can't go away.'

'It's all right,' he said tenderly, 'you'll be busy with the baby now. You'll see. You'll hardly have time for Robert, let alone me.'

It might have been said bitterly. In fact his eyes pleaded his love for her.

'Honestly,' he said. 'It'll be all right.'

Florence concentrated on smiling as Robert advanced into the hallway with two very tall champagne flutes and a glass of strawberry milkshake for her. 'Sorry, honey,' he commiserated.

'Thanks,' Thomas said, 'and congratulations!' He took a small appreciative sip. 'Delicious. I was just telling Florence I'm moving to California.'

'Early retirement?' Robert suggested.

'I wish. No, the new Wet Incubator Centre is rather under fire from Rita Morgan and her crew. They could do with some help.'

'God, that woman!' Robert agreed.

'She's about as stupid as you can get without actually being, you know, a hot water bottle,' Thomas said.

Sure enough, she was back on the kitchen radio within the half-hour.

'We have of course known for some days that the police were wrong to suspect Florence Brown. But were they wrong *in principle*?' Rita asked.

Then the two men Florence Brown loved most in this world moved together towards the door.

To: Thomas <thomas.marvelle@wic.california.usa.com>
From: Flo <florence.brown@gmail.com>
Subject: Re:

Hello you. I'm sorry I haven't written till now. I think you'll understand why. You know I had this idea, once, of writing you the longest love letter there had ever been. Every moment of the journey leading me to love you and then what happened after that. But I couldn't do it. I didn't want to put in all the sad bits. They tend to distort everything, don't you think? Mostly we were happy. That's what I remember. That's what I learned from you.

You remember when I wanted you to marry me? I think I'm glad you didn't. It would have broken Robert. And actually I knew, the very first time I went to your house, and saw all those books and papers and paintings, that you were never going to change your life like that for me. There had been too much of it already.

Before I met you, I had this idea of adultery as a sort of aesthetic blunder. Fat fingers and patent black high heels at the office party — something in incredibly bad taste, quite apart from the moral mistake. It had never occurred to me that people fell in love.

I think I'll always be in love with you, actually. I still dream about you. Perhaps you'll think this is sentimental but I already know that even when I'm an old lady, I'll still be dreaming about you. At the moment, to tell you the truth, there's a kind of security net for me in knowing that you are out there, somewhere in California, doing wonderful things, and it's not beyond the bounds of possibility that we might meet again. But I have a fear of the day when I'll read in the papers that you're finally gone. By the way, I wanted you to know that we called our son Thomas. Robert means it in gratitude for your help in discovering my chimerism. I mean it, of course, in gratitude for love.

Florence.

Thirty-six

The afternoon after Florence Brown had seen Thomas Marvelle for the last time, Helen Donald had been walking home. Across the road, the headlines behind the diamond panes of the newspaper stands read, 'Paxman Gets Pasting' and 'GP helps OAPs die'. The prospect of media heroism, of exoneration at last, felt remote to Helen. She had failed to confess to the mercy killing of Simon Long when she should have done, and now she was not sure what to do.

Crossing the street, she heard noises that she could not place. They were getting louder and seemed to be coming from at least two directions. Up ahead there was a crowd of people gathering at the foot of the steps of a university building where official ceremonies were performed – matriculations and degree days. Some of the crowd were chanting to the lead of a nasal loudspeaker, but she couldn't make out the words. Only the voices.

Inside Helen's head, there was a confession in endless rehearsal. *Richard Young was the doctor in charge. If you can call it charge.* Everything she said that morning about Simon's decline was met with an 'Uh-huh, uh-huh' or a thoughtful 'Ye-es' from the nervous new registrar that had not fooled her. *At one point I saw him looking something up in a textbook by the reception desk.* Everything boded well, better than the day before . . . *Then it wasn't your first attempt?* the voice asks, appalled.

She had, in fact, made several attempts. The day before the mercy killing, when Florence Brown came into the unit with a bottle of breastmilk and two other visitors, Helen had been feeding Simon for what she thought would be the last time. A good hour before the doctors were due with the new admission, she had got rid of these visiting relatives – and Sheryl, who was only too keen to do her Health & Safety tutorial – but then an auxiliary kept coming in. The next day, however, there was no one.

And then?

This is how it happened. This is where she is.

Standing by the end of Simon's cot. The blankets have not moved. He lies, as though obediently, tucked into the position another nurse gave him some hours before. Tiniest of the concentration camp victims, his left arm surmounts the bedding. So dark it appears suntanned. The cannula is in his hand – the left, she notices, as though for the first time. It's the left hand that's preferred, even for neonates, as though they might need their right for something urgent at any moment. She glances up at the glass door again. Nobody. Young is busy with a new Wet Incubation and Sheryl has gone to join him. She will ignore anyone who buzzes for entry. No one does. She readies the syringe and takes the baby's hand into her own. Finally she whispers, 'Goodnight.'

She remembers – she will always remember – how the small boy stirs when the adrenalin goes in, then lapses away again almost immediately. The monitors beep urgently and set off mild alarm bells as she replaces his weightless hand gently on the bedding. She detaches the wires and resets the machines with the push of three buttons. How easy it is! They work just the same as ever. She walks to the desk and calls Richard Young on the internal phone system.

Looking down the quietly humming room as she waits for him to pick up, she sees the ward as a funeral parlour again. When she gets through to Young she reminds him of the No Code. He sounds glad that she isn't expecting him to do anything.

'I'll be there right away,' he says confidently.

Next she reaches Simon's mother. Before she can say anything, a number of gasps on the other end of the line are followed by quiet weeping. Helen looks down the room again. Five babies left.

'Hello?' Mr Long says.

'Mr Long, Simon died just a few moments ago.'

'How was he – was he . . . ?'

'He was asleep. It was a very quiet end.'

Mr Long seems to be thinking. 'What happens now?'

'When you're ready, you can come into the unit and see him, if you wish. And then we can talk about what happens next. Burial and so on. I'll be here till eight this evening.'

'There won't be an autopsy?' Mr Long asks her later in the parents' room.

'No,' she replies. 'Not if you say you don't want one.'

'Do you think . . .' Mr Long says very carefully, 'that would be better?'

'I do think that would be better.'

'God bless you then,' he says, a look of grateful amazement transfiguring his face. 'For everything you've done.'

She takes a breath. She imagines going home later and how Joseph will be proud of her too. She tries out phrases. *I did a good thing today. A difficult thing. But the right thing. And I think that if anything* does *come to light, it's going to be okay.* She knows that medical professionals who assist in cases of euthanasia are avoiding prosecution by the police. Not only that, in the press they are being hailed as heroes. Helen

Donald, *heroine*. She intends to laugh modestly as she says the word. Joseph will like that.

For the rest of the day she is busy with bedding bales, feedings, bathings – and these encouraging thoughts. On the journey home they are, she thinks, quietly happy together. The gratitude of Simon's father is still warm inside her. Indoors she hugs Joseph with relief. It feels safe to do that now. There has been no further resumption of sexual intercourse. Joseph seems finally to have accepted the way things are. Perhaps he thinks as she does: that cessation is all for the best. Perhaps the actual experience has made him realize that she's right, that he should not expect it, that he should be grateful for what they have, which is more than many people. Whatever the reason, they can be happy again at last. While he showers she takes the photos of their baby out of the secret drawer and calmly arranges them on the bedspread. Looking at them, judging how she is reacting to the images, has become a kind of spot-check on her emotional well-being. This evening it is the final confirmation that she is on the right course at last. One day – it's not impossible – she may even be able to look at them without great pain. At least she is no longer tormenting herself with flashbacks.

'I've got something to tell you,' Joseph says, emerging in a towel and rubbing his hair hard with another.

'I've got something to tell you too,' she replies.

Then she sees his face. He looks sad, in fact, and impatient to speak.

'All right, you first then,' she agrees.

'There isn't any easy way of saying this.'

So they *are* back to sex, after all. And rather over-solemnly, if you ask her. Is that all?! If he wants sex tonight, well then perhaps they can have it.

'I'm leaving you,' he says.

'You're what?'

Now he has to be joking. But he's not joking. Her own husband is leaving her and she is listening to the prepared speech.

'There's no one else,' he says. 'It's just that I can see we're never going to have a sex life again. And I want one. Before I wake up and find I'm seventy-nine. So I'm going to be single again.'

'Surely we can – we can try again?' she pleads.

'It's not that I don't love you,' he continues, undeterred from the script by her question. 'Of course I love you. I love you very much. But the question is, do *you* love *me*?'

Now he waits angrily.

'Why would you even ask that?' she says. 'Of course I do. Love you.'

'Because I don't feel like you love me any more. I feel like you only love a baby we never had, and I can't compete with that.'

With this harsh mention of the baby, she is frozen. She can tell she's in a state of shock, not able to fully absorb what is happening. 'But you wanted the baby too,' she says from somewhere.

'Yes, and I would *still like* to have children. But you don't seem to want that any more. Don't you remember what we planned?'

She remembers.

'I don't want to live like a monk,' he's saying now. 'And I don't want to cheat on you either. If I found someone that I liked . . .'

Not – Kayleigh? she mouths. He doesn't hear. Of course Kayleigh. Joseph, Kayleigh and Jack – the ready-made family. Instant, off-the-peg fatherhood.

'. . . then I wouldn't want – it's not fair to people, Helen. I want the whole package with someone. And for that I need to be free.'

'Surely we can try again?' she repeats her first question.

'We have tried again.'

'All right,' she says ungraciously. She knows it sounds ugly, but he's hurt her badly this time. 'If that's what you want.'

'Of course it's not what I *want*! What I *want* is to have a whole life with you. But there's never going to be – with you, is there?'

She doesn't attempt to deny it.

'And I'm sorry the baby died,' he says heatedly, looking in the direction of the photos, 'I really am. But I don't understand where you've gone with this. For me it's like – it's like – all right,' he sighs, as though he is talking to himself, or deciding that it's better to confess belatedly than not at all, 'it's like a holiday we never had. We were going to have a baby, but then the holiday got cancelled, and it was a disappointment, a terrible disappointment. But I can't spend my whole life thinking about the holiday we never had.'

A cancelled *holiday*? She opens her mouth but again nothing comes out.

'I'm sorry if that sounds – if you're offended. I'm just trying to tell you honestly how it seems from my point of view. I know it's different for you. I really do. I wasn't the one who was pregnant. And I've tried to understand. But in the end . . .' He walks about and leaves his sentence trailing.

'Life goes on?' she suggests sarcastically.

'Well, yes.'

In the end, she was on her own with it. All of it. And she thought he was the only one who understood! They'd had a child, a dead child, and it ought to have bound them even more strongly than a living one could have done. But it hadn't. Later that evening he found her crying in bed. He said nothing as he held her. Even then it might have been salvaged. Enough love found, enough madness banished.

292

'I wanted to have your baby,' she said quietly.

'I wanted you to have my baby too,' he replied.

So she had not told Joseph – or Kayleigh – about Simon Long. She had not told anyone. Initially she had felt guilty when another woman was wrongly accused of the 'murder'. But since Florence Brown was, at that time, considered to be a baby kidnapper at the very least, Helen had been able to rationalize the situation to herself. However, Florence Brown was now known to be completely innocent. And now they might be coming for her.

The crowd by the university building was chanting much louder. Angry mutterings became shouts and screams of pain. She felt afraid. The sky was milk and the wind was up. People were watching the spectacle from the other side of the street. She fancied she could hear what they said. *She saved all the other babies. But not her own. Or killed all the other babies*, someone else replied. *Which comes to the same thing.* Then a new, robed graduate descended the steps rather quickly.

'Shame on you!' they cried. 'Shame on you!'

A woman graduate in high-heeled sandals with ankle straps was negotiating the steps with difficulty and there were four cries of 'Shame on you!' before she could make it to the bottom.

As Helen got closer she saw that the speakers were in fact animal rights protesters. They had arranged the march to coincide with a university graduation ceremony. One of the protesters had chained himself to the inside of a wooden cage. Another had tied himself by the wrist to the iron railings of the stone wall that encircled the building. The wall was punctuated by pillars, each surmounted by a stone head. They looked vaguely Roman but no one had ever been able to identify them. The students were being attacked, not because they had the slightest thing to do with the laboratory testing of animals themselves, but because they were now graduates of a university which did.

'Shame on you!' the cries continued.

A couple of policeman stood in complacent attendance, munching sausage rolls, on the other side of the road.

Helen walked by as quickly as she could. She longed to break into a run, but she was irrationally fearful of attracting the attention of the mob. In the other direction, a procession was surging unstoppably towards her and a tambourine was beaten relentlessly to the cry of 'Hare Krishna! Hare Krishna!'

No, a confession to the police was impossible. She realized that now. She would never be understood for who she was. She would merely become that thing in the public imagination – the killer of Simon Long. A chillier replacement of Florence Brown. She saw how it would go. Soon every recent death in the SCBU would be misattributed to her. Helen Donald: nursing's answer to Harold Shipman. There was only room for heroines and villainesses.

'Shame on you!' a woman screeched right in her ear.

Involuntarily Helen quickened her pace. Shame? She could not regret the scandal that now surrounded the Wet Incubator. Lives might be lost. But worse suffering might be avoided. There were other babies, other parents, she might yet be able to help. It was not the way Goldman would have gone about things, but she wasn't Goldman. What had taken place was a private affair between herself and the parents of Simon Long.

The loudspeaker roared again. Helen hurried on, plunged down the nearest side street, careless now where she was going, grateful for the semi-darkness that concealed her, listening to the chanting and the beating of the tambourine grow fainter.

And fainter. *His tiny bones, snap them like a fish's. His lonely, unnamed box.*

Acknowledgements

To see *These Are Our Children* published means a huge amount to me, so I would like to thank my agent, Peter Straus of Rogers, Coleridge & White, and my editor, Charlotte Van Wijk – formerly at Quercus, and now at Oneworld – for making it possible. Charlotte saw the point of what I wanted to do and her superb observations on the novel then enabled me to write a better version. Jon Riley and his assistant Rose Tomaszewska took excellent care of *These Are Our Children* after Charlotte's departure. I am also grateful to Bella Lacey at Granta Books for a shrewd suggestion about the plot line.

My brother Paul Maxwell was another wonderfully helpful early reader. He endured several drafts – and me. Thank you for the past thirty-seven years!

I was heartened when James Woodall accepted part of chapter five for inclusion in *Where We Fell To Earth: Writing for Peter Conrad,* a tribute to our brilliant former tutor at Christ Church, Oxford. Around the same time, two other tutors – Professors Christopher Butler and Peter McCullough – were instrumental in helping me to secure an academic teaching post. My warmest thanks!

I am pleased to acknowledge the financial assistance I received in the form of an Authors' Foundation Grant (Society of Authors) at an early stage of writing this novel.

I am indebted to the following publications for information and provocation:

Gena Corea, *The Mother Machine*; Fred M. Frohock, *Special Care*; John D. Lantos, *The Lazarus Case* and (with William L. Meadow) *Neonatal Bioethics*; James Le Fanu, *The Rise and Fall of Modern Medicine*; Armand Marie Leroi, *Mutants*; Robert and Peggy Stinson, *The Long Dying of Baby Andrew*.

Finally, and most importantly, I owe more than I can say to my husband Marius. These are our children: Baby Maxwell, Jude, Florence.

Reading Group Questions

Do you think Florence's theories about loving two men at the same time are selfish, or does she have a point? Could polygamy or open relationships ever be socially acceptable in Britain? How would this work with having children?

What do Florence and Thomas have in common? Do you think they would make a better team than Florence and Robert? What would Florence have done if Thomas was the father of the baby? Would that have altered Thomas's decision?

Florence and Helen have very different attitudes to sex. Do Helen's feelings stem from her bereavement, or from pre-existing tastes? How much is sex a factor in the make-up, and break-up, of each of their relationships – Helen to Joseph, Florence to both Robert and Thomas?

Helen believes a general anaesthetic would have made her recovery easier. Florence has a C-section, but feels detached from the birth, and afterwards, the baby. How could their experiences have been better? What takes priority over the mother's wishes?

How are the hospital staff depicted? What language do they use to describe pregnancy, birth and miscarriage, and how does this affect Florence's experience? Are any of the staff redeemable, in Florence's eyes? How does their miscommunication drive the plot?

What does Thomas value above all? What is his main motivation for promoting the Wet Incubator? How does his own personality impact on its trial and acceptance in the medical community? Is he a good leader?

Dr Rita Morgan believes Wet Incubators threaten women's role in pregnancy and childbirth. Do you think that progress in neonatal science preserves women's rights? Should it affect abortion law? Is medicine a patriarchal science? Do politics prevent doctors from saving lives?

Medical ethics teach that a baby, like Simon Long, should be treated as if he were a fully-reasoning adult when it comes to decisions about his care. How does this affect the parents' role of consent? What is the difference between these ethics and the ethics surrounding abortion?

Is Helen justified in performing euthanasia on Simon Long? Does she do it for his sake, his parents', or her own? His brain haemorrhage is an outcome of his prematurity, but without the Wet Incubator, he would not have survived birth in the first place. How does this alter the way you view the Wet Incubator?

For author interviews, articles and more reading group material visit

www.quercusbooks.co.uk/blog
Twitter/quercusbooks

Visit these websites for further information

Bliss, premature and special care baby charity: bliss.org.uk
birthtraumaassociation.org.uk
miscarriageassociation.org.uk
Lablit, science in fiction: lablit.com